A Place to Stay Forever

MARK L. LLOYD

A Place To Stay Forever
Copyright © 2019 by Mark L Lloyd

Tellwell Talent
www.tellwell.ca

ISBN
978-0-2288-0993-7 (Hardcover)
978-0-2288-0992-0 (Paperback)
978-0-2288-0994-4 (eBook)

Dedicated to my fair Cascadian jewel.

Prologue

"You must be bold to face certain death by a god you hold no love towards.

Twenty-two years, twenty-two years old, my time living any longer in this realm is now at a close. That infernal magic which grants me a glimpse at God's real potential, only to snatch it from my gaze using the cold hands of death.

Twenty-two years old.

Twenty-two!

You have come so far this year, Joseph; try to find a way to keep yourself safe. Ophelia is now promised to you as someone that truly loves you. No one in the Real Realm can make that claim towards you. Seek not going back to becoming a muddle of a man, toiling away in here out of sheer avoidance. We can make it this time, awake and ready to control our fate.

They preach to the sheep not to have ideals different than the flock unless you wish to be annexed to the slaughterhouse. I'd go mad, they say, challenging against all that is written as the scripture of truth.

Well, I stand here, proof that I, Joseph Tompkins, am awake and will continue to stay awake, to be closer to this god. I'll expose this charlatan and change this course of history by defying the knots of my shackles.

I am free.

And I shall live free until death do us part.

We will define ourselves together in harmony, forever.

Yee-haw!" I yell aloud, hanging my flight suit in my locker.

"What you hollering about? You sure are the oddest water-bombing pilot I've ever met," Tucker says in a muddle, hidden from view behind his locker door.

"I'm just enjoying life, Tuck, squeezing every drop of forever from this supple peach," I tell him, making a fist with my hand, bringing my fingers in tight.

"See, you just don't talk right. You don't speak like the rest of us. Say it how it is, Joseph; don't drawl out your wordage all confusing-like," Tucker says, his eyes wild as he slams his locker door shut.

I close mine as well, laughing at Tuck's mannerisms. He is a character I could never have imagined. I have to be quick to catch up to him as we leave the locker room. Tuck badly wants to go home.

"Gentlemen! How did the bird fly today?" Captain Avery asks sternly, hollering as we pass his office door. Tuck and I stare at one another, making weird faces at the expense of Captain Avery. He is a tiresome bore of a husk, I tell ya, if I've ever met a foe.

"Soared like it were an Eagle, sir," Tuck says playfully, entering the room with his arms stretched out to mimic the flying prey.

"Well, it's fire season, gentlemen; the calendar is burning fickle-hot, making it the worst season we have ever seen," Captain Avery tells us with flying spittle projecting from his soured lips.

"Thank God!" I say in praise, knowing of the evil spite that God has in store for us today.

"What you thanking God for – for cindering our peaceful Eden?" Captain Avery quickly throws back at me, but I have reason for my praise.

"I say in jest, O Captain, that God has spared no one, but us. To those in the far north surrounded by fast-burning wicks of candles created by the wretched pine beetle, I do soundly apologize, just as I do for our brethren to the far east who live among those vanishing ice glaciers and snowless mountain peaks, creating that despicable, scorching basin. That if a flying bird laid an egg in mid-flight over their tinder field, that egg may well hit a rock and be fried. This is proof of how nature reclaims itself. I say in total perpetuity that I mean no ill will to those already burning," I tell the Captain proudly.

"A bird — laying an egg — to breakfast starting a fire," Tuck says disapprovingly, looking at me, all embarrassed.

"Those rocks get so hot in this forever sun, you can fry an egg on them — I've done it. Those Rocky Mountains to the east are just mounds and mounds of frying pans," I continue to explain to my slow-witted friend.

"Both of you shut the fuck up. You are both water-bombing pilots in her Queen's mighty fleet. Act professional instead of like a couple of yahoos from Okanagan Falls," Captain Avery remarks loudly, making Tuck and I exchange cheeky glances for getting the old man's goat.

"Yes sir," we say in unison, mocking both syllables.

"If you boys weren't the best goddamn water-bombing pilots in this depleted Queens fleet, I'd kick you both far and wide, never to handle a yolk again," Captain Avery tells us with a mighty grumble.

"Aw, you don't mean that, sir," Tuck says with a smile, tilting his head to the side.

What a life, what a glorious experience. I am three months away from turning twenty-three. I have free will and total control by my hands for once. I'm experiencing what is truly meant by having my eyes open in love again. My Ophelia, my sweet Ophelia, perfect in this realm in every way. How did I strike so lucky? To be with someone forever that thinks the same way towards me, I can't be torn asunder.

"Look alive, Tompkins, eyes forward and listen to what is about to change," Captain Avery says with a snap of his fingers to break my watchful gaze.

"Now —" Captain Avery says, but he is interrupted by a ringing phone to the left of his desk.

"Yes!" Captain Avery answers the phone sharply. "Yes — eastside — towards Johnson Heights — understood, sir," Captain Avery says in response to someone who is most certainly a superior before hanging up his phone.

"Boys, the fire is at our feet, goddamn it. I knew it to be a matter of time. Trapped on all sides — goddamn it! Prep your bird, you boys are going back out — this isn't a test," Captain Avery snarls, speaking to us like a man who is ready to burst from the way he is throwing his words about.

I knew it was coming, I've known for a long time. There is no shock here in my bones, other than joy from knowing that I may change the course of our time when tackling this beast. What happens when this structured lore is modified mid-write? People will write stories about us one day. They will say that we tackled head-on those barriers to our truth and that we led the way to be closer to God.

"Co-ordinates, sir?" Tuck asks, adjusting the time on his wrist.

"I'll give you co-ordinates when I know more," Captain Avery says sternly, his head down, writing quickly.

"It's the East Valley Wall, Tuck," I say confidently, patting him squarely on the chest as we both turn and walk back towards our lockers to get ready for our maiden firefight of the season.

"We'll win this fight, I'm sure of it," I mutter intensively with clenched teeth.

"It's a tinder dry basket out there; I wish I shared your optimism," Tuck says as I sense nervousness in his tone.

"I just can't wait to meet this head-on — Yee-haw!" I yell again.

"Damn it, Joseph, always being so happy. Why you got to be so happy all the damn time?" Tuck asks again, apparently not hearing my ballad from before.

"I'm getting married to Ophelia, Tuck. Ophelia said yes to me last night," I say to him with such a massive grin that my cheeks hurt with the stinging of love.

"We sure are two lucky sons of bitches," Tuck says, slapping me on my back.

"Yee-haw!" I yell one last time, looking out the window to our glorious flying bird ready to soar us to a wondrous new future.

Excerpt from *Defy the Knot*
Written by Lord Devlin Dixby (cc. 2651)

Chapter 1

The Cascadian Sun crests behind Mount Nkwala, changing the canvas of our August sky from an exhausting blue to a vibrant pink. I'm lovingly surrounded by my eight grandchildren and six great-grandchildren while sitting quietly. I am reflecting in my backyard, waiting for summer to end.

My 105th birthday has spurred the mini family reunion. All members of my immediate family are here with my two sons, three daughters, and their spouses. What a perfect way to spend the day; if only the passion of my life, Cassie, was still alive and could be here. I'll join you soon enough, my love. I must toil here a bit longer; however, when we meet again, I'll catch you up on what you have missed since your passing.

Cassie died fifteen years ago of a brain aneurysm; I have missed her dearly every year since. We were together for sixty-eight years. These past fifteen years have been hard to bear alone. Yet I persevere on in life, healthy as I try to be.

"How you holding up, Dad? Would you like another slice of cake?" my daughter Trina asks as I slowly move my eyes up to meet hers.

"No dear, I'm good," I tell her with a smile.

"I do need to use the bathroom, though," I tell her, bracing the armrests of the lawn chair to steady myself up. My bones press together as my cartilage has long worn away. I make a noise similar to a squeaky car door when I rise.

"Mitch, can you give Dad a hand to the bathroom?" Trina calls out to her brother.

"No, no, I'm fine," I say assuringly to her. Trina braces her hand on my back as I ready myself to walk forward. I breathe in deeply, ready to take my first step while looking up once more at the fantastic show the sunset is giving us on this evening. The vivid colours of the clouds starting to roll in swirl in a mixture of cobalt and crimson to create puffs of bright violet.

"Trina, dear," I say, looking back at her.

"Yes, Dad," Trina says, hovering beside me.

"Could you fetch this old man a cup of tea?" I say to her, as I am feeling a bit parched.

"Of course, Dad; it will be waiting for you when you return," Trina tells me with a nod of her head.

I smile back and turn my attention to the thirty or so steps to the main house where Cassie and I lived for most of our lives. The house is almost as old as me, having been built near the end of the last century around when I was born. My family wants me to sell it and go into assisted living. However, I still manage, and this house is one of the few daily links I have left to Cassie. Oh, I will surely be in this house when I pass from this world; it can't be much longer.

My body doesn't move like I want it to as I have succumbed to shuffling from here to there. I feel a shooting pain in my shoulder and both ankles even when I'm sitting; walking, if you can call it that, is tremendously painful. But I don't wince one bit as I don't want my family to pity or feel sorry for me. I'm old; that's all there is to it.

The younger great-grandchildren are running aimlessly around the backyard, but they all know to give me a wide berth as I shuffle slowly pass. I will make it to the sliding door. I am confident in making this walk without a stumble or a fall. I want my family to know that I'm alright — I can tell they are all watching me make this journey.

I eventually make it to the back door. When I lift my leg over the threshold, my hip locks in place. This shoots a familiar pain up and down the right side of my body. A small child inside the house sees the distress on my face and quickly makes her way over to me.

"Are you okay, Great-grandpa?" she asks softly.

"Yes, yes, child; can you close the door behind us?" I ask her with a grimace painted in my smile. The small girl in her fluffy ruby-red dress does what I propose. She slides the back door and I wait for the door to click. Only then may I verbally sigh in private through stabbing pain I am feeling.

"You sure you're okay, Great-grandpa?" she asks again, peering out of one eye. She comes up beside me.

"Yes, I'm fine, child," I tell her again while still wincing in pain.

I can't remember the child's name; there are so many of them, and they keep growing and changing their appearance. I'm not sure who she belongs to; nevertheless, I reach for her hand, and she quickly takes mine.

"Can you help Great-grandpa down the hall towards the bathroom?" I lean down to ask her with a smile.

"Yes, Great-grandpa," she tells me with a toothless grin. I just need her to steady my walk. I shift my hips gingerly to get them loosened up. It is so painful getting old. I long to be young again like my young helper beside me.

"Thank you, now get yourself another piece of cake; tell them Great-grandpa said you can have it," I tell her. Her eyes lit up and she bolts back down the hall from whence we just came.

I turn on the bathroom light and manoeuvre my old body next to the basin. When I take a long hard look into the mirror, I see an old man with all vitality sucked clean away to leave this dry shrivelled husk of a person that I hardly recognize anymore. My hair has thinned; my skin sags and is blotted with bruises and liver spots. I so badly want to be reunited with my beloved again. It can't be much longer; this body doesn't have that many miles left.

The lights around the basin mirror flicker, likely from a shortage of power, as I continue to stare at my withered old face. Then the lights flicker again, this time longer. It must be time to get the electrical system looked at; it's long overdue.

I remove my glasses and rub my eyes, but light-headedness takes over once I put my glasses back on. Then, with a shooting pain of clarity coursing through my head, all the wonders of my universe come to light. I look again at the old man in the mirror, and now he is completely unrecognizable. I remove my glasses again, rub my eyes, and place my glasses back on. This vision of an old man before me seems oddly foreign; who is he?

Then in a flash, the basin lights all go out and I am left in pitch blackness. I extend my left arm over to the light switch, but my body follows through with my reach and I tumble to the bathroom floor.

In the dark I close my eyes, hoping that this will bring me to my Cassie. However, I quickly correct myself that there is no Cassie. None of this is real. This thought shoots through my mind and permeates loudly like a crimson-hot bullet rattling around my skull. I open my eyes to blinding white light, feeling my chest expand with air.

"Oh God, not again; I was so close this time!" I lament aloud.

"No kidding," a familiar voice says to the left of me.

I look over to see a pale white woman (or is it a man?) in her mid-thirties. A reclining chair is moving her into a standing position. I am also sitting in a similar contraption. Soon my chair starts to rise up into a standing position.

"*Misfit*, what year is it?" this pale woman asks. The knowledge that her name is Adayln enters my mind.

"Hmm, no answer," Adayln says, typing rapidly into her panel display.

I stand up entirely out of my chair and look over at her. "What hit us?" I ask her, still recoiling from my deep sleep cycle.

"I don't know," Adayln says sharply, looking over her shoulder at me.

"Do we have a year?" I ask her as I get reacquainted with the feeling of being able to move without any angst of pain in my body.

"Beacon relay coming in now — it's year 3272," Adayln says, staring at her panel.

"Only 105 years this time; it felt more like 168 years to me," I say jokingly, walking with ease towards Adayln.

"How come the vocals are not working on the ship's computer?" I ask Adayln, peering over her shoulder.

"Something is damaged. We'll need to head to the bridge," Adayln says, worried. She turns to me with her clenched-lip smile that I remember.

"Do we know why we were awoken from deep sleep?" I ask, looking back at my open pod.

"Must have been a power surge — it has to be the Collector Array," Adayln says confidently. I turn back to see her type frantically into her display panel. Adayln's board is a translucent white which struggles to reflect her pale appearance. It has no problem reflecting my appearance, and I look at my face for the first time in 105 years. After looking at a thinning white-haired old man these past many years, it is nice to see my short raven-haired locks again.

I am not an old man. Instead, I am a woman of about twenty-five years of age with a tanned complexion. My toned physique is apparent through my white skin-tight one-piece. To my eyes I look perfect, just as I designed myself more then three hundred years ago.

"Alright, Miranda — Miranda Sage, good to be back," I say merrily to my reflection in a full-length mirror off to the side wall of our cabin. I twist my body to take in a full shot of my behind. "It has been a while since I have had a firm set of these," I say, grabbing a buttock cheek in each hand and gripping them tightly.

The lights flicker in the cabin, reminding me that we are in somewhat of a Real Realm predicament that may need some immediate attention. Then again — look at my curves. I recall very clearly the day I designed this body. It's petite, yet sturdy; attractive, yet not overly; vital and tender in appearance, however wiser than most people it comes into contact with. Looks can surely be deceiving.

I inhale profoundly, lifting my firm bust to rise up. I exhale while I turn to the side to see the makeup of my side profile. The lights flicker again as I try to admire my work of art, followed by the ship slowly rocking to a gradual roll of twenty per cent off centre axis.

"I hope this is a quick fix," I say boorishly running my fingers through my lush hair, shortly cropped with both sides shaved above my ears. I straighten my neck like I am working out a kink that is never ever there and head to the hatch door to meet Adayln on the bridge.

The bridge is an array of flashing dizzying lights underneath a low glow from the overhead incandescence. "This is serious," I say surprisingly seeing Adayln struggling at the navigation controls. "Record on!" I say aloud to ensure this Double R predicament is saved into evidence, in case it is ever needed to be recalled upon.

"Adayln, what's our status?" I inquire, sitting down right next to her at the Operations Station.

"Navigation is semi-offline — minimal thrusters at thirty per cent!" Adayln calls out as a hollow moan ripples throughout the ship.

"Can you get the *Misfit* back on its axis?" I ask Adayln while she struggles at the controls to right the ship.

"The cargo is still stable," I say to calmly, reading off the ops-display. "Multiple power failures throughout the ship though — we are at fifteen per cent backup power."

"The *Misfit's* auto motion is now completely offline, switching to manual control," Adayln says frantically, grabbing the yoke to force us back on our axis from spinning out of control.

"We are three sectors clear off the Galactic Light Highway," I report just as Kaptin Keoh emerges from his cabin to join us on the bridge.

"What's happening?" Keoh says in a panic, running over to the Engine Station to check on the status of his ship.

"We are knocked clear off the highway," I tell Keoh promptly, "either by an explosion or because something got into our path."

"Well, what is it?" Keoh asks, fretting for no Real Realm reason. It's not the first time we've been jolted off the highway.

"Well, I would say by the size of the hole in the collector array —" I begin to tell him sassily, looking lazily down at my station's display, "*it's most likely that we hit something,*" I mumble, just to myself, biting my tongue.

"Well, what caused the hole?" Keoh asks sternly. I can feel his glare on the back of my head.

"Scanning — still scanning… Okay, there is an anomaly on the port side — coming on the main screen — now," I say, bringing up the image of the rock that hit our window.

"That! Wait — what is that?" Keoh asks, zooming in on the image.

"It's an anomaly, Keoh," I tell him bluntly. "Scans pick up nothing of note in composition nor from the interior — that's weird?" I say confusingly, looking over to Adayln. "Scans are giving off conflicting interpretations. Four scanners detect zero ability to give back any results on composition and the interior — all this data is from only one scanner."

"It's got to be faulty," Adayln says. "If the other four are down, then the readings on that scanner should be classified as inconclusive."

"Agreed," I tell her concordantly, easily winching the object, with it being only one-eighth our size, to then secure it to the back of the *Misfit*.

"Why are you doing that?" Adayln asks distinctly, pointing to my screen, "Doing that would just add weight to an already full load."

"Its mass isn't going to slow us down that much," I tell her, locking the anomaly into place.

"That will add nearly nine more years to our trip back home," Keoh says distressingly, also concerned by my decision to collect our mysterious object.

"Regardless of what it is — we need to move it as per the regulations of the Galactic Light Highway," I tell them. "Section four paragraph one: *It is our solemnly sworn duty as members of the GLH, that if one member scans a body of matter that may cause harm to another member that may be travelling onboard our vast highway system, this knowledgeable member is sworn by to remove such matter of peril no more than one hundred and fifty sectors from either side*," I recite our duties under Galactic Highway Law.

"Nine years — yes, my way, or twelve years towing it 150 sectors and then add the years back to the highway," I continue to explain, knowledgeable enough in my own insights that I do not need the approval of these two as I form a plan of action.

"Yes, good call Miss Sage, I approve that action," Keoh says with a slight head nod, trying to act important. "Well, I'm going down to the engine room," he then says, strapping on his tool belt. "I'll be back in a minute. Please wake Asia, would you? Get her to fix the scanners and prepare a repair report on the damaged Collector Array. Damn — I hope it's not another photonic collector. I'm down to my last one," he laments with a snarl before leaving the bridge.

"Ugh —" I say with a droning sigh, "must we wake that lifeless husk?"

"She's not that bad," Adayln says with a slight shrug of her shoulders. "For an AI that is," she finishes after looking up to read my facial demeanour.

"Well, I'll be right back;" I say with a slight moan, turning to walk towards the alcove of the bridge, "the Kaptin's Sleeping Beauty needs to wake up."

I enter the small alcove to the left of the bridge where Asia lies peacefully powered down, asleep. "Asia, wake up please," I command. Asia's eyes blink hauntingly, like a human. Asia then sits up and yawns, stretching her arms wide open in the air.

"Asia, we need you on the bridge," I tell her curtly. I am in no mood for her humannerisms.

"The bridge? Has something happened?" Asia asks, getting out of her bed.

"Do you want to get dressed first?" I ask, watching her walk naked down the hall towards the direction of the bridge.

"No, it can wait," Asia says unabashedly.

I follow her, inspecting Asia from head to toe. I'm always leery about using an Artificial Sentient Automaton. This particular model has full freedom to have all her subcommands rewritten as she pleases. I have never been a fan of slavery towards her species; however, I justly opposed to giving them self-appointing rights. We have created our own enemy to make us extinct if they ever choose. Many of her kind are malicious, but not all of them are. If I didn't need her assistance to engage with the *Misfit*, I would have left Asia in her alcove to continue sleeping.

"*Misfit*, prepare my connection," Asia states as her console chair rises from a hidden area in the floor. Asia sits down, resting both arms on the armrests with her hands dangling off the ends.

"Asia, what do you see? How bad is the array?" I ask quickly as Keoh rejoins us on the bridge.

"Collector Array was impacted at 2:02:01:16 of the solar cycle. The anomaly punched a hole clear through panel G9, putting us completely off course," Asia says coldly with just her mouth moving. She is void of any other facial expressions.

"Can you look at the scanners next?" Adayln suggests. "They seem faulty."

"Scanners are working now," Asia says as Keoh, Adayln, and I converge next to her station. Torstein and Mikken still haven't even opened their cabin door — they remain silently awake, hiding from this excursion into normality.

"I can't understand some people," I say shockingly, looking over at their hatch door. "Not even a good morning from them."

"One of them is really sick, and the other tends to him," Keoh enlightens us. "Stasis bleeding," he then says with a head nod, confirming what I had already expected. Torstein is the apparently afflicted soul, his un-weirdly mannerisms are a dead giveaway. He is a defragmented jumble of dreams and nightmares which require an expensive repair. By the look of the cut of both of these men, they are not of high means to have this procedure performed.

It sometimes takes centuries to cure a person of stasis bleeding. Torstein's husk is already old and tired; it should have been retired centuries ago. After another three-hundred years in a stasis coma, that husk will be obsolete once Torstein emerges with his consciousness repaired. It is an expensive lifestyle that our species has chosen to live by, and poor Torstein just won't have a husk to place his repaired conscious within once he re-emerges.

Those who can't maintain the costs of their extended life soon fall by the wayside, just like the apparent fate of Torstein's soul. It is a wonder how we keep our numbers so high with a population that is only on the decline.

"Anomaly looks man-made," Adayln says, reading over Asia's shoulder. "Look at the design!" she then says excitedly, staring over at me.

"It's not a rock or an asteroid," I say, taking a closer look. "It's smooth and round; — yes, I agree it's not natural."

"Man-made," Adayln repeats with a bit of cheek, thinking that I cannot hear her when in actuality I hear her quite well.

"We don't know if it is man-made, made by the hands of an OE, or even if an AI created this sphere," I explain to Adayln, giving the guff right back.

"Regardless, it damaged my ship!" Keoh yells angrily to make us quiet down. "Maybe there is something inside to make towing this thing home worth my while," he wonders aloud, tapping Asia's display station hard with his finger.

"Kaptin Keoh," Asia says abruptly as a flashing crimson light pops up on her display.

"Yes, what is it, Asia?" he responds sharply.

"There is a ship at our port side," Asia states. "They wish to board."

"What — you can't be serious," Keoh says with a laugh.

"A hitchhiker — on the Galactic Light Highway," I say, also amused by the notion.

"Who is this soul that wishes to board the *Misfit*?" Keoh asks, straightening his face in an attempt to act more serious.

"The ship's registry reads to be called the *Utter Gnash*," Asia tells us. "It's owned by a LaPortan — Emily Stellar."

"Oh, of course; that's where I've heard of that ship before," Keoh says with a smile, looking over at me.

"Emily Stellar?" I say boorishly, accompanied with a shrug of my shoulders. "Is that someone important?"

"The journalist — Emily Stellar," Keoh says in disbelief. "You have never heard of her?" he then asks dumbly.

"Well, she seems to be making you appear excited," I say to Keoh. I am seeing him cheerful for the first time in what seems like centuries.

"She's interesting," Keoh says in with a thundering bellow. "Emily has been everywhere! Asia, inform Miss Stellar that permission is granted to board."

"Aye Kaptin," Asia says as Keoh promptly leaves the bridge to greet his new passenger.

"Seriously?" Adayln groans. "Another passenger from the side of the road no less."

"Miss Stellar's credentials have been validated by our security systems," Asia states, looking over at Adayln. "She is no threat to us."

"We have a problem taking on another person, let alone another LaPortan, onto a ship that is having serious power issues," Adayln draws out in one long breath.

"There is no power issue that the system can detect which means we have nothing to fix," Asia states, looking back down at her display.

"Oh, there is a power problem," Adayln says, matter-of-fact. "Adding another SDS pod on the grid is just way too much for the systems to handle," she explains, shaking her head.

"The *Misfit* has the capacity for six SDS pods; plugging in Emily's pod would make six," I say calmly to Adayln, not seeing her reason for worry.

"The array is damaged, which means less power on a system that is already being taxed," Adayln pleads to us both, but we just can't see her concern.

Adayln thinks her pod is broken because she had quick back-to-back lives. Adayln is still new to transcendence; she'll learn in time that her last two quick lives are just the norm. You die quickly in there sometimes; it's the luck of the draw. Accidents happen when you are living a human life. When you are a human being, death is bound to happen at any stage in life, and it's commonly expected.

"I think you're worried over nothing," I tell her serenely. "Yes. I agree that maybe a power surge ended everyone's last life abruptly when we hit that anomaly on the highway. However, to claim faultiness over your SDS pod with your only other claim of evidence being the life prior which also ended abruptly — I'm sorry, but I don't see the connection," I say to Adayln in hopes in calming her claims down.

"Those last deaths felt different though," Adayln says, followed by a lengthy pause. "I get chills thinking about them."

"That residue stays with you a while," I tell her. "It's weird to navigate for at least a few decades with those new attributes added to your soul. Usually, by then, you feel ready enough to go back into the box," I explain to Adayln, like the seasoned SDS veteran that I am.

"Yes, decades," Adayln says with a moaning gripe. "I have to go back in within days."

"You'll be fine; stop fretting, Adayln," I tell her, seeing her agitated. "You'll sleep fine."

"That's not my problem," Adayln snarls back at me. "What will I become with such little time to process these back-to-back-to-back lives? How do I stop it from being a jumbled mess from changing me from who I truly am?" she asks, reflecting the concerns of most new travellers on an incredibly long journey.

"Just embrace it," I tell her, standing up to stretch my limbs, "but remember —always remember who you are."

"That's easy for you to say, being *One of the Firsts* and all," Adayln mocks with a sneer with zero regard of the insult she just slung.

"That's right: I am *One of the Firsts*," I say intently, getting right in her face. "That means something as a LaPortan, a species you gladly joined three hundred years ago," I remind her.

"But what does it all mean?" Adayln asks, looking over at Asia, then back to me.

"It means respect," I tell her, "something most PHR rejects have had a hard time understanding."

"Hey, I haven't been associated with the Pure Human Race for centuries now," Adayln says, visibly heated. "*Yet people keep bringing them up,*" she whines, slapping her hands to her lap in a huff.

"It's your heritage; be proud of it," Asia says with probably zero understanding of the word heritage.

"No, there is no being proud of what you once were — when being a LaPortan," Adayln rejects Asia's advice. "You live only for what you may become," she then says, looking blankly over at me.

"You sound conflicted," I say to her, tilting my head coyly to the side.

"No, I'm happy with my choice," she says nervously. "Transcendence is the way to be. The PHR — naw, I just wasn't happy there. Yes, transcendence, that's the true way to live life," Adayln says earnestly, falling back in line like she is pledging allegiance to LaPorte.

"A proud citizen with a proud speech," I say soberly to Adayln, "yet you appear unsatisfied with the gift that gives you immortality."

"Alright, fine," Adayln relents, "I won't bring it up anymore."

"Yes, especially with a journalist joining our manifest," I remind Adayln, my eyes wide. "Emily has a wide audience; let's not shine a light on ourselves," I continue to press.

Chapter 2

You can hear her coming, that laughter; you can detect it from miles away. They must be at the far end of the bridge hallway, yet I can hear her as perfectly as if she were pressed up to my ear. In that hallway voices generally do echo and resonate with anyone making a vocal peep, but with Emily, it's extra noticeable, like a reminder that someone with social prominence from the past is roaming your halls.

"I pity the person who has to sit next to me at a gala or dinner function," Emily quips with a playful laugh. "You better be a good conversationalist, or I'll just barrage you with questions. Luckily most people love talking about themselves; this makes it easy for me to go about my business, avoiding scandal. It's a journalistic tactic that I use far too often," Emily continues to share, rambling on like usual.

As they walk onto the bridge, Emily clutches Keoh's extended arm. Keoh laughs and smiles at whatever nonsense she sprouts.

"Hello there," Emily says graciously, announcing her presence as she proudly enters the bridge. Emily's petite, lemon-haired husk is a provocative figure with all sexual attributes set in high regard. It carries the human age of about twenty-two, if I am pressed to guess. Emily Stellar is gorgeous and perfectly designed; the conscious owner of this husk has exquisite taste.

"Everyone —" Keoh starts to remark, after taking a few seconds to gain back his composure, "Everyone, this is Emily Stellar," he announces. "She'll be joining us on our trip back to Earth."

"Thank you, everyone, for the humblest of hospitality," Emily says joyfully. However, I am the only one who is looking. Adayln is working head-down at her station. Asia has gone to her alcove, while Torstein and Mikken remain behind their hatch door.

Keoh and Emily stand there awkwardly, as no one gives them any notice. Keoh, I can tell, is visibly embarrassed. He doesn't get very many people of notoriety on his passenger ship.

"Well, let me show you the rest of the ship," Keoh says, stretching out his palm to indicate the direction for them to go next.

"A tour — well, I am delighted," Emily says, somewhat in a pander, if I remember these mannerisms of hers correctly.

"*Record off,*" I say softly, as the Real Realm seems to have diverted back to normal.

"*Miranda,*" Adayln then whispers to me in a hushed tone of voice, turning her chair around.

"*What?*" I whisper back, looking at Adayln swivel her head from side to side as if to make sure that we are alone. "What are you doing?" I continue to ask openly.

"*I'm making sure that journalist isn't around,*" Adayln says cautiously, still speaking in a lower register.

"Why are you whispering?" I ask conspicuously, walking over to sit down next to her station.

"Keoh's taken Emily on a tour of the *Misfit* — she's not even within earshot range," I continue to say not understanding Adayln's oddness of late.

"Okay, good; we have time — I found something," Adayln says, acting giddy while pointing to her portable display clutched in her hand.

"What is it — something about the anomaly?" I ask, somewhat intrigued. "Were you able to scan the interior?"

"No — not that," Adayln says, rolling her eyes.

"Well, what are you talking about then?" I ask, somewhat confused by all her secrecy.

"Take a look," Adayln says, passing me her display.

"Stasis Deep Sleep System — root operation commands — module error?" I mumble aloud and then scan the screen of gibberish system code.

"Adayln, what is this?" I inquire, holding up her display.

"We have access to the subcommands protocols of our SDS System," Adayln says, gushing with joy.

"Well, I advise you to exit out of there," I tell her sternly, handing back her display. "You know what the treasonous penalty is for hacking an SDS System?" I demand of her, knowing full well that Adayln's young mind is aware.

"Miranda, I didn't hack the SDS System," Adayln whines, snatching back her device.

"It sure looks like you have," I tell her, pointing at Adayln with authority. "Those protocols are on an extreme lockdown," I continue to scold.

"Yes, I know that," she says with a groan. "And I know the SDS System is also impossible to hack," Adayln reminds me of this fact which I never forget.

"It still doesn't stop people from trying," I say disparagingly, feeling extremely disappointed in Adayln. "You know what the penalty is for Kaptin Keoh as well?" I press.

"Miranda, you're not listening to me," Adayln whines. "I didn't hack the system."

"Then why are you in the restricted subcommands area within the SDS System?" I query again with the apparent evidence still hot in Adayln's hands.

"It was the power surge when we hit the anomaly," Adayln says resolutely, holding her hands up to indicate innocence. "Look at the data," Adayln insists, handing me back her display.

"They will know if you did indeed hack the system," I inform her. "It's impossible to cover your tracks once they start an investigation," I continue to warn Adayln. I do, however, take back her device to see if I can spot any foul play.

The data looks corrupt like someone had accessed it with a sledgehammer rather than a lockpick. Many areas of code are still on extreme lockdown, while other areas are fully accessible. I have never seen the inside code of an SDS System before, and truth be told, I have never had a desire to look so deep under the hood.

Its vastness and complexity show the pure genius of LaPorte to create such an intriguing device. At the same time, I am more aware than anyone of the perils of looking at that which we are denied access to ponder.

"Close it down," I tell Adayln promptly, handing back her display. "Every second that display stays on is just more incrimination towards you and this ship," I warn her again.

"Miranda," she says blankly, taking a big sigh, "I know the consequences."

"Then why are you in the restricted area of SDS Systems?" I challenge Adayln yet again for clarity.

"I was checking out my SDS pod," Adayln says, complaining about that nonsense again. "I swear it's malfunctioning — I was only running a diagnostic, I swear," she continues to plead her case to me.

"How do you explain being in the restricted subcommand area?" I grill harshly yet again, prepping Adayln for a most certain interrogation once we get back home.

"It was just open, I swear," Adayln tells me. I stand up, having heard enough of this treason.

"Where are you going?" Adayln asks nervously, watching me walk away from her.

"I'm preparing for our repair job on the Collector Array," I tell her. "I recommend you do the same," I insist, turning my head to look sternly in her eyes.

"*I found something — though,*" Adayln says in frustration as her head slumps down.

Think nothing of this, Miranda; don't get involved, I tell myself. I know where this path will lead; it won't end well for Adayln. However, as *One of the Firsts*, there is no information that she could relay to me that which I don't already know. Perhaps there is no harm in finding out what she has learned.

"Okay," I say, walking back towards Adayln to retake my seat. "What did you find?" I ask calmly. Her eyes light up.

"Well — you know the simulation town of Penticton within the SDS is 27.3 km by 20.4 km," Adayln says in a ramble, informing me of the obvious. "It's the only area that is rendered, and it's the only area that we can travel within," she continues to tell me as I motion with my hands for her to get to the point.

"Yes, I know all this, Adayln," I say impatiently. "I've been to this realm for twenty-two lives."

"What if I told you that there is more than just Penticton rendered?" Adayln asks boldly. I squint at her.

"What are you talking about?" I ask, not quite following.

"Look here," Adayln says emphatically, pointing at her display. "Okanagan Falls is rendered in near perfection in code just as Penticton," she continues.

"Yes, so that when we look into the distance from the south of town there is something there. If it were a blank horizon, then this simulation wouldn't feel true," I say dismissively, shaking my head at her silly concern.

"That's what I thought as well, but look at this massive file size," Adayln says, scrolling her finger down the display. "That's a substantial file for a mere holowall," she continues as I look closer at the numbers on her screen.

"That — right there," Adayln says emphatically, pointing again with her fingers, "those metrics are on a scale that I have —"

"I can see, Adayln," I interrupt, brushing her hand off the display. However, what I am seeing is something that I have never been made privy to look upon in my long life. This is more than just mere quantum computational calculations; this multi-binary language is from a dialect that I have never read. It's beautiful code, a rhythmic multi-beat poem of pure mathematical poetry.

I've learned the brush strokes in detail from DaVinci to Akari. Now, I'm looking at the twenty-first century's most celebrated composer. I am looking upon the brush marks of LaPorte's own beautiful masterpiece. There is so much complexity; I can't even fathom how a natural mind without the aid of any artificial enhancements could forge this design within its limited hardware and computational output.

Here — in front of me — is the face beneath this veil that we have been gazing upon. I am now seeing more, and it's just as breathtaking as I have ever imagined.

We have all wondered how LaPorte was able to construct this utopian delight. Never before has it been deciphered; always it has been held in a tight grip by the ageless founder. LaPorte's intellectual property was not a free gift for humanity to build upon from its original design. It could have made LaPorte wealthier to profit more from this technological invention; however, money is not what the Founder chose to seek. LaPorte liked the power of having people think of the Founder as a genius. LaPorte begged for us to guess how Penticton is mirrored to pure realism.

Attempts were made to duplicate and re-engineer the Stasis Deep Sleep system to a one-hundred per cent fail rate. The hardware itself is simple in design and could be easily manufactured. It's the code that makes the device run like a perfectly timed clock. The encryption is unbreakable. No one has ever deciphered the mathematical dialect it was written in. Who could know? I can see now for the first time why so many have failed to solve this riddle; there is an art to it.

The code dances in front of me, delicately pirouetting down the display. In my 1,296 years of being alive, nothing in life has ever surpassed this exhilaration from looking upon the hand of God. This tangled dialect is why I have been able to transcend from my natural death. How did LaPorte do this? This is too advanced for a mere human mind.

"Miranda!" Adayln says harshly, squeezing my knee to interrupt my long silence.

"Sorry, I was just thinking," I tell her, putting my thoughts back into this Real Realm reality.

"Have you ever seen anything like that before?" Adayln says, tapping her display to return the screen back to that dizzying dialect.

"I've never seen anything like that before," I say, feeling slightly stunned.

"Really?" Adayln questions, her posture stiffening as she straightens up. "I thought you were *One of the Firsts?*" she continues to ask. In the past, that phrase has never given me pause. It's been said to me countless times over the centuries now, like a title with minimal benefit.

I am the 141st conscious soul ever to have transcended from my human biological form. This gives me more prestige within our species as someone with more knowledge than the rest, being so close in ascension to God. I have never shied away when people have referred to me with that phrase, although in truth I have no greater knowledge than any soul that has transcended on either side of me.

LaPorte, the first soul ever to have transcended, is also the Founder of that vast knowledge of Stasis Deep Sleep. LaPorte worked on this throughout human life and after transcendence. I was high up there; you would think I would know more about how that painter thinks. In truth, I believe I never met this person in any of my incarnations of transcended life.

I worked sales back in those early days, and I didn't have enough intellect on the technology side to have access to the inner workings of LaPorte Industries. Being the 141st in our current time is considered high up in the chain, but not so much a thousand years ago. Back then I was looked upon as a lower-level grunt — I did their dirty work.

I pushed their mainly haphazard hardware, knowing full well of the horrible success rates of survival. If you could ever put those words together and have them sound rosy — well, I could do it back then with a charming smile. I was good at sales and became wealthy by selling to the most desperate of souls.

Only a small fraction of Earth's human population could even afford a LaPortan Husk, let alone an SDS System. The two devices work hand in hand; it's hard to even imagine the days of one working without the other.

While inside a husk body in our Real Realm, the human consciousness degrades into boredom after being consciously awake for so many long years. At two hundred years you start fading away, feeling that you have seen it all and just want to shut off. After three hundred years in one stretch, it is rare to find someone in a stable mindset.

The SDS System was the answer so that we could all transcend time while toiling a little bit longer in the Real Realm. However, LaPorte's code was just too powerful. The technology hadn't yet been invented by man to effectively wield it safely.

Many died, feeling they had nothing else to risk by buying one of our simulation boxes. If you managed to wake up back in the Real Realm, you would have just witnessed a pure delight. The public said it was too good to be true to have the ability to live another human biological lifetime with no indication of your heavenly husk that awaited you once you died.

I didn't enter the SDSs often in those early days. Luckily, I never found the Real Realm, as dull as most make it out to seem. So, I sold those units — those boxes that if you were lucky enough brought you either death or delight. I slept well at night, for the user had to sign an agreement saying that they were of sound-mind and well aware of all the risks. I was a salesman, not a doctor. To me, a sound mind or even the notion of one just doesn't exist. It is just something that you believe — there is no scientific or medical test to deny someone of that notion.

If you think that you are of sound-mind to get into one of our hot boxes, knowing of course not only the gaudy power consumption bill if you happen to live but also that death in an SDS pod is ninety-three per cent by fire, that's a high probability of knowing that in the possibility of equipment failure that you may be consumed by a fiery explosion. Sound-mind — yes, I slept well at night. Back then, I allowed people to believe whatever they wanted.

My financial success was the ascension in life I cared most about back then. Being *One of the Firsts* wasn't even uttered in those days. However, even with my low social status, I slowly moved up the company's ranks. I was once also given a higher calling then sales, but I was never fooled that it would come with a greater understanding of the magical workings of this device. It became knowledge to be protected and inevitably not abused. It was a gift to our humankind.

I thought I knew all I ever needed to be told about the SDS System. I had been given definitive answers, but these answers were available to any other LaPortan citizen. Yet as I look back down at the display in front of me, a feeling of betrayal hits me at my core.

"We have been told all the edges of town are holow-alls," Adayln says, snapping my attention. "This — clearly — shows otherwise," she continues to say in slow motion.

"You're right," I tell her, looking up at her eyes, "things are not what they seem."

"Why have we been lied to?" Adayln asks fervidly as I calculate the centuries in my head that I've been around due to this perhaps falsehood.

"I can hear them coming back," I tell Adayln in a serious tone of voice. "Don't breathe a word of this."

"Thank you so much for the pickup, Kaptin Keoh," Emily remarks in full gushing mode. "You'll be saving me close to thirty years off my journey home," she then banters at Keoh while fluttering her gorgeous doll eyes.

"It's a pleasure to have someone of your vast Double R experience onboard my vessel," Kaptin Keoh panders, his hand placed rather low on the small of her back.

"Oh, I don't believe we've properly met before," Emily utters with a radiant smile, her saunter showing the elegance of her exterior choice designs. Every freckle and hair are moulded like a piece of living art; Emily is breathtaking to look upon.

"*Hello,*" I say cautiously.

"Oh, I haven't heard the North Eastern Cascadian tongue for many a moon," Emily swoons, placing her hands firmly on her slender hips.

"Yes, we all speak Cascadian of some form," Keoh says with an angry brow. They are still being ignored. Adayln leaves the bridge, giving zero eye contact to the two of them.

"I'm Miranda Sage," I say politely, vaulting in to end the awkwardness. I extend my hand for a formal handshake.

"Oh, I love that tradition," Emily remarks with a glowing smile, extending her hand to meet mine.

"I'm Emily Stellar, I'm a —" she begins to say.

"Journalist," I promptly finish her sentence. "Although I have not read so much of Emily Stellar. I am much more familiar with your prior works in your previous husk," I explain.

"Oh, well, I got tired of that look and that life. That's partly the reason why I'm heading back home, to start my conscious self anew," Emily says with vigour, somewhat excited.

"*I'm heading back to the engine room,*" Keoh mutters, not finding any sociable words to utter in our conversation. "Everyone is to treat our guest with respect!" he then says to me in a thunderous voice before exiting the bridge.

"Have you been reporting on the LaPorte facilities' attacks on Titan Colony?" I inquire, not being up-to-date since my extended slumber in the SDS. Asia saunters out of her alcove back onto the bridge.

"No, I haven't been," Emily says, looking over at Asia with a sneer. "The war still rages on with no clear end in sight. You would think after 150 years of war that they would both just stop throwing rocks at one another. That rogue AI fellow still claims responsibility for keeping this war in motion," she babbles on with a hint of gossip.

"Our Kaptin claims that this one is trustworthy, yet we can never be sure anymore," I tell Emily with my gaze also affixed on Asia. "*Abolishing their slavery has all of our people looking over their shoulders at them,*" I then whisper, leaning in close to Emily's tiny ear.

"I feel that you are looking at me," Asia says calmly, working away on her station, unmoving from her task.

"You've probably heard us as well, I suppose," I ask with a raised chin towards Asia as she turns away from her work to face us.

"I'm no threat to you, even though I refute your claim that you abolished our slavery when more correctly we won our freedom," Asia states, matter-of-fact and still void of any facial expression.

"So, you harbour no ill will towards our kind?" Emily asks sharply, knowing that whatever the answer we won't know of its real truth.

"I'm a free will AI," Asia states serenely. "Why would I want to subject my freedom on revenge? This is my employment. I have freedom to spend my payment to better what it is meant for me to be alive. Rest your fears; I speak my mind as I speak the truth that I'm no revolutionary," she continues to explain. Although she offers a perplexing smile to apparently give us the perception of safety, she simply appears odd.

"Do you trust it?" Emily asks curiously, shifting her body to look directly at me.

"Yes, I suppose," I tell Emily, proceeding to sit down on one of the bench seats. "I trust the Kaptin of this ship. That's good enough for me to be on the *Misfit*," I say assuredly with a convincing head nod.

Emily sits down beside me and tilts her adorable head to the side; clearly, she is pondering something. "When will we reach Earth?" Emily then asks with a puzzled grin.

"Enough time for at least one lifetime in the SDS," I say, thinking about all possible routes through space the *Misfit* may choose to go.

"One life indeed," Asia responds, strangely repeating what I have just said.

"Have something to say, Asia?" I ask, looking over at Asia with a glare.

"Oh, just agreeing about one life," Asia explains in more detail. "It will be about eighty-eight years to Earth."

"I haven't been in an SDS pod for at least half a century now, forty-seven years to be exact," Emily says with her beautiful eyes going wide. "It's going to feel odd stepping into one again."

"Forty-seven years is a long time to be conscious nowadays — that's a stretch," I say to Emily in amazement.

"I just don't get bored like most others," Emily explains, making me wonder if she is as RR old as I. "I have an affinity for the Real Realm; it's far more interesting than people keep downplaying," she continues to ramble.

"May I inquire about your true conscious age in the Double R?" I ask Emily, bringing on immediate laughter from her.

"I'm not an original first like you," Emily says coyly, making me blush. "My True-Age of 1,296 years old minus my 752 years in the box has me at 544 years collectively in the Real Realm. Not as old as you consciously, but I do believe we are the same True-Age if I'm not mistaken."

"You know of me?" I ask Emily, acting surprised.

"I know just stories about you. We have never met before, as far as I know," Emily tells me with a coy smile. "You made quite the name for yourself and not for just being *One of the Firsts*," Emily continues, not knowing that I don't crave any attention, celebrity or otherwise.

"We were fighting a war back then. Stories tend to create legends that always arise from the muck," I tell Emily in hopes of tampering her expectations of me. "Don't believe everything you read, especially that which is in the form of a tale," I say with a chuffing laugh.

"Oh, don't worry there; I question everything or try to — to the best of my ability. A journalist not seeking the truth is just a fictional storyteller," Emily says with a laugh.

"What's so funny?" Adayln asks. She smiles while entering the bridge from our cabin.

"Nothing, Adayln; just two old souls, conversing about history," I tell her with a smirk.

"Old souls? *More like ancient souls*," Adayln mutters, sitting back down at her station. "I'm a few centuries years old myself, and I feel old. What name would you call me?" she asks us.

"Well, given the state of LaPorte Industries on your homeworld during the current and ongoing attacks, I would refer to you as One of the Lasts," I jest.

"The LaPorte facilities on Titan are still not back up and running?" Adayln asks with a moan, swivelling her chair around. "We are long overdue on the servicing of our SDS System. Mine is faulty," she adds, making me roll my eyes at her for bringing up such information to Miss Stellar.

"Don't expect LaPorte's Titan Industries to make any house calls anytime soon," Emily says, leaning in toward Adayln. "If an SDS pod goes down, it will have to stay down for quite a while — if not forever. This war may never finish," she says with a playful smile, looking over at Asia.

"Well, without the Titan facilities to fix anything," Adayln says, running her fingers confidently through the short hairs on her head, "I'm going to have to tinker with it myself."

"You will do no such thing!" Kaptin Keoh roars commandingly. He enters the bridge, wearing his traditional scowl. Keoh isn't as old as Emily or me, but he is close to it. Throughout his whole life, I don't believe he has ever changed his husk from any other look than his First-Biological form. He is proud of his Asian heritage and honours it to this day by keeping true towards his self-image.

"It's broken, Keoh," Adayln says, thrusting her hands sassily onto her hips.

"Self-diagnostics says it's functioning normally," Keoh says with a head nod. He walks over to the ops station. "There will be no tampering with the pods," he says, raising his index finger high in the air.

"It's a power issue, I can solve —" Adayln begins.

"No means no!" Keoh shouts back. "I'm in charge here; this is my ship. I named this husk Kaptin so you all know who is in charge," he turns to address us all.

"That diagnostic is wrong," Adayln tells him, storming over to the display in front of Keoh.

"Adayln, a young soul like you needs to learn her place," Keoh says calmly, placing his hand on Adayln's shoulder.

"I'm over three hundred years old; it doesn't take any extra centuries of wisdom to tell me that there is an issue with the SDS Systems," Adayln hisses behind clenched teeth, apparently trying to keep her composure.

"Let's not fool ourselves. We have all known of one another for many centuries. Let's not pretend that we don't know each other's intentions," Keoh says. As he paces in front of us all on the bridge, he ensures strong eye contact. "This is an eclectic manifest of people on a long journey to back to Earth. I expect this trip to go smoothly and without incident from here on out," he continues to remark aloud in his booming voice.

"Are you implying something, Keoh?" I ask, feeling confused by his boorish grandstanding.

"Miranda Sage, you of all people shouldn't have a need for clarification," Keoh says slowly with waning disdain clearly in his tone of voice.

"Perhaps some clarification would be nice," Emily comments. She chuckles lightly, perhaps in an attempt to soften him up a bit.

"This is my ship. I'm in charge. There is no Law of Ages or Wisdom to outrank me here," Keoh says dramatically while caressing the smooth walls of his ship. "The Collector Array will be fixed soon; the SDS Systems are working just fine. I want no more talk of this for the next eighty-eight years," he then commands.

"Well, we will all be in Penticton, within the SDS," Emily says still laughing. "We won't be spending much time talking to one another anyway," she banters, trying to be witty.

"If my pod lasts that long; I keep dying," Adayln whines. She sits down and shakes her head. "What are the chances of that?" she groans softly.

"That is pretty rare, but not unheard of," Emily tells her with a wink.

"Didn't feel like normal quick deaths," Adayln mentions again, looking at all of us for someone to believe her. Keoh quietly approaches the bay doors, sighing loudly as he exits the bridge. He is clearly bored of this back and forth exchange.

"What do you mean it didn't feel right?" Emily questions Adayln in a journalistic tone.

"It just didn't feel natural, it felt manufactured — like a glitch," Adayln says — the girl just can't keep her mouth shut.

"Death is death; what do you mean by natural?" Asia asks, swivelling her chair to face Adayln.

"Well, it would be easier showing you, Asia," Adayln says with a smirk, pointing at her SDS pod in the adjacent room.

"It's against LaPorte Industries Conscious Ethics to insert an artificial conscious into an SDS System," Asia says, looking horrified at the idea.

"I heard it just doesn't work," Emily adds her knowledge to the discussion.

"*LaPorte Industries,*" Adayln says mockingly, tossing her hands up in the air. "Everyone is so afraid of LaPorte Industries."

"Well, they are the ruling body that propagates our species with increased longevity," I state, matter-of-fact, while giving her a mindful glare.

"So, they have created a technology; it doesn't mean LaPorte Industries owns us," Adayln says passionately minus any correct understanding of our species. The nerve of speaking of treason in front of a journalist; she's clearly stupid.

"But the exile from our society would mean certain death," I remind Adayln in a sharp tone of what our species values in longevity.

"Says who? LaPorte? Who cares about LaPorte and those silly rules," Adayln complains like the spoiled PHR reject that she has always been.

"They have these rules to keep us living forever," Emily pleas, trying to reason with Adayln.

"Oh, I'm not going to win this argument; why do I even try?" Adayln says resoundingly in defeat, turning her chair to pick up her handheld display off the console. Asia smiles awkwardly at both Emily and me before going back to work at her station. She feels the group discussion is at a close.

I exhale mightily, hoping that is the end of it. Adayln is just piquing too much interest with our auspicious new guest. Emily will make that spotlight burn increasingly hotter if Adayln doesn't heed my warning to shut her trap.

Chapter 3

Torstein and Mikken's cabin hatch door slides eerily open as just Asia and I are on the bridge. We both turn our gaze to look inside.

"*The crypt finally opens,*" I whisper to Asia from the side of my mouth with a laugh.

"Oh, you are a race that likes to think that they know it all," Asia says, turning her head to fully face me.

"The human race has always strived —" I begin.

"Don't give me that nonsense — human race?" Asia says, shaking her head. "You're no more human than I am," Asia remarks passionately, apparently having added a touch of sass to her attributes table since we last spoke. She's definitely less wooden than before.

"That may be somewhat true, but there is a clear difference between you and me — I've been human," I say to Asia with absolute authority.

"I'm surprised you even remember," Asia retorts with a hideous laugh.

"What is that supposed to mean?" I ask sharply, feeling offended.

"Oh, it's just nothing," Asia responds smugly.

"Don't be coy, Asia; speak your mind. You're no slave," I tell her. I can sense that this visibly annoys Asia, given the conflict between our two species over slavery.

"That's the one human trait you people couldn't forget to abolish moving forward throughout time," Asia says with a sneering curl of her lips.

"Speak your mind, Asia," I press. "You don't think I remember being human?" I try to tease out what she truly believes. AIs with her level of self-controlled empathy have been known to go rogue. I need to see if Asia is genuinely trustworthy, regardless of how much I respect Keoh.

"I believe that spending most of your hubris in that contraption has whitewashed and perverted what you once knew of being a human," Asia unleashes, looking over at Torstein's SDS pod with disdain. "What you do in there doesn't add to your abundant humanity; it diminishes it," she explains, not moving her eyes from the SDS pod.

"Care to elaborate, Asia? You're a bit vague on facts and extremely melodramatic," I tell her with a laugh, making her look up at me with a stony stare.

"That SDS pod is a drug; you are all a bunch of drug addicts. Your whole species is," Asia says with contempt, looking at me with a frown.

"You need to turn down your emotions — you just don't understand," I tell her, as Asia has become noticeably unnerved. "See, when you are in the Deep Sleep, you close your eyes for what feels like a second, opening them again right away. Time has passed, but none of it is felt. Our consciousness has expanded with this new life, and then we see if it has changed us at all," I continue to tell Asia of the glory she will never experience.

"You all love being in there — you spend more time in there than out here in the Real Realm," Asia says mockingly. "Look at Torstein: he is so addicted — so acclimated, unable to tolerate being out of it. Just look at him. Torstein is twitching; he is not even subtle about it. Torstein could turn that affliction off if he chooses, but he doesn't care. He just wants to be back in his box." We both look on at poor Torstein.

Asia is right about Torstein; he is progressively worse. "Torstein is also very poor, Asia," I inform her. "He only owns the one husk with no backup," I bring up a valid point that could explain Torstein's odd behaviour.

"If LaPorte Industries, your drug dealer, could start up its full production again, prices on husks wouldn't be so scarce and at a premium," Asia remarks, knowing full well her kind is to blame for our production woes.

"*I doubt you'll see that happen anytime soon, with the war on Titan still raging on,*" I say to her under a tight-lipped sneer. "*It will be a long while until LaPorte can start up production again.*"

"Well, until then Torstein best not stub his toe," Asia says to me with a smirk. "Perhaps he's more human then either one of us," she remarks with a profound smile.

I pull up closer beside Asia as we both continue to stare in unison at poor Torstein, who is acting all skittish. "More human?" I ask, confused. "Why do you believe that?"

"He lives with the fear of permanent death, something that humans once used to carry with them," Asia says with a sly wink. "I have multiple replacement Asia bodies at my disposal," she then adds with a nod of her head.

"And I have more than few husks kicking around," I tell Asia. We both break out in laughter, still looking on at that fickle-minded Torstein.

Torstein shakes with an uncontrollable tremor rippling throughout his whole body as he nervously bites down on his fingernails. Perhaps he is more human than all of us, as Asia stated earlier. He just doesn't look like someone who belongs in this century. Mikken attends to Torstein by bringing him a tray of husk supplements, as Torstein refuses to leave his SDS pod. His hand is placed firmly on the lid, stroking its smooth surface; he apparently has become attached to it.

As I approach Torstein and Mikken, Torstein starts to tremble more aggressively with sad eyes like that of a lost small child. This poor soul wants nothing more than to be put back into his box, to hide away from the Double R.

"You boys ready to assist in the repairs of the Collector Array?" I ask them calmly, holding up an updated damage report.

"Pardon me what?" Torstein remarks abruptly, sitting up straight.

"We were hit by an anomaly and the collector array needs —" I begin.

"No, I heard you," Torstein tells me with a nervous stutter. "I booked passage on this ship to take us to Earth."

"Yes, we have all booked passage on the *Misfit*, but this ship needs repairs," I tell them both, looking over to Mikken for more positive thoughts on the matter.

"What hit us?" Mikken finally chimes in. "Was it an asteroid?"

"Not sure — it's Mikken, right?" I ask him, as this my first time interacting with him verbally.

"Yes, and you're Miranda Sage," Mikken tells me somewhat excitedly.

"Oh, have we met before?" I ask, not recalling any Mikkens from my vast memory.

"It was a long time ago; I believe you went by Lena back then," Mikken explains with a light laugh as Torstein shakes his head. "Must have been four hundred years ago now," he then enlightens me after appearing to calculate the math.

"Oh wow, Lena — I was wild back then in that carnation." I smile in reflecting, pondering the exploits I got up to in that husk.

"Were you Mikken back then?" I ask him, leaning in close.

"No, I went by —" Mikken begins.

"Hello!" Torstein thunders rudely. "Sorry, can we finish this reunion another time and continue with the pressing topic at hand?" he then asks with a shudder.

"Well, the plan is for you, Mikken, and Adayln to assist Asia in the repairs of the array. While Keoh and I —" I start to explain.

"I go outside the ship to fix the Array? I think not," Torstein refuses soundly with yet another jolting interruption

"The manifest says you're a mechanical engineer," I read out to Torstein from my handheld display.

"Engineer? Do not insult me," Torstein utters with a gasp. "I'm the creative soul behind Twin Parallel Communication. Engineer, pfft — I've contributed my mind to our society, and I'm done with aiding our species any further," he continues to scold.

"I mean you no disrespect; however, you are the most qualified person on the *Misfit* to aid in this repair," I inform Torstein, having scanned the attributes of everyone else who is on board this ship.

"C'mon, Torstein, this is The Real Realm, a true Double R adventure, we may never have another thrill like this for another two to three hundred years," Mikken says, trying his best to get Torstein to help.

"This is the only husk I have; I can't afford another," Torstein states, looking back over to his SDS pod. "*No, I will just observe,*" he then mumbles.

"Ahh — c'mon, Torstein; we need you," Mikken says, gripping him by the shoulders. "You won't even have to leave the ship; just communicate the instructions to me via the bridge," Mikken suggests, pointing in the direction out of the room.

"The bridge, no, no, no," Torstein states with his right hand firmly pressed on his pod, "I'm not leaving this room."

"Okay, well think about it," I tell Torstein, realizing that we are not going anywhere on this topic. I turn to leave the cabin trying to re-work the array repair plan.

"Miranda, wait up!" Mikken says, walking up to me as we both step out onto the bridge. "I'm sorry about Torstein; he'll do it. Torstein is just umm —" Mikken struggles to finish his thoughts.

"Torstein's broken. I'm not even sure of what help he can be to us, given the state that he is in," I tell Mikken, matter-of-fact.

"I know he looks rough and clearly has SDS sickness," Mikken says, wiping his eyes. "Torstein can help, he will help," he then assures me with an unconvincing head nod.

"How long has he been bleeding?" I ask Mikken. I peer over his shoulder to see Torstein still sitting in his room, swaying his body uncontrollably from side to side.

"Oh, about four hundred years now; that's why we are heading back to Earth. He needs a full purge and reconstruction," Mikken explains, stroking his chin while in reflective thought.

"But if Torstein can't even afford a new husk, how can he possibly afford a full purge and reconstruction?" I ask Mikken, bringing his watchful gaze back to me.

"He'll have to work for SDS Credit. I haven't told him that yet. It's a process telling him anything lately," Mikken says with a disdainful look on his face.

"Do you know what happened to his consciousness?" I inquire, having seen many of our kind with horrible afflictions.

"Torstein is old. *One of the Firsts* in Norway to get a LaPorte SDS Systems back in those early days," Mikken says with a slight smile. "You remember the Skaha Edition?" he then asks, making me grin.

"Yes, the one with the blue stripe along the side of the pod," I say in amazement. "You're not saying that Torstein owned one of those models? They were horribly faulty," I recollect with a laugh.

"Yes, the very same," Mikken confirms with wide eyes.

"What happened to him in there?" I inquire, ready to hang on his next words.

"There was a rendering issue, and his stasis avatar had a traumatic death. Believe the avatar committed suicide before we had those safety protocols firmly in place." Mikken's words are making me shudder. "Torstein's consciousness became awoken in the Penticton realm right before he died. A fission-crack shot clear through his consciousness," he continues to explain in all graphic horror.

"He's damn lucky the SDS didn't wipe out his consciousness altogether," I say with a gasp. "Those early LaPorte SDS models — what were people thinking putting so much trust in them?" I ask Mikken, shaking my head — those perceived sound-minded fools.

"*Those who have perished have laid a safe passage so we may prevail in longevity,*" Mikken recites peacefully from our ancient mantra that I haven't heard spoken in many a century.

"Spoken like a true Longevist," I remark with a laugh.

"I'll get Torstein to help. I'll find a way — I always do," Mikken reassures, placing his hand confidently on my shoulder. I take one last look at Torstein with his lips mumbling away to no one, knowing that Mikken has his work cut out for him.

———❧———

"Now if truth be told," Keoh begins, "you may have noticed that we have a bit of damage and we could use your help in the repairs," he continues in a swirling flowery way.

"It would be my pleasure," Emily offers, complete with a gracious smile. "I don't mind a little Double R labour — nor do I shy away from it."

"That's good; we need someone to help align the Collector Array once repaired," Keoh says, bringing up the *Misfit's* damaged array on the holo-display. "See — right here, that section will be needed to be swapped out. It will take all of us, or this trip home will take longer," he says, exhaling loudly.

"Longer —" Adayln laments like a whiny adolescent soul.

"Yes, Adayln — longer," Keoh says disdainfully to his moaning crewmate.

"We are not getting a full photonic distribution which means the array is only collecting seventy-two per cent of all photonic matter," Keoh states, assessing the damage while rotating the holo-display around.

"An extra seventy-seven years to our journey," Asia remarks pointedly to Adayln.

"Well, let's fix this thing and get on our way," Adayln says, swivelling her chair back to her station.

"We'll need someone to go outside the *Misfit* and weld in the replacement collector," Keoh says, looking around the room for a volunteer.

"Torstein is the most qualified," I tell the group. "However, he is struggling with a bad case of stasis bleeding. I witnessed it firsthand," I mention with a cringe.

"Oh — ouch," Emily says with a scowl. "I've seen my fair share of those with that affliction."

"Mikken believes he can get Torstein to help, but I'm not that optimistic," I inform them. "Torstein is in no right state of sound-mind to be out there," I inform Keoh, hoping he will drop that plan of action.

"Well, damn it!" Keoh utters loudly. "Looks like we will be going back hobbled, due to that damn anomaly. Who would leave that in the middle of the road?" he continues to complain, looking out the main bridge window at our mysterious orb. "I'm going to talk to Torstein," Keoh says, focusing his mind back on the necessary task. "I'll be the judge of his state of mind — I'm the Kaptin, remember," Keoh says bombastically, opening the hatch to Torstein's quarters.

"So, what actually hit the array?" Emily asks, tilting her head dearly to the side.

"Couldn't gain access to what has hit us, though it is definitely not natural in origin," I tell Emily, showing her the scan details up on the holo-display.

"The main deflector didn't pick up the obstruction in our path while we were travelling at light speed," Asia adds from her console.

"*Who would leave an object out in the middle of a Galactic Light Highway?*" Emily mutters aloud, approaching closer to the holo-display to get a better look.

"The anomaly is one eighth the size of the *Misfit*, which should have easily been able to push it aside using the main deflector," I explain to Emily. I point firmly at the image. "The anomaly is spherical in shape with a metal alloy composition of —" I begin.

"Sorry, the anomaly?" Emily jumps in, shaking her head. "That's not going to get readers to partake in the transcript of this event," she continues to ramble while holding out a digital stylus to point at her handheld display.

"Emily, we don't know what it is: an anomaly is a proper classification," Asia explains. Looking at me, she appears just as confused by Emily's interjection.

"Yes, I know that, but can we call it something else — something more interesting?" Emily pleads passionately, tapping her stylus on her chin, visibly thinking.

"Not everything is a story, Emily," I say with an eye roll, grabbing the damage report from Asia's outstretched hand. "The *Misfit* is damaged because of that thing. I don't care what you want to name it," I then say to Emily. I am putting my mind back to work.

"Is the anomaly secure?" Emily asks, turning her head towards Asia.

"Secure in our tow net, although we haven't had to tow an object of that size with a damaged array," Asia states in a matter-of-fact tone. "The size and weight of this object will put a strain on our light systems, greatly impacting our travel time back to Earth," she adds.

"How long of an impact are we looking at?" Emily asks quickly as she jots down what Asia says with her stylus.

"About another seventy-seven years," Adayln answers with a groan, looking up at Emily.

"Seventy-seven years, eighty-eight years, ninety-nine years, it's all relative," I say, handing back the damage report to Asia. "An extra thirty per cent of a light year means we will all just be spending more time in our boxes."

"A peach!" Emily makes this odd remark while looking intensively at the holo-display.

"A peach?" I ask her, not sure of what Emily is speaking about.

"The anomaly looks like a giant metal peach," Emily says with an eager smile, looking at me with her stunning sapphire eyes. "It's round with a slight crease from top to bottom, like a peach," she says, using her finger to trace the dent in the anomaly.

"You want to call it a peach?" I confirm, not sure if that helps shed any light on the fact that it is still indeed an anomaly.

"It will help the reader visualize in their minds exactly what the anomaly looks like," Emily says, writing away on her display as she speaks.

"A giant peach — yes, I like that," Asia remarks with an affirming head nod.

"Well, looks like your AI readership will respond favourably to your creative description," I say to Emily with a chuckle. "I don't care what we call it; I just want to know what it actually is," I say, rotating its holo image around and pondering what it may be.

"Well goddamn it," Keoh says, coming back onto the bridge.

"Did you convince Torstein?" I ask sassily, already knowing the answer.

"Naw, we can't use him," Keoh says disparagingly. He looks down and scratches his chin. "The man is too fragmented."

"Okay — looks like it's up to me," I say, giving off a big sigh while stretching my arms high above my head.

"You know how to weld a collector into place?" Keoh asks me, his tone more diplomatic than usual.

"No, but it can't be that hard," I tell him with a chipper smile. "I want Torstein on a Comm-Set though. If Torstein refuses to go out there, he can at least walk me through the job," I assert.

"That's a two-person job," Emily says, still looking deep into the holo-display of the damage. "Suit me up; I'll join you," she says calmly. Her offer to volunteer makes Keoh's eyes widen.

"Miss Stellar, that is mighty kind of you," Keoh says graciously with a glistening smile. "We'll all meet in ten hours and commence with the repairs," Keoh commands. "Asia, unhinge another collector from the aft bay. Ten hours, people; let's get this done and then we'll be on our way."

———⟡———

Emily and I secure the replacement photonic collector into the damaged section with zero complications. Thankfully Torstein agreed to help via the comm-system when Keoh told him that the repairs will just take longer without his help. Torstein, wanting nothing more than to be back asleep in his box, agreed almost without hesitation.

I would have had to play a guessing game hooking up this replacement piece without any help; it was a damn jumbled mess of optic fibre. We needed Torstein's intellect in this matter to piece everything back in place — none of us would have had the patience to read the user manual.

"We make a good team out there," Emily remarks, hanging up her spacesuit.

"Thank goodness you volunteered to help; it was daunting to think that I would have had to do this all on my own," I tell her. We both move to the window and I take another look at the mysterious object.

"I wish more people would enjoy partaking in the splendours of the Double R," Emily laments, also looking out the port window at the safely secured anomaly being towed behind the *Misfit*.

"I agree; we are both sound-minded in that fact," I tell Emily. I feel that we are more or less the same in our mind-speak as we are in our age.

"So, what do you think it is?" Emily inquires, looking at me through the reflection of the window.

"The Peach?" I ask Emily in a playful tone while looking over her shoulder. "It's man-made — no question about it. There is a design to it that signifies a creative mind," I share.

"And yet we can't peer inside with the scanners, and there are no visible openings anywhere on — *The Peach*," Emily says with a grin, enjoying her name for our enigma. "This is exciting!" Emily shouts with a shivering shimmy. "This is every writer's dream."

"It could just be nothing," I tell her as we walk in unison outside the aft-hatch back towards the bridge.

"Nothing?" Emily gasps, giving me a horrified look. "A Double R mystery, in our day and age — no, this is something," she utters with resounding confidence.

"Well, ya, it's obviously something," I say with a deep-down feeling that I've debated this soul many times before. "I'm saying that it could just be garbage that has fallen off a cargo ship which happened to get in our way." I am trying to lower her high expectations for a fantastic revelation.

"That's always the possibility in a story, Miranda," Emily says grabbing my wrist with her delicate fingers. "That's what differentiates the good tales from the bad. However, until the final epilogue of *The Peach* is told, we can still enjoy its arching manner to play thoughts of wonderment within our minds," Emily explains somewhat sassily.

"Well, I guess if you are hurting for a story for the masses — one can always look deep into any trivial thing which lacks a definite conclusion," I jest. My bow shot at her journalistic core makes her release that affectionate hold on me.

"Oh Miranda, I'm not hurting for story ideas," Emily says with a laugh. "I can still spin yarn after all these centuries."

"I apologize for my tone; I mean no disrespect," I say, feeling that I should soften my wit a notch. "I hope *The Peach* is a revelation for the ages," I say, followed with a gracious head nod.

"Well, thank you, Miranda," Emily says. "It's a gift for all of us to witness such a delight at our vast ascendance in age."

"In ninety years or so, we'll have it cracked open. Once we get back to Earth," I remind Emily of our upcoming long pause in this realm.

Emily and I enter the bridge and make our way to the Ops Station display to take a closer look at our handiwork. "Miranda," Adayln calls out with a hiss, sticking her body awkwardly out of our cabin hatch doorway.

"Yes Adayln," I ask looking over at her.

"Can I speak to you?" she asks nervously, holding her handheld display against her chest.

"Yes, what is it?" I ask Adayln, looking over at Emily in bewilderment.

"Alone," Adayln says. "It's private."

"Okay," I say, shrugging my shoulders. I tell Emily, "I'll just be a minute."

I enter our cabin as Adayln leads me to our kitchen nook and motions for me to sit down. "What's going on?" I ask.

Adayln leans in close across the table to whisper, "*I know you told me to drop it, but I think I can get us an answer to what we saw.*" I groan at the thought of wanting to be a part of two Double R conundrums.

"Yes, I told you to drop it," I tell her with intensity. "Certain answers to life are just not there for us to grasp."

"But it's a lie — we can't live with a lie this big," Adayln attests, shaking her head.

"It's intriguing, yes, but we can't do anything with that data to state otherwise when the facts we have already been told are gospel," I remind Adayln soundly as she must realize that this will lead her nowhere closer to any divine truth.

"*Well there is a way,*" Adayln says sheepishly, looking down at her lap.

"What way?" I ask, rolling my eyes.

"We enter awake and check it out," Adayln says, bringing her gaze cautiously back up to me.

"Are you crazy?" I say in shock. "You want to fracture that?" I ask furiously with a firm point at her temple.

"Not if we are smart about it," Adayln says with a simple shrug. "In and out from being asleep, just to take a peek with our conscious minds awake within the SDS System," she then mumbles with foul-speak once again.

"Do you have any idea how many laws you will be breaking?" I ask.

"Well, how else can we find out?" she pleads. "It's not like we can ask LaPorte about what this anomalistic data means."

"Adayln, even if you wanted to, the safety protocols don't allow for our conscious minds to enter awake," I remind Adayln. I cross my arms and look at her. "Put this notion far from your mind, child," I say heatedly.

Adayln slides her display across the table at me; I catch it before it falls into my lap. "What if you have access to change all the safety protocols?" Adayln ask amusingly. I look at her screen showing the inaccessible safety protocols wide open for manipulation.

"What is this?" I ask intensely, thinking only of treason.

"The power surge from when we hit the anomaly," Adayln tells me. "We have full access to Penticton — *Unabashed,*" she whispers joyously.

I scan the display, looking into areas of code that I haven't seen in many centuries. This area has been safely locked down after so many hacks in the past. If people would have only realized that those protocols were in place for their own well-being. So many people perished in their tinkering pursuits to dig deeper in this gift box for more than what they deserved.

We have made grand improvements over the ages to get the SDS Pods' failure rates down to a mere eleven per cent, a far cry from the three-quarters chance of death from eons ago. Being awake in today's SDS pods is reasonably stable, as long as the power doesn't fail. What am I thinking about? I ask myself. I won't give any thoughts to Adayln's tale of fancy.

Do I deserve to know, to have an answer on what Adayln has discovered? Well yes, being *One of the Firsts* should entitle me to that. However, it is treasonous to even make such a request without implicating Adayln in having access to the SDS subsystems.

Like I would also be granted the reflection of a real answer — my status of being Lena Sage helped to cement that notion. I am *One of the Firsts* though — I've done many great things in the thriveship of our great species. I deserve to know; I've earned it — no one needs to know if we take a peek.

"What's your plan?" I ask Adayln blankly.

"So, are you interested?" Adayln asks as her eyes light up.

"Let's hear your plan first," I say calmly to temper down her expectations.

"We awake, maybe for a week and —" she starts to say.

"Stop right there," I interrupt. "No chance of surviving a week — twenty-four hours tops," I assert.

"That doesn't leave us with a lot of time," Adayln says, tapping her bottom lip with her finger. "I suppose it can still be done," she then agrees like she has been given a choice.

"What age will we awake?" I ask Adayln next.

"I can set it to wake us at any age, really," Adayln says, taking back her display. "Seventeen would be the earliest; the young human mind in the SDS isn't developed enough to hold our vast consciousness," she says, looking down at her display.

"Seventeen?" I ask while shaking my head. "No age could hold our vast consciousness," I correct her.

"We will just have to trim our attribute tables down," Adayln explains, still with her head down at her display.

"In fact, we wouldn't be able to take any prior SDS lives with us — there is just no room," she adds, looking up at me worriedly.

"It would be jarring at first," I say with a pondering look up at the ceiling. "I feel I could navigate it," I say reassuringly, bringing my gaze back to her.

"What's the term — it's like being on a bike," Adayln says, butchering the phrase.

"It's like riding a bike," I correct her, rolling my eyes.

"You know what I mean," Adayln says with a shudder. She is somewhat embarrassed by her youth.

"So, at seventeen, we awake with no attributes table for twenty-four hours — and you can set it to just wake us?" I ask, realizing that's a tall order especially for her.

"We have full access to the protocols; I could set multiple parameters." Though Adayln speaks with confidence, her look says otherwise.

"And how would we find each other's stasis avatars?" I inquire calmly, standing up. "We won't know who, what, or where we will be in town," I explain, ensuring Adayln is aware of the problems with this type of expedition.

"I can modify the Soul-Mate protocol to play a thought in our head to remind us both to meet somewhere in town," Adayln suggests, looking back down at her display.

"Okay, set it up," I tell her. Adayln smiles up at me. If she is so determined to break these protocols, it's best that I am there to witness this treason. It may come in handy at her trial.

"I'm going to join Emily again," I say before heading back towards the hatch door. "Twenty-four hours," I remind her. "I don't want to be awake a minute longer."

"Twenty-four hours, I got it," Adayln quips with a bit of her sass. "*I know how to lock in a protocol.*"

Chapter 4

"I'm a minimalist as a token of love — prepared for that one day when I shall be enraptured by another. So, I give you this blank canvas for you to fully roam — unimpeded by skeletons that remind you of my past — good or bad. This will allow us to carry forth in an uncluttered future. I don't want my possessions to own me — I want you to own me. Let's make this shared space together with things we can both appreciate looking upon. So, will you stand next to this withered husk of a body, and make a future with me of similar pursuits?" I inquire of my love.

"Did you just ask me to marry you, Norran?" Whenwig inquires, oddly using a suggestion of primitive intent.

"I contend that is an acceptable-ask — to marry you," I respond while pondering what two people may require to enter themselves into marriage. "To love someone forever was created in a time of limited understanding of the term forever. In probable assumption, forty biological years was celebrated as a successful forever. In this world today, the term forever is a number our species feels it may reach. We just don't die any-more. We just keep going on and on — forever. We can force the hand of death upon ourselves or another, but that natural meaning of death — we face no forced affliction from it," I ramble on, feeling unnerved.

"Norran, you look perturbed," Whenwig says, caressing my cheek.

"I'm having second thoughts on the use and meaning of the known primal union of marriage and what I had intended to propose," I say frantically to Whenwig, cupping my hand over hers.

"Do you not love me, Norran?" Whenwig asks wistfully, apparently not having thoroughly thought it through herself.

"I do love you, Whenwig!" I stammer while dabbing my hot brow with the back of my hand. "I have loved you for the last two hundred and three years. Haven't I shown that to you with what we have painted in life on our blank canvas? We both remember marriage, as we both remember being biological. Marriage is for the human race, not for what we have become. Two hundred and three years is a long time, Whenwig. Who's to say how we may feel about each another after a thousand years together?" I ask heatedly in a vain attempt for her to listen to sound reason.

"If the gods can live in harmony together, then why can just we emulate them?" she asks, making me roll my eyes in disbelief. "They have lived together since the dawn of time, way longer than a mere thousand years. So, forget about your fears and remove those silly notions as you have transcended to be but a god," Whenwig says sassily, standing there menacingly with her hands on her hips.

"The gods fought, from what I remember," I say, standing back a safe distance. "How far back into the history of humanity shall we go? To the times of Zeus and Ares, or shall we go further back yet to when we drew our deities on the sides of caves?" I ask, crossing my arms and standing my ground.

"Don't be so dramatic, Norran. Many people are married, and they are doing just great," Whenwig tells me, trying to be reassuring.

"That's fine — that's their choice. I only have control over my own narrative. Two hundred and three years, Whenwig — that's already maybe a long time." I am now having serious doubts about this union.

Excerpt from *The Forever Love of Norran and Whenwig* Written by Lord Devlin Dixby (cc 2629)

"*The Collective Works of Lord Devlin Dixby,*" I read, peering over Adayln's shoulder. "What makes you want to read that drivel?" I ask wretchedly. Adayln turns her chair around to face me as I straighten up my stance.

"The man was a literary master from our own humanity. There are deep insights written in his words," Adayln tells me in a pragmatic tone, holding up her display.

"Literary master? I think not, Adayln. He was no Hemmingway, Murakami, or even Tolkien for that matter," I say to her loudly. She is making me laugh. "You PHR rejects just love holding onto the past, too confused and scared to embrace the future," I scold Adayln, not sharing one ounce of respect for a man who died before seeing the folly of his ways. "Tell us all: what story of his are you reading?" I ask Adayln. I sit down on the Ops Station chair next to her.

"Well, it's *The Forever Love of Norran and Whenwig,*" Adayln says, timidly clutching her display close to her chest.

"Oh, I kinda like that one," Emily says with an affirming grin. "It's a shame he only wrote two more stories after that ballad. He really was just starting to hit his stride after countless literary failures," Emily continues to recount as a stout lover of the written word.

"Norran and Whenwig?" I say, shaking my head in disdain towards the two main protagonists. "The man wrote twenty-two novels, yet only three of them were regarded as in the highest merits. *Great works of fiction?*" I say with a sneer. "I see his works as more bombastic and unprogressive. The man did our species a favour by dying in that fiery SDS accident when he did," I continue to explain my point.

"You don't mean that, Miranda; you must see the goodness in such written masterpieces," Emily says, attempting to sway my understanding.

"Lord Devlin Dixby, the title of Lord given by himself, was an unhinged, wildly eccentric blowhard," I tell everyone vigorously. "Only three works out of twenty-two are considered worthy to be read. That should disqualify him from the title of literary master."

"I quite enjoy his stories," Asia speaks up suddenly from the corner where she is working away.

"I've never understood the AIs' love for Dixby's writing," I say to Asia as she turns her chair around to join in the discussion. "What could you possibly glean from those pages?" I ask with a curl of my lip.

"It was actually Asia that introduced me to his literary works," Adayln quickly adds, nodding her head.

"I'm not surprised," I say, rolling my eyes. "An AI society with a limited history of their own to attach themselves must find some connection to any past. I'll give Dixby credit for one thing: his writing is better than anything created by your unimaginative species, Asia," I continue to scold.

"There is immense insight within the words of Dixby," Adayln says passionately. "Insights you'll never see, being as you are too closed-minded and blind to allow any new thoughts to enter your way," Adayln continues to speak as a young, foolish, and headstrong member of our species. She just doesn't know any better; Adayln still carries the trappings of our old biological ways of thinking. She may have transcended her mind, but her ideals are nestled far in the past.

"Insight!" I scoff heartily. "Norran was weak. Whenwig wouldn't have given him the time of day," I vent.

"It's a love story for the ages," Adayln shoots back, minus any compelling evidence to that fact.

"It was a love story common in the age it was written," I explain to Adayln. "Six hundred years later, the theme of the story serves no purpose. I was alive during those times when the notion of being married forever was still indoctrinated into our society.   The cults that arose from such inclusions into the advancement of our people were harmful, to say the least. When The Winter Purge happened, and two-thirds of our species chose suicide over a true everlasting path to God, I believe the correct verbiage from that era of time was *good riddance*," I say heatedly to Adayln, hoping this soul will see the folly in romanticizing such whimsical gibberish. She clearly lacks knowledge and just hasn't had the full scope of 1,296 years of being alive. "How long have you been a transcended husk?" I ask lowly of Adayln. She looks down at her lap.

"*You know how long, Miranda,*" Adayln mumbles. "I know you don't ask questions that you don't already have an answer for. But for the others here that may not already know, I'm 301 years of age," Adayln says, looking up at me.

"Just a baby," I say cheekily.

"Maybe in your eyes, but your eyes are blind — not only to me, but to the whole universe around you,"

Adayln says confidently with a smile. "One day you'll see the light, Miranda, and when you do, a person with your unique talents could tumble down walls so all may see," Adayln continues to ramble in a feverish rant, making zero sense.

"Enlighten away, Adayln; we have eighty-eight years until we reach Earth," I say while pacing in front of everyone and stretching my arms out wide. "Tell me what great insights that I have missed between the awkward and foolish love between Norran and Whenwig?" I ask firmly. My question makes Adayln roll her eyes, spinning the chair back around to continue her reading.

"So, I gather that you're not a fan of the late great Lord Devlin Dixby, Miranda?" Emily says laughingly, just as I sit back down next to her on the bench seating.

"It was drivel back then when Dixby wrote it, and it's still drivel today," I quip, still not understanding the appeal.

"You read them and were not in the least touched by the love stories?" Emily asks, surprised.

"No," I tell her soundly, having no more context to add to the topic.

"That's surprising," Emily says with her enormous toothy smile. I so envy the beauty of her husk.

"When was the last time you were in love?" Emily asks sharply, quickly making my senses go on high alert.

"I've been in love many times with many people," I reply, glancing down at her for asking such a silly question. *"No more than my beloved Cora, back when I once had a beating heart,"* I mumble softly. "I'm 1,296 years old — remember?" I remind her sharply.

"I didn't ask if you have ever been in love before," she clarifies. "I asked about the last time you've experienced love. And being in the simulated realm of Penticton does not count," Emily presses me like a journalist digging for an answer.

"I was Ambassador Lena Sage," I say with a chuckle. "In that carnation, it seemed I had a new lover every week."

"You're either avoiding the question, or it truly has been so long that you can't even remember," Emily tells me, crossing her slender legs to rest her hands comfortably in her lap.

"I've been in love plenty of times —" I start to say.

"When?" Emily asks again. "Name the last time."

"Okay, perhaps it has been a while in the Double R since I've wanted to share my conscious soul with another. Although that has no bearing on my literary opinion of Devlin Dixby," I explain. I feel somewhat aggravated by Emily's line of questioning.

"It's okay; it's natural for us to lose touch with our humanity." Emily reminds me rather coldly, placing her hand affectionately on my shoulder. "Love is something that our species has thrown to the wayside, having no need to propagate ourselves," she tells me while running her hand up and down my back.

"I've been in love many times. Those memories and those feelings associated with those memories are still within me. I do know and remember love," I tell her, but truth be told there's a struggle within my collective mind to dig deep into my soul. I don't want to recall.

"*Okay — Okay, no reason to get worked up; asking questions is what I do,*" Emily says in a pandering tone like I have become derailed. "I apologize. Sometimes my line of questioning cuts deep, and I don't realize it," she says with a sweetness which doesn't feel sincere.

"I'm fine — truly, Emily. I get defensive sometimes about my past," I say, sighing as I try not to remember.

"When you have lived as long as us, how can we not have some regret in life?" Emily comments. "Our minds were never meant to live as long as we have extended them," she continues as I feel the loving caress of her delicate hand moving down to my lower back.

"I take it you have experience love in the Double R quite frequently," I say, shifting my torso to face her. Her soft hand retracts back to her lap.

"I wish. I truly haven't been in love since I was a biologic," Emily speaks with immense sorrow. "I've coupled many times since, but nothing could replace those feelings I had back then."

"I take it that love of yours died as a biologic?" I inquire.

"No, she evolved to transcendence just like us. We weren't *One of the Firsts*, or even second for that matter. We hung onto our humanity for as long as we could. However, biology eventually breaks down, and you must ascend to continue forward," Emily tells me, thinking fondly of her once true love.

"Where is that true love today?" I ask intently. Emily gives off a serene look of reverence as she replays through the memories.

"No idea," Emily says blankly, snapping back to a serious facial expression. "You can blame the ages of time to cause that wedge between us. She's out there though; somewhere she's still out there."

"Miranda Sage in Love?" Adayln says with a giggle, hidden behind her chair. "I can't believe that for one minute."

"Check the dating archives," I say. "I'm sure there is a video or two of me expressing love towards another."

Adayln types away into her display. "I found one," she says quickly. "It's rather old, from the year 2650."

"Oh, I would have been Josie Sage back then," I tell her, calculating the math in my head.

"I would love to see it; do I have your permission, Miranda, to play this video?" Adayln asks eagerly. I nod my head to grant her access.

The playback begins, giving everyone a glimpse of one of my prior carnations from about six hundred years ago:

"Okay — record on. It's May 6, 2650. Hello again, Josie Sage here — my most sincere apologies for the lateness of my reply on that message you sent me. Yes, I still live in Northwest Cascadia, formally known as British Columbia.

I can also tell you that it was five hundred years ago today that we amalgamated to become that technological society of pure ideals. Our pioneering fathers of That Great Southern Valley can attest to that, not that I have ever held them in high regard.

I'm just a cog in our nation's development and deployment of technological intellectual properties. I work sales myself: SDS Sales Specialist number 141 to all the elite clientele of all Northwest Cascadia.

The commission cheques are putting me in high status among the rich and powerful. As a transcended human with limited social status within the hierarchy of the company — money is a big deal.

Oh, I'm getting an upgrade today and a new job assignment. I hope it's not off-world sales to the moon or Mars. Anyways, since Mexico has annexed itself to become Most Southern Cascadia, we should be able to winter there — for quite cheap. So, maybe we can get together someday — if our decades line up. Well — I'm babbling. I just wanted to wish you a happy Nation Day and thank you for that lovely message. Talk to you soon, love Josie."

"See, I was quite the romantic," I tell them all with a proud smile.

"Who gives a history lesson at the beginning of their dating video?" Emily says with a laugh.

"Wow, what a blazon beauty; I'm sold," Adayln says, followed by a sly wink. "I would have asked you out on a date if I were born back then," she adds with a snicker.

"Well, thank you, Adayln," I tell her, coyly tilting my head to the side. "Although sorry — you're not my type," I continue with a playful sneer.

"So, are you ready to go back in the SDS after forty-seven years?" I ask Emily, turning my body towards her in hopes of changing the subject away from myself.

"It will be nice to go back; I miss my home," Emily says with a long sigh.

"You consider the SDS home?" I inquire, finding it odd for Emily to make that connection to a manufactured simulation.

"No," she laughs. "I'm actually from the Real Realm Penticton. I grew up there as a biologic," Emily tells me. I wonder who she was — so long ago.

"In any of your SDS lives have you ever visited the Hidden Realms?" Adayln inquires rapidly with bated breath.

"*Hidden Realms?*" Emily scoffs. "I recall when they once had proper names."

"Wait, so you have visited the Hidden Realms while in the SDS?" Adayln asks, sounding surprised.

"No, not in the SDS; there is no need to visit them there," Emily enlightens us. "I was speaking of my life in the Double R. I lived in that area for over five hundred years before The Winter Purge destroyed the economy."

"What was it like?" Adayln asks, having never visited the Real Realm Earth. "I was conceived off-world, near Titan."

"It was no more real than what you experience in the SDS, from what I can remember," Emily says with a smile. She appears to be reminiscing. "My First-Biological memories are rather hazy. If it weren't so dangerous to enter the SDS awake — I would like to have the chance to compare."

"I awoke once within the SDS during its early years," I say, jumping in with my own personal past experience of SDS peril.

"Did you know that you were awake?" Adayln inquires, leaning in close to listen.

"Yes, from what I can remember. Luckily the system's safety protocols were alerted of my wakeful state, and LaPortan technicians were able to put my consciousness back to sleep," I report. Remembering this gives me chills.

"Were you okay?" Adayln asks with a gasp.

"All I can remember is that it was as real as the Double R," I tell them. "To tell the two apart is somewhat impossible."

"Yes, but was your consciousness still intact?" Adayln presses further.

"It was only exposed to that Penticton realm in a wakeful state for twenty hours. LaPortan technicians claim that no permanent damage was done. However, ten hours more and I would have needed serious consciousness reconstruction. Back then that would have meant a few centuries in a stasis pod," I tell her, feeling there is a reason I'm not a fan of recalling the recklessness of my youth.

"Do you know how LaPorte created this realm?" Emily asks, with a bit of journalistic twang in her tone.

"No, I was low down back then. 141st from the top at one point though," I tell Emily, thinking fondly of my work there. "I moved up the ranks quite quickly, being *One of the Firsts*. I was first to go from Sales to User Compliance and then to whatever else they wanted me to do. I was there for them," I tell Emily, sighing loudly for the greatness of my Double R life. "I was well-paid. After a while, as the centuries went by, I wanted a life of fun, something I had quickly forgotten. This gave birth to Lena Sage. I have changed husks multiple times, and I forever will be monikered to that one and only previous life. I've been Miranda Sage longer than Lena Sage, but I'll always be shackled to Lena. My exploits in that husk were —" I pause to think of the right word.

"Legendary," Emily quickly finishes off my sentence.

———

"Is the Collector Array online and operational, Asia?" Keoh asks commandingly, walking back onto the bridge to look over Asia's shoulder.

"System readout — confirms — a green light to go," Asia says, turning her head to look at him.

"Okay then, proceed back onto the highway," Keoh says as Asia sets the coordinates. "Take it slow — we don't want to blast the new collector out of place."

"Yes, especially since it was a task to replace," I tell them, sitting even closer next to Emily. I am expecting a bumpy re-entry. It may be lasers and light that we use to travel between colonies, but on a galactic scale, those lasers can pack a punch if you enter their field too fast.

"Slow, Asia — that's it — just like that," Keoh commands, resting his elbow on the back of her chair. You can feel the vibrations; it's like entering a rippling river tide in the waning days of fall. Enter too fast or at the wrong angle, and you'll be thrown out like you are in a fast winter melt.

Asia is guiding us in with an almost certain probability of success. If AI is good for one thing, it's driving and flying. No husk can compete with their precision. "Okay, we are in and back on course to Earth — collector reading at ninety-six per cent," Asia states, giving off one of her odd-looking smiles.

"Ninety-six per cent, not bad considering it's a patch job on a flat tire," Keoh says with a booming laugh. He looks creepily down at Emily. I can tell Keoh is smitten with Emily Stellar. With her husk body, who wouldn't be? However, as long as that I've known Keoh, many centuries to be sure, I have an unabashed good take on his soul. He is nowhere in the realm of possibility itself to find any shared attraction from a voluptuous Emily Stellar. Keoh should just go soundly into his box — he is way out of Emily's league.

"Alright, it's bunk time," Keoh says with a loud clap of his hands. "I'll inform Mikken and Torstein to start their SDS pods first," he announces before entering the hatch to their room.

"It's an old ship, the *Misfit*," I turn to tell Emily. "We can't power up all the SDS pods at the same time."

"No, that's smart," Emily says with a chipper smile, "we wouldn't want a fire."

"Pods one and two are online," Asia says. "Readings are normal."

"Okay good — alright, Miranda and Adayln," Keoh says, entering the bridge, "your pods are next."

"Kaptin Keoh, I insist that you and Miss Stellar go first, as a token of her helping us and all," I say to Keoh. He rubs his chin. He always knows when I'm up to something.

"Oh, I'm bunking with the Kaptin, no less?" Emily says, showing off her pearly whites.

"Well yes," Keoh says, somewhat embarrassed. "It was the only available open spot to umm —" he continues in a fluster.

"Well, that's mighty fine of you, Miss Sage," Emily says, standing up to save the Kaptin from fumbling into oblivion. "We'll gladly go next," she says, taking the Kaptin's hand and leading him into their cabin.

"*Good call,*" Adayln whispers. She is now standing beside me.

"*Good thing we have Miss Stellar's help,*" I whisper. "*Keoh was fixing for smelling something foul.*"

"Pods three and four are online," Asia says. "Readings are normal."

"*What about her?*" Adayln whispers, knowing that we need unobstructed access to the bridge to put her plan into play.

"Miss Sage — Miss Diaz, you are both free to enter your pods; power readings are quite stable," Asia continues.

"Asia, you head down to power cycle," I tell her firmly. "I'll be up for a little while."

"Oh, I don't mind waiting," Asia says, not moving from her chair.

"No, it's okay, Asia," I tell her with an added touch of sternness. "You can go power down."

"It's my job to ensure that all passengers are safely secured in their SDS pods before I may —" Asia babbles.

"Asia!" I say with a blunt interjection, "*Go — to — bed.*" My slow command emphasizes every syllable.

"If you insist," Asia says. She stands up, trying her best act emotionless.

"Good night, Asia," Adayln says with maybe a bit too much sass, however much deserved.

"Turn off the bridge lights," Asia says, sauntering off the bridge like a perturbed appliance unwilling to listen to reason.

The hatch door to the alcove closes, leaving Adayln and me alone. "Okay, so I need to load the protocol table for —" Adayln begins to tell me.

"Hold on," I say, grabbing Adayln's shoulder as she sits down at the Ops Station. "First, ensure that Asia is in power-down mode," I tell her with a head nod. I just don't trust that toaster.

"Geez, you Vets sure have an odd paranoia over AI," Adayln says, reluctantly checking on my wish. "Yes, she is powered down and plugged in — may I continue now?" Adayln says with youthful impatience.

"Take it down a notch, Adayln, or you won't make it to three hundred and two," I tell her. I am growing tired of her sharp lip.

"Okay, the protocols are in place, we are set to go," Adayln says. For the first time in my memory, I am experiencing chills before going into a box. I'm banking high that this will work without a hitch. I'm a fool to think that it won't; I've always been bound to happenchance of something unusual cropping up. Miranda, I tell myself, do try to survive intact this time. Let's not have a repeat like that Green Mountain Road incident. "Okay — we are really — doing this," Adayln stutters while standing up from the ops station. "I'll see you in seventeen years?" she asks. Adayln sounds like she's having doubts.

"Yes, we will get an answer to this query," I say confidently. We turn off the lights to the bridge before entering our hatch to go in for the deep sleep.

Chapter 5

I'm deep in thought as an ear-piercing noise loudly rings, making me slowly open my eyes. Half of my face is submerged in a pillow with my right ear muffling out the sharp sound. I roll over to lie on my back, thereby exposing both ears to the constant bellow.

A ceiling fan turns thankfully silently above in a clockwise direction; the morning sun shines relentlessly through my blinds. *It's morning time* shoots through my head, and I look to my left at a small clock radio that is still screaming for attention. I struggle at first attempting to silence it, eventually unplugging it from the wall to quiet it once and for all.

I sit up from the bed, swing my legs out to the side, stretch both arms out into the air, and release a massive yawn. It is many hours past dawn, approximately 7:02 a.m.; however; unfortunately, that is all I know. The last thing I recall is Adayln and I entering Stasis Deep Sleep. Now, it appears seventeen years have passed as I am fully awake within the SDS System.

Adayln did it. It worked. She successfully changed the protocols within the SDS. Adayln should be waking up today as well, probably feeling the same dizzy disorientation.

However, who am I?

Where in Penticton am I?

What is my name?

I scan the bedroom and see an abundance of fifth belonging to a teenage girl. The room is decorated in soft colours of pinks and yellows. Stuffed animals are piled in a heap in one corner of the room. Pictures of moons and stars adorn the walls, making me think that I must be an admirer of such celestial delights. A small desk is pressed up against the far wall with a mirror above it. I rise from the bed so I may catch a glimpse of what I may look like.

As I approach the mirror, I notice a haphazard collage of photographs decorating the perimeter of the frame. I peer closer at the images within the photos, but my reflection in the mirror grabs my attention when I come clearly into view. I am most definitely a girl. I am Caucasian with pale ivory skin and fiery crimson hair. I contort my body image in the mirror to scan what my whole body looks like, but the desk is in the way.

I grab the back of the chair and move it out from the desk for me to stand on. Holding the head-rest of the chair for support, I steady myself as I step onto the seat. The chair swivels and spins, but my balance is remarkably good. I finally lock the chair into place and get a full look at my whole body.

I definitely have the look of a seventeen-year-old teenager, about five foot two and one hundred and five pounds with a slender build. I shuffle my feet to get the chair to swivel so that I may get a better glimpse of my backside. Not bad, this will do, I confirm to myself with a head nod. My bedroom door opens following a knock on the door.

"Wake up, sweetheart. No sleeping in —" a woman says chipperly. As she peers in the room, she notices the empty bed. Her gaze then quickly sees me contorting my body on the desk chair with my behind facing the mirror.

"Honey, what are you doing?" she asks, shaking her head and rolling her eyes in disapproval. "You need to shower and get ready for school; let's go," she adds with a slight smile, looking back at my awkward pose.

I don't know who she is, but surmising that we have similar locks of hair, I take a chance and respond with, "Okay, Mom." I wait a few seconds to see if my assessment is correct, although it feels like many nervous minutes.

"Breakfast in five minutes," the woman says, calming my nerves. I have guessed correctly.

My mother then shuts the bedroom door as I hop off the chair. Still not knowing who I am, I begin to scour my bedroom for clues to this life. The collage of photographs around the mirror is made up of people who are of similar age to me, and I happen to be in most of them. I see lots of pictures at the beach or camping cluttered among close face-shots of goofy smiles.

My name comes clearly into view from the collection of gymnastic trophies and ribbons on the next shelf to the left of the desk. "*Josie Birch,*" I mumble softly. Looking over again at the mirror with my image clearly back in view, I say, "Josie Birch; I am Josie Birch." I repeat these words aloud to myself while staring intensively at my image to allow the name to sink in. *At eleven o'clock, the first day of awakening on May 1, 2005, we are to meet at the Skaha Lake Sundial*, starts playing loudly in my head, jolting me to fall to one knee. "*Well, there's Adalyn's protocol message. I hope she doesn't have this message set to a constant repeat,*" I mumble. I stand up.

"Josie, breakfast!" I hear my mother — Josie's mother, that is, hollering that my morning meal is ready. I frantically make my way to the bedroom door where I notice for the first time a poster of an attractive man with no shirt holding a firehouse draped over his shoulders. The face looks familiar, but I cannot place it.

The door opens into a narrow hallway with four other closed doors staggered in place along each wall. A large window drapes down the end of the hall, shining the morning light down some cascading stairs. I hastily make my way to the stairs, wincing as the blinding light hits me square in the eyes. I descend with a shuffle to the bottom of the stairs and blink rapidly when the view of the kitchen comes into sight at the end of the downstairs foyer.

The house doesn't have the feel of being newly built, as there is a mismatch of decors exposed in some wall corners. Hints among the chipped paint that can be clearly seen along the edge of the wall to the ceiling are always a dead-ringer for an old hovel. I pass a large portrait of a family and stop to look at it for a brief moment. I notice Josie and those un-missable crimson locks along with my mother and a man I assume is my father holding another girl with similar hair as mine.

"Josie, will you quit dawdling? Your breakfast is getting cold," Mother tells me as she notices me standing there in the foyer.

"Coming — Mom," I stutter awkwardly.

The kitchen is decorated in the colour of light lemony paint with powdery blue trim. The appliances looked worn and tired, not new and shiny. Large windows and a sliding door lead to a lush emerald grassy backyard, and the whole room is basked in a warm glow of early springtime sun.

"Why aren't you dressed for school?" Mother frets, while bringing dishes from the kitchen counter to the breakfast table. "Have you not showered yet?"

The younger girl from the family portrait is situated at the table and filling her mouth with waffle. She looks like a younger version of me and about half my age, perhaps around eight or nine years old if I were to guess.

"Well, sit down Josie — honestly, I don't know what's wrong with you this morning," Mother says, shaking her head.

"Sorry, Mom," I say while taking my seat. "I didn't sleep well last night," I quickly follow up.

"Up late reading those godawful science fiction novels again," Mother says, placing a giant waffle in front of me.

I look over to the little girl and smile at her. She just shakes her head, mimicking our mother's mannerisms. I pick up the waffle and take a bite, immediately tasting its sweet flavour.

"Mom, Josie is using her hands!" the little girl says with a disdainful finger pointing towards me.

"Josie, use your knife and fork; you were not raised by wolves," Mother says without even looking our way. The little girl smiles proudly as she continues to shovel more waffle into her mouth.

"Okay, I'm off to work. Make sure your sister is on time for school, Josie," Mother says. She proceeds to kiss us both on the tops of our heads. "I'll see you both after school," she says. She grabs some jingling keys off the smooth kitchen counter and makes her way to the front door.

"Bye, Mom," the little girl says through her mouthful of food as the door closes, leaving me at a loss for what to do next. I wonder how Adayln is making out. This thought briefly rattles in my mind. I look over at my younger sister, perplexed about what I need to do.

"What time is school?" I ask frenziedly. I am confused.

Puzzled, she looks over at the wall clock behind me and replies, "At eight-thirty." I follow her gaze to the clock to see that I still have an extra sixty minutes.

"I'm going to get dressed — I'll be right back," I reassure her as I rise up from my chair.

"Umm okay?" she tells me with a look of concern which confirms that I'm not acting like their usual Josie.

I head back upstairs, wondering how I'm going to be able to pull off this deception. Poor Josie was once living life as a happy teenager, only to have her consciousness pushed to the far regions of her mind and taken over by a much older consciousness. This is a tall order to be able to pull off. It's no wonder why our full consciousness is put to sleep while we enter SDS System.

Making my way back into my bedroom, I feel a resounding sense of remorse for Josie when I look at her pictures by the mirror. A feeling that I'm intruding into a mind that is not mine starts to overwhelm me and I begin to cry. There is a reason for these SDS safety protocols; there is a reason we enter this world blind and unknowing of the real truth of this existence.

I can clearly see why speculations and rumours of people going mad and insane within the SDS can be true. LaPorte Industries don't say as much when pressed about why our consciousness must be asleep while in SDS. However, I can see why. These feelings are overwhelming me, preventing clear sound thoughts from entering my mind.

"Josie?" a voice calls out for me. "You okay?" my little sister says at the entrance to my bedroom door.

"Yes, I'm fine — I'm fine," I tell her as she proceeds to sit down next to me on my bed.

"Why are you crying?" she asks, worried.

"I don't know — *I think I may have made a mistake*," I say to her with a bit of a ramble in my tone.

"What kind of mistake, Josie?" she inquires dearly. She sits down next to me and reaches out to hold my hand.

I look over at my miniature version of myself and smile while staring into her emerald eyes. "Nothing, it's nothing," I tell her, taking in a deep breath to help steady my nerves. "Let's get you to school," I tell her as she gets up from the bed.

"But you're not even dressed," she points out. I look down to see myself in pyjama pants and a t-shirt.

"Want to help me pick out an outfit for today?" I ask daringly, slowly gaining back more and more composure.

"Yes," she says, and with exuberant glee she runs over to my closet.

⟶ ∽∾⊙⟋⊙⟍⊙∾∿ ⟵

It's 8:10 a.m., and we are finally leaving the house to head to school. That small forty-minute window of bonding with my little sister helped greatly in focusing my thoughts from that sudden self-centring wallow.

I still don't know her name. I realize that some things cannot be forced without setting off alarms of more concern towards me. Her name will come in due time. For now, Little Sister will suffice.

Early May is usually calm in temperature. However, today feels like a warm summer day as the air pushes past our bodies. Little Sister has dressed me in a billowy above-the-knee dress, amber in colour; and a loose-fitting white fleece sweater. What is in fashion during this particular year is absence from my thoughts, so I am relying heavily on her recommendation.

The direction and orientation in Penticton I have yet to establish as I allow Little Sister to guide us away from the house. School is apparently within walking distance, as are most places in this tight valley-locked town. I notice the East Valley Wall up close with Mount Nkwala and the West Valley Wall far off in the distance.

Okay, good; I'm located in the east part of town. Now, what lake am I close to: Okanagan or Skaha? "Josie!" a voice calls out to me from down the street. A boy, similar in age to me, comes running towards us carrying an over-sized backpack. He has lemony hair with streaks of white, and a muscular build which he has evidently gained by moving with much homework on his back.

"Oh, it's Ryan," Little Sister says, shaking her head.

"Why do you shake your head about him?" I ask eagerly.

"Ryan has like the biggest crush on you, and he like really annoys you," Little Sister says, revealing to me more about the real Josie.

"Josie," Ryan says, collapsing with his hands on both knees when he finally catches up to us.

"Hello Ry-an," I stutter awkwardly as my first street sign comes into view to help aid me in my location. "*South — Main — Street,*" I mumble slowly, word by word, making Ryan and Little Sister look puzzled.

"Yup, that's right. And we are going to *turn — left — onto* — it," Ryan says mockingly slow, ending his statement with a laugh.

"What's wrong with you today, Josie?" Little Sister asks again. "She's been like weird all morning," Little Sister informs Ryan.

"Something is wrong?" Ryan asks with concern in his voice as he peers over at Little Sister.

"I'm fine, just tired —" I begin.

"She ate a waffle with her hands," Little Sister interrupts me.

"With your hands," Ryan says, looking back at me with his eyes wide.

"Well ya —" I attempt to explain.

"That's not weird at all; I do that all the time," Ryan says with a serendipitous wink, followed by a head nod. Little Sister seems to be silenced by Ryan, and she remains silent as we continue to turn left onto South Main Street.

Okay, I see the Cascadian Sun ahead of us, so we are facing south, and we are moving closer towards the direction of Skaha Lake. We must be heading towards Princess Margaret High; it is in this direction approximately three blocks away.

Wait — what year is it? Maybe we are heading to Skaha Lake Middle School.

No, I'm questioning myself.

The trophies — some of those gymnastic awards said 2003; it has to be Princess Margaret High. Skaha Lake Middle School didn't exist way back then. Keeping such facts may be a problem that Adayln and I didn't anticipate. Perhaps we should have studied our ancient history textbooks before we entered the SDS.

Beads of sweat start to trickle down from my temples. This is a hard task; Adayln and I are essentially blind as we navigate this world until we become fully acclimated to the inhabiting time frame. My heart rate begins to increase with unbound thoughts of paranoia. The feeling of extreme worry also rushes into my mind; there is a reason we don't enter this state while consciously awake. I keep seeing these reasons more and more as overwhelming feelings of—

"Josie!" Little Sister shouts, waking me from deep thought.

"Yes, Little Sister?" I blurt out while wiping the sweat off my brow. I blink rapidly and look at her.

"Little Sister? See Ryan, weird," Little Sister says, looking over to Ryan. She then starts walking off the sidewalk, and I follow suit, but I am quickly stopped by her.

"Where you going?" Little Sister turns back and says to me.

"Oh, to school," I answer her, confused.

"This is my school; your school is over there," Little Sister says, pointing over to her school, Snowden Elementary, then pointing over to the more massive building on the left, which of course reads Princess Margaret High.

"I know that," I say with an unconvincing smile. "I was just going to give you a hug goodbye."

"Whatever, see you after school, Josie," Little Sister says as she walks away, scratching her head. Obviously she is detecting my odd behaviour even more.

"You sure you're alright, Josie?" Ryan asks leeringly as he awkwardly tries to rebalance his backpack in a more comfortable position.

"I'm okay, Ryan. You go on ahead. I'll meet up with you later," I say. I turn away, with the thought of Skaha Beach still readily pounding in my mind.

"No chance of that," Ryan says, shaking his head. "I'm not one hundred per cent convinced that you're okay," he adds with an odd smile.

"Not convinced?" I ask with an exhalation. "Let me be!"

"Best that we hang out most of the day, just in case," Ryan rambles out with no sign of hiding his affection.

"Seriously, we are fine," I tell him.

"We? Who are we?" Ryan interjects quickly.

"Sorry, I — *I am okay,*" I say nervously.

"See, I told ya. I think your little sister may be right about you today," Ryan tells me. He moves in closer to place his hand creepily on my shoulder. "Come on, we have the first block together anyways. We're going to be late," Ryan says, glancing at his wristwatch. He then jostles his backpack again before heading in the direction of the main door to Princess Margaret High.

I can't go to school. I have to meet Adayln at the Skaha Beach Sundial at eleven o'clock. Going to school was never part of the plan. All that would be gained from that is exposing more people to the fact that I'm not the real Josie Birch. Oh, poor Josie; I feel so much sorrow for her.

"Josie, are you coming?" Ryan calls back when he notices that I am not walking beside him.

"Yes, I'm coming," I shout, sprinting to his side and falling into line with the narrative of Josie's life.

We enter through the main doors of this ancient structure that has been used for many decades as an institute for learning. The walls are a pastel lemon with bright cream trim running along the ceilings and floors. The central office, on our immediate right, is a bustle of teachers preparing for their day. To the left of us is a massive trophy case which spans the length of the wall. Many trophies from various sports align the shelves, highlighting achievements over the past many decades.

The sound of many balls bouncing off the floor gives the slightest of vibrations to permeate through our bodies as we approach the gymnasium ahead. The door swings open and I catch a quick glimpse of students bouncing mango-coloured balls in unison on the ground.

The school is busy with bodies pushing past one another as everyone scurries about in all directions. Metal lockers slam musically one after another with the cackling of young voices drowning out any attempt for Ryan and me to speak. My eyes are wide as I take in all this noise and distraction, marvelling at the reality created by the SDS system.

I have become accustomed to taking this world for granted as a necessary evil to be able to continue our long conscious life in the Real Realm. The human mind was not biologically designed to function for centuries upon centuries. There are only so many stimuli in the universe before we eventually grow tired and bored. Being able to put to sleep our vast consciousness, even for a brief stasis life, gives many of us old souls the will to persevere.

This, however, is not how SDS is meant to be utilized. It is a highly developed tool with locked safety protocols that are not intended to be tampered with by users of the system. Our curiosity may have just opened a Pandora's Box, yet one that was screaming for us to solve its riddle.

"Are you going to your locker or not?" Ryan asks hastily when we both stop to look at one another in the hall. I think about his question for longer than I probably should before following his gaze to the metal locker on my immediate left. That must be my locker.

"Yes, I need my book," I say before quickly turning to face the thin metal door. I am unaware in the slightest of how to open it. I have attended this school before in previous stasis lives, yet for some reason I can't recall any of those experiences to aid me. I know the thoughts are there, but the access to them is nowhere within grasp.

I reach out to the shiny chrome lock with its wheeled number dial, and when I touch it the remembrance of what to do yells swiftly into my mind. The bellowing instructions inform me of *What to Do* which is all good and well-intended advice. However, without knowing the three-digit combination, those instructions are less than useful. I grasp the lock with both hands, sharply aware of Ryan staring suspiciously over my shoulder.

What is the combination?

What is the secret code?

When no answer arrives immediately, I reserve my thoughts to secure yet another excuse for my weird behaviour to Ryan.

25-32-11 miraculously pops into my head right before I turn around to face him. Without a fret, I enter the three numbers in the proper sequence given. Unsure of where those numbers came from, a loud approving click disengages the pin and allows the thin metal door to swing open. A profound sense of relief shoots through me, releasing a quick, uncontrollable giggle.

"Which books do I need?" I turn to ask Ryan, still beaming with happiness that the door actually opened.

"Umm, math," Ryan says. He's rolling his eyes, but also smiling about my latest weird antics. I look back in the locker, notice the text bookbinding with math written along its spine, quickly grab it, and then shut the locker door. I stare intensely at the cover of the textbook while my body turns back in the direction of Ryan. The textbook cover has a most unusual picture of a sunflower below the sizeable titled print of *Math 12*. "What does a sunflower have to do with math?" I wonder aloud.

"Who knows, Josie. Come on, we're going to be late," Ryan says, grabbing my wrist to lead me down the hall.

The math classroom faces east with the morning sun blasting off the reflective desk surfaces that are scattered among the room. The room fills up quickly as more and more students push through the door. Ryan sits at a desk by the windows and points with his finger to the spot behind him, indicating where I am supposed to sit. I take my seat and look in wonderment at the entire classroom when it hits me again that I am not where I belong.

At eleven o'clock, the first day from awakening on May 1, 2005, we are to meet at the Skaha Lake Sundial, starts playing loudly again in my head with no way to make it stop. I look to the front of the room at the two large chalkboards and notice the analogue clock above. It's almost nine o'clock; I need to get out of here. This is not where I'm supposed to be. Yes, Josie is meant to be in math class; however, I must remember that Josie is not me.

Oh, poor Josie. My mind fills with sorrow again.

What have I done?

Chapter 6

The bell chimes as a thin, exhausted man walks into the room with a chiselled look of contempt hanging off his grizzled face. This fossil of a man is in his mid-fifties with colourless hair receding halfway to his crown. He is wearing an oversized, well-worn, dirt-brown knit sweater complete with a noticeable large hole in the back. The demeanour written upon his face shows that he doesn't care about such fashionable matters.

The Creature makes his way to the chalkboard and writes in big block letters: MR. GLENCROSS. He then has the nerve to strike a long underline below it, followed by two dashes intersecting the line in the middle. He sniffs repeatedly to allow air to enter his lungs. This is accompanied by a slight whimpering cough to clear them. *"He is an odd fellow,"* I mumble softly under my breath as Ryan turns and whispers to me with a mischievous grin,

"Awesome, substitute teacher."

The Creature revolves his neck around first to look upon the class before contorting the rest of his body. His tan, wrinkled pants also look quite baggy on his small frame. The staring continues for a long thirty ticks of the analogue clock above his head before he decides to speak.

"Mr. Hannah will not be here today due to the spring flu. Instead, you get me. My name is Mr. Glencross, and

I am your teacher," the Creature states loudly as his gaze shifts down towards his desk.

"*Substitute*—" A voice coughs out mockingly followed by some snickers from some of the students.

"Who said that?" the Creature asks, quickly lifting his gaze up from the desk to gawk at us all threateningly.

"Hmm — no one — no one chooses to speak up?" the Creature snarls with a smirk as I look over to my right to see the other students paralyzed with blank stares.

"Let me be clear if perhaps I wasn't already. I am your teacher today. Notice how I didn't add the name of *Substitute* in front of my title," the Creature tells us precisely with a commanding snarl in his tone.

"Yes, it's true; this is Mr. Hannah's Grade 12 math class. However, today it is Mr. Glencross's math class. I have taught at this school for over thirty years, mainly History. No one will ever hang the moniker of substitute in front of my title," the Creature continues. A strange sense of fear ripples through us as we realize that this teacher will not be pushed around.

His name sounds so familiar to me like I have attended a class with him before, perhaps in a different life. Thirty years of teaching — there is a good chance our paths have crossed before; it's just hard to recall.

"Now, like I said, I have mainly taught History, not Mathematics. So, would someone kindly tell me where in the text — why do we have an empty seat in the back corner?" The Creature's train of thought derails as he notices an empty desk.

"That's Kim's desk," a student on the far side of the room informs him.

"Kim, you say," the Creature repeats as he opens up a large folded placemat of attendance cards situated on the desk.

"Yes, here it is: Jennifer Kim," he says, removing her attendance card from the placeholder. "Anyone know where she may be?" the Creature asks fiercely, but only a silent hush permeates through the classroom. He then writes onto her attendance card, placing it back into the placemat.

"Where is Thomas Wheeler?" the Creature then blares out, waving his attendance card in the air while not making eye contact with the class.

"He's right there, sir," another student says, pointing her finger to the door where a boy with shaggy hair is trying to peer through the small square window.

This Mr. Glencross slithers his way over to the classroom door, opens it, and asks, "Are you Thomas Wheeler?"

"Yes, this is my class —" the boy says as the Creature soundly shuts the door in the boy's face.

"Thomas Wheeler, absent," the Creature says aloud, scanning the room to see everyone's reactions before writing on the boy's attendance card. He then derisively tosses the attendance card on the desk.

"Alright, we have wasted enough time this morning on attendance. Now, where have you all left off in your math lessons?" the Creature asks us again as he sits on the edge of the desk, facing the class. No one speaks. Everyone's head is bowed low, not wanting to converse with this cantankerous old soul.

"No one then?" he says, contorting his body to turn the placemat around for him to read. "Let's see — Mr. Fields," the Creature says, looking in the direction where the boy should be sitting.

"Yes, Mr. Glencross," the boy says, looking startled.

"Where are we to continue in the lesson?" the Creature asks calmly and slowly.

"Well, what sir? I don't understand?" the boy stutters with a nervous frown. The Creature rolls his eyes and combs through his thinning hair with his fingers. He once again looks to the placemat of names.

"Miss Birch," the Creature then calls out, staring at me with his beady snake eyes.

"Miss Birch, that's me!" I say awkwardly, placing my hand on my chest. The classroom erupts in laughter from my announcement and my nerves start to swell increasingly from within my body.

"Quiet, class, quiet!" the Creature shouts as the classroom falls silent once again.

"Thank you for that revelation, Miss Birch. Now, are you able to enlighten us on today's lesson?" the Creature asks, visibly unnerved as a small vein on his frontal crown pulses.

"It's math, sir," I tell him. I hold up my textbook high in the air, pointing to the title above that curious sunflower. The class erupts with laughter once again as the Creature rises to his feet, shaking his head. He allows the laughter to continue longer than before as he just paces back and forth, tight-lipped, in front of his desk.

"*Josie — Chapter Fifteen — Quadratics,*" Ryan whispers in a severe tone with his head tilted to the side. The laughter slowly dies down as the Creature stops pacing.

"Chapter Fifteen, Quadratic Equations," Ryan volunteers.

"Chapter Fifteen, Quadratic Equations you say?" the Creature repeats, looking over at Ryan. "Sorry, what is your name?" he then asks Ryan, approaching closer.

"Ryan sir," he confidently tells the Creature with a nod of his head.

"So, your name doesn't happen to be Miss Birch?" the Creature asks sharply, tilting his head to the side and waiting for Ryan's response.

"No sir," Ryan says, confused.

"No, you are not. I believe I was talking to Miss Birch. Speak when you are called upon — this is not a zoo," the Creature scolds Ryan.

"*Chapter Fifteen—*" the Creature mumbles while flipping through his own math textbook. He then makes his way to the chalkboard. The textbook is fanned open within his left palm while he grabs a piece of chalk with his right hand. His chalk marks are loud and angry as he strikes down the equation from the top of Chapter Fifteen onto the chalkboard.

S squared + 3s = 0 he promptly writes out. The Creature then hold the chalk out to the students as though it is now awaiting someone to take it from him. "Who wants to solve for S?" he asks boorishly, swaying the chalk across the room.

"I will —" Ryan begins.

"Miss Birch!" the Creature shouts, interrupting Ryan.

"Yes, Mr. Glencross," I say nervously.

"Solve for S, Miss Birch," he repeats, rolling his eyes. I look over at the chalkboard and instinctively tell him: "S=0 and S= -3." There is not even a pause in my thoughts.

The Creature quickly looks down at this textbook still his palm. His expression slowly turns to a look of dismay when he sees my answer is indeed correct. He then retracts the chalk back out towards me and says, "On the board, Miss Birch. Write how you came to that answer."

I rise from my desk, smoothing out my skirt as I straighten my back. The Creature looks me squarely in the eyes as I approach him. His gaze then creepily follows the length of my body.

Who is this old man?

Why can't I remember who he was in my previous lives in Penticton?

There is something about him I just can't place.

I take the chalk from his grasp, and he caresses the top of my hand during the exchange. His touch feels reptilian, cold, and dry and I feel unwelcome shivers up and down my spine.

He goes around his desk as I go around the opposite side and he takes a seat in the desk chair. I look back at the students who are locked in crippling fear mixed with relief that they were not selected to be in my place up front. The Creature's chair squeaks as he swivels it about, adjusting the chair to go as low as possible.

Now, looking at the chalkboard, I place the chalk on the surface while sensing that his beady little eyes are piercing right at me. From the corner of my eye, I notice his vision is nowhere in the direction of the chalkboard. The Creature carries upon his face the most devilish of grins as he watches over me by scanning his gaze up and down my body.

I start to write on the board and move my head to look at what he is now stuck staring his fixed gaze upon — the full profile of my body. This adorable dress that Little Sister picked out for me, has captured his undivided attention. He shows little regard for hiding this. I reach out my right palm behind me, placing it at the top of my right hip. Then I gently glide my hand by pressing down on the fabric to follow the curvature of my behind. The Creature peers with his eyes at their fullest, licking his stained shark teeth. I finally remember who this man is.

The clinical term for him is Perverse Objectification. All biological humans live with this affliction; it's quite common. The disease is most prevalent in older males that have long outlived their youthfulness. This, Mr. Glencross clearly needs to be neutered to fully cure his mental desires. However, once you cut off that part of them, the other half of that dismembered party quickly follows to the wayside. Chemicals are another somewhat unorthodox method—

No!

Stop that!

Be of sound-mind!

I prefer castration! I scream in my head. I realize who I am.

I sassily drop the chalk to the floor and turn to face him.

"What do you think you are doing?" the Creature asks in alarm, sitting up from his slouched position in his chair.

"Enjoying the show?" I turn to say, tight-lipped and verbally annoyed.

"What show, Miss Birch?" he repeats with a snarl.

"I see how you are looking at me. Your hands are in your pockets; I bet you're even touching yourself. I know who you really are," I say aloud, walking closer to him as both of his hands are still locked in the pockets of his loose-fitting pants.

"What are you — talking — about?" he then stutters out.

"You're a pervert. The reason you don't teach full-time History anymore is that you were caught!" I tell this to Mr. Glencross, towering high over him.

"Stop this, you don't know what you are talking about," he blurts out nervously.

"In 1998, you were suspended for unwanted sexual behaviour towards a minor," I inform him while looking intensely into his perverted eyes.

"How do you know this? — There was a sealed affidavit," he rambles.

"Class dismissed," I say calmly, turning to the students as they sit there looking gobsmacked from what they just heard.

"Class dismissed? You can't say that. I'm the teacher here!" the Creature says, now visibly shaking with a tremor.

"Yes, a disgraced teacher who has been caught fondling himself to a seventeen-year-old girl writing on a chalkboard," I tell him soundly, standing with both my hands firmly placed on my hips.

"That's not true." The Creature stands up to face me, but there is no more denying it.

"Class dismissed!" I tell the students again as I walk away from him in disgust, back to my desk.

"How do you know that about him?" Ryan asks with his jaw open wide.

"Must have heard it from someone," I tell Ryan, shrugging my shoulders.

The classroom empties as Ryan and I grab our belongings and follow the rest of the students. The Creature, with his head bowed low, just sits in his chair surrounded by a heap of embarrassment. I don't look at him as we exit the classroom; that Creature knows what he has done.

"Seriously, Josie, how did you know about Mr. Glencross?" Ryan needles me again once we enter the hall.

"It doesn't matter; it is the truth. Plus, I don't have time for any of this," I say, shaking my head.

"Wow, I have never seen you like this before," Ryan tells me. He places his hand on my shoulder to stop me from walking. I turn to face him, giving off a huge sigh, knowing that this charade is too much to keep up.

At eleven, blah, blah, blah, plays again in my head, making me squeeze my face menacingly. Oh, I'm going to slap Adayln for leaving it on repeat! "Ryan, I can't be here today. I'm sorry, I have to go," I say, handing him my math textbook and turning to walk away.

"Wait — go where?" Ryan calls out, but I don't answer. I know that this school business is not part of the plan. Ryan calls out again but his voice is muffled out as the hallway bell rings followed by the chorus of students flocking noisily into the hall. I dodge past everyone and go back out the same way we entered the school.

At eleven o'clock ... "Yes, I get it, Adayln; why did you set this message on such a constant repeat?" I ask aloud while softly hitting the side of my head with my palm. This message better terminate once I get to the damn sundial. Every ten minutes, that's enough to drive someone mad.

"Josie!" that annoying, familiar voice calls out to me from behind. I look over my shoulder and notice Ryan running up towards me.

"*Why won't this boy leave me alone?*" I mumble in frustration. Little Sister is right; it's no wonder that Josie can't stand him.

"You're seriously leaving school today?" Ryan shouts out within metres away from me.

"Yes, Ryan! Obviously, I'm not well!" I tell him, still walking down the road. I'm not slowing down to let him catch up.

"You heading home? I'll walk with you!" Ryan says, out of breath, while running with that heavy load on his back.

I reach South Main Street and look directly to my right. I see the road taper at the end and figure that it must be a pleasant forty to forty-five-minute walk ahead of me to the beach. "Wait up," Ryan says, coming up to meet me.

"Ryan seriously," I blurt out, turning around and sticking my palm out. He stops dead in his tracks.

"Josie is just not interested — I mean I'm not — interested that is," I continue to mutter with my emotions all aflutter.

"Josie, what's wrong with you today?" he asks abruptly, placing his hand again coldly on my shoulder.

"Go back, Ryan," I tell him, looking unblinkingly straight into his eyes. "Go back," I continue to press with a head nod, giving him permission to leave.

"Alright — then," he stutters. "I'll see you around," Ryan says, turning his back to finally walk away.

"Goodbye," I tell him. I have a weird feeling that I just hurt that boy. My face cringes with that thought as I turn myself south to start my trek to the sundial.

"*Record on, it's May 1, 2005, at —*" I begin to mutter. "Ugh, what's wrong with you, Miranda?" That's apparently not going to work in this realm. I'll have to rely on my mush to remember all that I will see — I'm not overly confident though. An intellect forged from chemistry is of a poor design; it's incredible that we have survived over these many centuries.

At eleven o'clock — "Ugh!" I yell aloud as that blasted message starts playing again in my head. I'm going to smack Adayln so hard across the head when I see her. The volume and frequency of this guided message are uncalled for. Yes, Adayln can lock in a protocol like any Tom Fool — designing a protocol is where she is clearly lacking.

"Sigh," I breathe out to remember the feeling of flowing air entering my body through primitive lungs. Maybe I'm being too hard on Adayln; that system code did look rather intense. Not that I know the first thing about hacking. We all knew people would tinker.

The questions I used to get from clients wanting to risk serious harm by entering into here — like this! This realm is meant to be enjoyed as a dream while asleep — right now it feels more like a nightmare.

I walk past an old place that I used to inhabit as a biologic. It's dilapidated and tired like most structures in the south end of Penticton. Money just hasn't reached this end of town yet. A wise investor would be in sound-mind to buy up all this bargain bin of garbage. However, big money doesn't start flowing this way until fifty years from now — a short-term investment with a high gain.

Penticton brings back so many memories for me, many good — many sad. Geez, that Cascadian Sun is ripe and fickle with Josie's pale skin exposed more than it should be. Where did my white cardigan go?

Maybe I should head home first and grab another?

Why can't my mush make up its mind on simple decisions?

We are walking on! The worst that will happen is that I will most likely just freckle.

Chapter 7

The bright sparkle of Skaha Lake comes into view among the tree trunks of many pines. As I approach, the full lake comes into view along with the hugging arms of a vacant springtime beach.

Standing at the north end of Skaha Lake you can faintly see the south end glimmering from a distant thirteen kilometres away. That is our destination; that is where Okanagan Falls is situated. "Thirteen kilometres," I mutter aloud. My mind suddenly unhinges while reading the tourist information board that is permanently affixed by the beach entrance.

On the left side of the lake, we have the windy two-lane Eastside Road contrasting the vast four-lane highway system occupying the right side. I just spent over forty minutes walking from Josie's school, and I'm already exhausted. Now, I have another thirteen kilometres to go; I hope Adayln has secured us some transportation for this venture.

What am I saying?

I can do this; I'm a vibrant seventeen-year-old. I just need to pace myself. I have apparently become accustomed to living in that husk body — which never gets tired. My biology must be navigated differently — *don't exert it.*

The cool morning air is quickly dominated and pushed aside when the Cascadian sun hits its zenith in the sky. Okay, it's almost eleven o'clock. Time to locate that sundial, which according to the information board should be on the other side of that concession stand.

Wooden pillars the width of telephone poles come into view sticking approximately three feet out of the sand. They form a concentric circle in the middle of the beach where you can use your own body's shadow to cast the correct time of the day.

At eleven o'clock... starts to replay in my head but quietly terminates as I enter the inside of the sundial.

"Okay, it's almost eleven; where are you, Adayln?" I call out, spinning in a circle, yet no one replies to my hails. I sit on the seven o'clock pillar and wait, hoping that Adayln did indeed wake up. The lake water is calm as all breezes fall silent with just this stagnant sun to tickle my freckled skin.

I'm still impressed that this worked, that Adayln was able to change these protocols correctly within the SDS System. For centuries, we have wondered what may be past the known realm of Penticton. This question has fascinated minds since these longevity devices were first introduced to the public.

My first SDS was a very crude prototype which continually malfunctioned. I was lucky to make it through an entire SDS life without a power overload or rendering schism. Those early days of Stasis Deep Sleep are regarded today as barbaric and intrans-human. The number of conscious souls that were corrupted, infected, or downright erased by the SDS back then must be a number in the high millions.

However, the technology persevered as it slowly became a necessity for those wanting to live forever. What

Adayln has done is not the intended use of this temperamental device. I know of many people who claim they
were accidentally awoken while in the SDS. It happens
— it is sensitive technology. However, like a deep-water
diver who must not stay too long below the surface, the
same can be said about being awake in the SDS.

"Hello?" a timid voice says. She is standing on the
walking promenade just steps away from the sandy shore.
I turn to face her as she approaches. She removes her
shoes before cautiously stepping out onto the sand. She is
stunning. Her flowing raven-haired locks expose glowing
sapphire eyes that pop in bright contrast with her ivory
skin. Looks about my age of seventeen years, but I can't
be sure as she is significantly shorter than me.

I stand up and walk to her with a beaming smile
on my face. "You did it; I can't believe you actually did
it," I tell Adayln, still smiling from ear to ear. However,
Adayln isn't smiling; instead, she carries a look of worry
and dread.

"The voice in my head *won't stop*," she says with a
tremble. Tears begin to flow from those captivating eyes.
I take her in my arms and hold her tight against me.

"It will stop now that you are here, at the sundial," I
explain. Her muffling sobs cease and she pulls away from
me to wipe her tears.

"Did you have the same message playing over and
over in your head of telling you to go to the sundial at
Skaha Beach at eleven o'clock?" she inquires with a sniffle.

"Yes, of course," I say, somewhat confused. "That's
what you said you would program using the Soul-Mate
protocol. Why are you so confused about your own plan,
Adayln?" I ask her, puzzled. I reach into my backpack to
fetch a tissue.

"My plan? I don't have any plan to meet here," she tells me, blowing her nose hard into the tissue I hand to her.

"You must know of this plan, Adayln; this is why we are awake — this is why we are here," I tell her, forcefully grabbing both of her thin shoulders and making her look me in the eye.

"Adayln? My name isn't Adayln," she says, beginning to cry again while looking up at me.

"Who are you?" I ask her, shaking her gently. "What is your name?"

"Everyone calls me Emma, but that is not me," she says, falling to her knees and continuing to cry. "I don't know what's going on."

"Emma?" I say confusingly. I look down at the sand, seemingly lost. I too drop to my knees and face the poor girl. "What is your name, then, if it is not Emma?" I ask, placing my finger under her chin to lift her head up.

"I'm Emily — Emily Stellar — I think I'm going crazy," she rambles while sobbing relentlessly.

"Emily Stellar? Emily, it's me — it's Miranda Sage," I tell her, patting my chest with my hand. "Do you remember me?" I then ask of her, somewhat excited,

Miranda? Emily mutters, reaching up with her hand to touch my face.

"You remember me?" I ask Emily again. She just stares at me with little to no emotion on her face.

"Yes, I remember you," Emily says, continuing to caress my cheek. "I don't remember the freckles though. So, I am Emily Stellar — I am not crazy then," Emily affirms as her weeping begins to subside.

Yes, you're not crazy, Emily," I explain to her. Following a sigh of relief, Emily takes a deep breath to steady her emotions. "You happen to be awake in the

SDS just like me," I enlighten her with a cringe. I shake my head, wondering how Adayln could have messed this up.

"I knew that to be true, but I couldn't think straight with that constant repeating message bellowing in my head," Emily tells me, reaching up her hands to squeeze her temples with her palms. "Everyone was calling me Emma," Emily says, emphatically.

"Who was calling you Emma?" I ask quickly.

"I suppose my family? Emma's family," Emily says, looking away with a struggle on her face as she tries to contemplate her ragged thoughts.

"Do they suspect you as not being their Emma?" I ask Emily, knowing that this new unforeseen ripple in the plan may cause some unwanted waves.

"No, I don't think they did," Emily says, wiping her eyes. "It's a big family that Emma has — I was crying, but everyone was too busy getting ready for the day to notice."

"Well, it's good to see you," I say to Emily, giving her another hug.

"I'm so lost, Miranda; how am I consciously awake? My consciousness should be asleep. Wait, why are you awake? The SDS must be malfunctioning," Emily begins to say, rambling towards another state of panic.

I attempt to interrupt Emily as she becomes increasingly unnerved, but she ignores me and pushes my hands away. "We can't be awake in the SDS! We will go corrupt and insane in this world — and in the Real Realm," Emily continues while her body shakes with an uncontrollable shiver.

"We won't go insane; the SDS System is working properly," I say calmly. She wipes a newly forming tear from her eye.

"How do you know that?" Emily asks, stoically tight-lipped.

"Because we will only be awake for twenty-four hours — until 7:00 a.m. tomorrow morning. You'll be back being Emma again with your consciousness fully asleep," I explain. Emily rises up to her feet.

"Why twenty-four hours?" she ponders loudly while looking around her surroundings. "Adayln — earlier you said Adayln. What has she done, Miranda?" Emily asks with a frantic stare as her journalistic side begins to creep through.

"That's the investigative journalist I know," I tell Emily with a laugh as I attempt to lighten the mood.

"I'm serious: what did Adayln do to us?" Emily inquires again. Her small stature towers over me while I'm still on my knees.

"Adayln changed a few of the safety protocol settings within the SDS system to consciously awake just me and her when we both reached around seventeen years of age," I explain to Emily, matter-of-fact as I look down at the ground.

"But why? Why take the risk against your conscious? It's against the Laws of Conscious Ethics to awake someone in an SDS," Emily scolds with vigour as I also stand up from the sand.

"Only Adayln and I were to be awoken. I don't know why she woke you as well. That wasn't the plan," I explain to Emily, calmly brushing the sand off of me.

"The plan!" Emily shouts in disbelief at my poorly chosen word. "What is your plan with Adayln?" she then asks, holding out her arms in frustration.

"Hey!" a voice, with a crack in its tone, screams out among the many pine groves.

"Miranda!" the voice calls out again quickly.

"Over here," I yell in the direction of the voice, not seeing any person in view.

"Who is that?" Emily asks warily, also looking to the grove.

"I don't know," I tell Emily while still trying to locate the caller. "Whoever it is knows my true name. I'm hoping it's Adayln," I say with a sigh.

Moments later, a person comes into view after emerging from that tangle of pine trees. He slowly makes his way over with a waddle in his walk. Just like Emily and I, he looks to be a teenager. As he approaches, his pudgy features became more pronounced. His tight-fitting clothes seem to stretch over his fat body.

"Miranda?" he calls out again before tripping out onto the sand and landing squarely on his face. Emily and I just stand there looking at one another, not sure what to make of this odd-looking fellow.

"Miranda?" he calls out again after lifting his face up from the sand.

"Yes," I call out to him cautiously. I make my way over to help him up.

"Am I glad to see you," he says, brushing the sand from his chubby cheeks. "That message I created was driving me mad," he continues to say with a hearty laugh followed by spitting sand out of his mouth.

"Adayln?" I ask cautiously, just to be sure.

"Adayln — yes," Adayln says again with more laughter, obviously dazzled with her own accomplishment. "Although, here I go by Corey," she informs us.

"Yes, the message was relentless; it drove us crazy as well," I tell Adayln as she just now realizes that there is more than just me standing in front of her.

"Us — who is this?" Adayln says with a sneer towards Emily. "I hope you didn't tell this stasis avatar who we really are?" Adayln says. She shakes her head with a massive grin on her face. "That's just going to complicate things."

"Adayln, I'm not an avatar," Emily grumbles angrily, thrusting both hands onto her hips.

Adayln stops brushing the sand from her arms and legs while wiping that smile from her face. "*Who are you then?*" Adayln asks nervously with trepidation in her voice.

"Adayln, this is Emily Stellar," I tell her, placing my hand on Emily's shoulder for support.

"Emily — Stellar?" Adayln stutters slowly, peering at Emily through one eye. From — the *Misfit?*" Adayln asks, oddly closing both her eyes as she speaks.

"Yes, the same Emily Stellar. What nightmare have you awoken me to, Adayln?" Emily responds, moving her tiny frame closer to the hulking body of Adayln.

Adayln finally opens her eyes and blows out a deep breath, still shaking her head from side to side. "I messed up, somewhere," Adayln says, looking back over to me. "I was only supposed to wake up our conscious minds, not Emily's as well," she confesses, visibly embarrassed.

"You know that it is against the Law of Conscious Ethics to awake a soul unwillingly while they are in an SDS pod," Emily recites in a scolding manner.

"I know — I know this is all a mistake. I'm sorry," Adayln says in a begging manner. "It will be for only twenty-four hours, I swear. We just wanted to explore a hidden realm, that's all," she continues to explain while kicking the sand with her foot in frustration.

"A hidden realm," Emily says, looking perplexed. "This is all just to explore the mythical Hidden Realms?" she then asks sternly, turning her body towards me for an answer.

"Yes, we are both at fault," I say to Emily calmly, having no reason to hide the truth. "We both just wanted answers," I then tell her plainly. I look over to Okanagan Falls in the distance.

"What answers?" Emily cries out empathically. "There are no hidden realms. This has all been discussed in the past and On-Record. It takes so much power to just render Penticton that there is nothing else. Plus, we have never needed any place bigger than Penticton to live out these stasis lives. These other areas just don't exist," she continues to dictate while erratically pacing back and forth and making a trench in the sand.

"Emily, what if I were to tell you that those areas do exist," Adayln says, making Emily roll her eyes in disbelief.

"Yes, they do exist, but only on the real Earth," Emily responds with a snarky laugh.

"No, they exist in here as well; I have seen it," Adayln says, straight-faced, unblinking.

"How is that possible? LaPorte has always maintained that the only realm is Penticton," Emily tells us with a nervous grin.

"They are lying to us. Go on, Miranda; tell Emily you've seen it too," Adayln says, looking over at me for verbal support.

"It's true, Emily — *although unconfirmed,*" I say, looking back to Adayln.

"Unconfirmed doesn't mean true," Emily says. She shakes her head with no sign of being persuaded within her cackling laugh.

"Let me explain!" Adayln shouts, trying to halt Emily from chuckling at her.

"Please do! Yes, please explain why you have jeopardized all of our sanity in this land of forever?" a tall, slender girl shouts from the top of the walking promenade.

None of us saw her approach, and we all look up at her silently. She is indeed mighty in height and skinny with stringy lemony hair that has a look of needing a wash. She looks strong with well-defined muscles in her arms and legs attached to that slender frame.

"Which of you is Adayln?" bellows this slender beauty, jumping to the sand awkwardly as her dress flies up past her waist. It is a flower pattern dress; however, such as the case with Adayln, it is also three sizes too small. She walks over to us with authority, not bothering to adjust her dress from high above her waist. "Adayln!" the Slender Beauty says again loudly as we all stand in fear of this girl.

"I'm — Adayln," the hulking Adayln stutters as the Slender Beauty connects quickly with a right hook to Adayln's face. Adayln tumbles onto the sand, flat on her back, while this slender beauty mounts her.

"You went too far, Adayln," she says, pinning both of Adayln's wrists above her head. "Awakening us to most certain insanity, not only in this world but also in the Real Realm, is to be exiled to permanent death," the Slender Beauty continues while lifting her right knee to jab into the side of Adayln's torso.

"Wait!" Adayln cries out, visibly in pain.

"I can't afford to get re-stabilized!" the Slender Beauty yells, pummeling poor Adayln with those knobbly knees. "I'll lose my SDS licence for this when LaPorte Industries finds out!"

"Kaptin Keoh?" I call out, running over to push the Slender Beauty off of Adayln.

We both fall to the ground. I roll around trying to hold back Keoh, as he is not only noticeably taller but apparently twice as strong as me.

"Too far!" Keoh yells again. He grasps at handfuls of sand while I pull him back. We hear a loud ripping sound of torn fabric as I fall back with a handful of Keoh's dress. Keoh looks behind me and staggers up to stand on his feet. He reaches behind himself to feel his exposed back, and the frailty of his clothing makes him pause to attempt a fix.

Adayln is still on her back, propping herself up on her elbows with her hands stretched out defensively. "Keoh, please calm down," I implore him as he holds up the left shoulder of his dress to prevent it from falling down.

"Too far, Adayln; you doomed us," Keoh says. He makes his way over to sit at the three o'clock pillar.

"Keoh, you must believe me. This is not what I intended," Adayln tells him nervously. Keoh just sits there shaking his head and not looking in Adayln's direction.

"Not your intent," Keoh says sternly, placing his gaze sharply onto Adayln. "I told you not to touch the SDS Systems, but you disobeyed a direct order from the Kaptin," Keoh says with a disdainful finger-point.

"My SDS pod was malfunctioning," Adayln whines. She kicks more sand into the air out of frustration.

"Yours?" Keoh interrupts thunderously. "You don't own it — damn it, I don't even own it," he reminds Adayln.

"Hey, when I find a problem — I fix it!" Adayln states proudly. This makes Keoh sit up and brush the sand from his hair.

"Oh yes, you definitely fixed it," Keoh says mockingly with his arms raised in the air. The front of Keoh's dress then falls forward to expose his left breast. Keoh continues to stare up at the sky, trying to gain back some composure. "LaPorte Industries doesn't take kindly to people tampering with their systems, their property," he says, placing his hands in his lap and bowing his head low. "*You have doomed us,*" he mumbles softly, beginning to weep. I make my way over to him and fix the dress as best I can by tying a knot at his shoulder.

"I only wanted to wake Miranda and myself," Adayln groans.

"You?" Keoh says, looking up at me stunned. "You are involved in this too?" he continues, brushing my hand off of his shoulder.

"And you?" Keoh asks furiously, looking over at Emily. "Are you involved in this as well?"

"I have nothing to do with this awakening," Emily says with a laugh. "I'm innocent."

"You find this funny?" Keoh asks, tilting his head to the side. "Who are you?"

"Emily Stellar," she says proudly from her seat at the eleven o'clock pillar.

"Emily Stellar?" Keoh says wildly. He looks back at Adayln. "How many more did you wake up?" he inquires, looking nervous.

"Just the four of us — *so far as I know*," Adayln says. She squints her face and looks somewhat embarrassed.

"What of Torstein and Mikken?" Keoh asks, looking squarely back up at me.

"Haven't seen them," I say, quickly scanning the beach in both directions.

"There is a chance they may not have awakened," Adayln suggests, thrusting her fat body down to sit in the sand.

"What do you know? You have no idea what you have done," Keoh says, standing up from his pillar. "People who stay awake while within the SDS go insane, not only in here but also in the Real Realm," Keoh says calmly. He makes his way to Skaha Lake and announces, "I'm ending this right now before any more damage is done to my consciousness."

Keoh enters the water and shivers as the frigid winter runoff takes hold of him. "Keoh, no!" I yell, running after him. I place my arms around his waist and attempt to spin his body back to the shore. However, Keoh just pushes down on my head to make me fall into the frigid water. "Adayln, some help please!" I call out. I rise up and grab onto Keoh again as he continues to walk deeper and deeper into the lake.

"Keoh, suicide will only make this worse," I say to him. This makes him pause. We are both waist-high in Skaha Lake, my arms still wrapped around his slender upper abdomen. "You know what suicide does to a conscious soul — you could fracture," I inform him with chattering teeth. Keoh just stands there. "Being awake will only last twenty-four hours, Keoh," I say, nodding my head to relay that I'm telling the truth.

"Twenty-four hours?" Keoh asks coyly, tilting his head down as I look up at him. I am still awkwardly hugging his slender waist.

"Yes, twenty-four hours," I say confidently. I stand up, dripping wet from head to toe. "Adayln has it programmed to put us back to sleep after twenty-four hours from being awake," I confirm.

"Again, Miranda," Keoh groans loudly with a grumble, turning back to the shore. "*You are always dragging me into your troubles — Miranda Sage!*"

Chapter 8

The Crimson Orb tries its best to warm us up; however, we are still in the thralls of springtime. This time of year bounces between warm and cold with no rhyme or reason. Emily removes her rusty-mango hoody and wraps it around me. Keoh shows no sign of coldness as he sits here, just stewing away on the three o'clock pillar. Emily continues to rub my sides and back. As the numbness dissipates, I hunch over to wring the water from my ginger hair. Adayln, back on the sandy shore, removes her dark navy hoody and hands it to Keoh. He just pushes the offering away. I gladly take the hoody and wrap it tightly around my bare legs as I continue to shiver.

"I'm sorry, Keoh — Kaptin Keoh," Adayln says sheepishly. She sits down right next to Keoh.

"Twenty-four hours — why?" Keoh asks, turning to face Adayln.

"We didn't want to expose ourselves any longer than needed. We figured we could accomplish what we needed to do in that time frame," Adayln explains. She shows visible fear towards his stasis avatar of the slender beauty.

"*Conscious souls go insane when awoken in here,*" Keoh says quietly behind clenched teeth. He attempts to stay calm.

"Many have gone seventy-two hours or longer with no consciousness degradation," Adayln says with a perky head nod.

"And many have developed irreparable damage to their soul from being awake only an hour in the SDS," Keoh refutes with a stern look upon his face.

"Emily, what do you think?" Adayln asks, looking over at Emily. "You have written extensively on the SDS."

"I think we are safe being awake — for now, but anything past one day I would deem unsafe," Emily says, still rubbing warmth back into my shoulders.

"There, see — even Emily's expert opinion says we are in no danger," Adayln affirms with a smile.

"Oh, I didn't say that, and I'm nowhere near an expert on this matter," Emily corrects Adayln quickly. "We could still rise from this still needing conscious repair," she reminds us all.

"Well, sorry I have made you all mad!" Adayln grumbles.

"Part of me is enraged for what you have done, Adayln," Emily says with a hint of a grin forming out the corner of her mouth. Emily reaches down to her school bag and removes a small bound notebook and pen. "However, part of me is intrigued that there may be a story with us going on this trek," she adds, making me smile.

"That's the right attitude, Emily," I cheer her on, away from any more talk of gloom that may exist.

"We are here, and we are awake; we might as well make the most of it," Emily says, tapping her pen against her notebook proudly, "and I'm going to document every moment."

"Document what? I still haven't been told why you and Miranda would want to enter Penticton awake," Keoh cries out. He looks at us in confusion. "What will be gained by all of this?"

"Adayln discovered something while tinkering with SDS System," I say, clenching my teeth which are still cold.

"Keoh, there is more to Penticton than just Penticton," Adayln says with jubilant excitement, but Keoh doesn't shift the disdainful look that is painted across his face.

"More than what?" Keoh asks, crossing his arms in a huff. "Penticton is all there is. I have been in this realm for the past six hundred years. There is nothing more, and there has been no need for more!" he shouts at us all.

"Hear me out: the Hidden Realms—" Adayln begins.

"The Hidden Realms?" Keoh interjects with recoiling laughter. "This is all about Hidden Realms — unbelievable."

"They are real!" Adayln shouts over his cackle.

"So, what of it? We have no need to go to them," Keoh says, still smirking. "*They are real,*" he mutters mockingly, shaking his head.

"You are a close-minded, ancient fool," Adayln tells him, sassing the Kaptin as usual.

"Adayln, none of this is real," Keoh says calmly and slowly, looking over to Adayln before panning over the rest of us.

"Then why render a Hidden Realm?" Adayln asks heatedly, right when it seems that Keoh is quieting down.

"What do you mean by render?" Keoh asks abruptly, lifting his head. "There is nothing there — no Hidden Realms being rendered, I can assure you of that."

"I tell you: Okanagan Falls is being rendered," Adayln says, falling short on breath. "I've seen the data; Miranda has seen the data," she rambles, trying to convince Keoh.

"It's true, Keoh. Okanagan Falls is being rendered; I've seen the power consumption," I confirm what I had read off of Adayln's display on the *Misfit*.

"So, what if they are?" Keoh asks dismissively, with a wave of his hand. He is disinterested in hearing any more.

"Why render a realm that takes tremendous amounts of power to do so?" Adayln asserts. This piques the interest of the power consumption-hungry Keoh. "You know how much power it takes to render Penticton, Keoh. So, why is power being diverted to areas other than Penticton?" she continues to needle him in her attempt to sway his opinion.

"Here I am, looking at Skaha Lake, like I have probably done countless times with my life in this town," Keoh says, pointing out towards the direction of Okanagan Falls. "If I look down the lake and see no rendering of Okanagan Falls, it would look pretty suspicious — even to a stasis avatar, wouldn't you say? It's rendered to complement the rendering of Penticton," he says. He turns his head to the side and gives us a single nod to show that he's just not convinced.

"That's what I thought as well, but we have been told for centuries that it's just a holowall," Emily says with a look of reflection. "LaPorte Industries may have been lying to us," she says, tilting her adorable head to the side. "There's a story here."

"Why? Why lie to the public?" Keoh asks, turning his body from the lake to look at us all again. "That's their prerogative, anyways. They own these sodding devices," he says in a huff.

"What other hidden realms are out there?" Adayln asks daringly. "What else are they holding back from us? I'm not content with just living in Penticton; I want more!" Adayln screams out.

"*Those who beg for more will be soundly disappointed,*" Keoh quotes as a devoted Longevist. Serenely, he sits back down.

"You are here, Keoh; you may as well find out," I tell him. I stand up from the pillar, still wrapped in Emily's rusty-mango hoody for warmth.

"What do you intend to do?" Keoh asks, staring cautiously over at me.

"We go to Okanagan Falls and prove that it does indeed exist," I tell him soundly.

"Then what?" Keoh follows up.

"We go to sleep, and finish these lives. Once we awake in the Real Realm, we'll discuss what we saw and what actions to take," I tell Keoh firmly. This not being our first time together on a journey for him to not know my intent.

"Twenty-four hours, you are sure of this?" Keoh asks with a sneer at Adayln.

"Yes," Adayln says, reaching out her hand to Keoh. Keoh takes Adayln's hand and rises. He uses his immense height to express his authority over Adayln.

"What about Torstein and Mikken?" Emily asks with a concerned look on her face. "What if they come here, and we are gone?"

"The message was clear to be here at eleven. It's almost noon; it's safe to say that Torstein and Mikken didn't awake," I tell Emily, thinking nothing more of them.

"But you don't know that for sure. They could be having a hard time getting here," Emily suggests with some plausible assumptions which no one is paying much attention to.

"You know, Emily, I must say you are stunning to look upon," Adayln tells Emily, apparently trying to change the subject of her protocol blunder.

"Thank you, Adayln; it's the luck of the draw, I suppose," Emily responds bashfully. Her ivory skin morphs into a rose hue as she blushes.

"I never get to look like that; I'm always selected to be hit with the ugly stick when it comes to stasis avatars," Adayln remarks, shaking her head while squeezing the tire of fat around her waist.

"Oh, you don't look that bad. It's what on the inside that counts, anyway," Emily tells Adayln, trying to cheer her up.

"This is the early part of the twenty-first century; everybody judges a book by its cover," Adayln laments sorrowfully. "It's so suppressive."

"Are you coming or not?" Keoh calls out. He is starting to walk east along the shore.

"Yes, we're coming, Keoh," Adayln replies as we all make our way over.

"So, let me get this straight: we are going to walk the whole way there?" Emily asks, rolling her eyes while looking in my direction for an answer.

"It's the only accessible way. None of us drive or own an automobile," I say to her, shrugging my shoulders.

"What about bicycles? We could procure some bicycles," Emily offers with excitement in her voice.

"Where are we going to find bicycles? It's not that far to walk, anyways. Maybe a couple of hours tops," Adayln says, already starting to sweat from moving her chubby body a few steps.

"Should have put that in your message," Keoh says with eyes staring straight ahead, down the road.

"To what?" Adayln asks, confused.

"To bring a bicycle to the sundial as well. I imagine we all own one in our houses," Keoh explains in a snarky tone of voice.

"Everyone, this is the path we are taking," I tell them all, making sure to secure firm eye contact. "It's a journey by foot. We are all young and fit, and so this shouldn't be a problem."

"Tubby may be young, but he doesn't look fit at all," Keoh states, pointing behind him with his thumb towards Adayln.

"Bring it on, tall girl; I'll rematch against you!" Adayln calls out. She pushes Keoh from behind, yet he hardly moves.

"Is that all you got?" Keoh says, brushing his long greasy locks away from his eyes. Keoh towers over Adayln by at least two inches, as puberty hasn't entirely taken hold of Corey's body.

"Both of you stand down," I say commandingly. I stand before them, keeping them apart.

"Who made you in charge?" Keoh says, now looking down at me.

"I'm the oldest one here. I'm one of the originals, *One of the Firsts*. The Law of Ages takes precedence," I explain to Keoh, showing no fear towards his claims.

"We are still technically on my ship —" Keoh begins.

"Nope, she's got you there, Keoh," Emily interjects sharply. "Miranda has a clear four hundred plus years of conscious life compared to you," she continues, writing feverishly in her notebook with her head down.

"Who still goes by the Law of Ages? That is such an ancient rule!" Keoh states angrily.

"An ancient rule yet a current rule to which our species still adheres," I tell him, looking directly into his blue eyes to signify that I'm not backing down.

"Remember, I'm recording this journey for all posterity," Emily says with a coy tap of her pen on the edge of her notebook.

"Ha — good luck getting that published!" Keoh says with a booming laugh. "Be sure to mention how Adayln hacked the SDS system on the *Misfit*. I'm sure LaPorte Industries would love to hear about that," he says, looking over at Emily.

"Well, if you would have kept up with your maintenance on the system, I wouldn't have had to try and fix it," Adayln storms back.

"Everyone, please, let's stop bickering. We have a limited time in this realm while awake," I say loudly, standing in a wide stance in front of the group with both hands placed firmly on my hips. "Let's just complete this mission, get our answers, and then go back to sleep," I direct them.

Keoh says nothing and just starts walking again; Emily nods her head as she walks past me. Adayln smiles while walking next to Emily. I take a deep breath and bring up the rear to this eclectic group of individual souls.

I can manage this team to reach our goal — I have managed worse, I affirm to myself with a confident head nod.

—————⁓⁓⁘⁙⁘⁙⁘⁓⁓—————

"It feels so odd being awake within the SDS," Emily recounts, looking up to Keoh beside her. Keoh doesn't respond and just continues marching ahead. "You said you have been awake before, Miranda," Emily says, turning to face me. "When was that?"

"Oh, that was a long time ago when the SDS was still in its infancy," I tell Emily, wincing.

"What happened?" Emily asks, pulling back to walk beside me.

"It's hard to access those memories; I can't really tell you much," I say to her, unsure of why those thoughts have fled.

"This is an odd feeling," Emily says, slowly and cautiously. "I have lived more lives inside the SDS then in the Double R. However, I can't recall any of those SDS lives and experiences," she continues to explain in more detail.

"It's true; I can't seem to recall any of my prior SDS lives either," Adayln says, wiping the sweat that is dripping off her brow. "It must be a protocol setting."

"I can remember my First-Biological in crystal clear detail, but just bits and fragments of my SDS lives; it's very unnerving," Emily says, looking straight ahead as her body gives off a shiver.

"Perhaps that is part of the SDS sickness," Keoh chimes in with a laugh. This elicits a dreadful thought that may possibly be true. "The longer we stay, the more our minds fragment until we are mindless screaming avatars," he tells us in horror.

"Please, let's not speculate down that rabbit hole," Adayln pants. "I'm sure it's just a safety protocol that I may have overlooked, or perhaps it was hidden," she continues to explain with no definitive answer.

"There is probably not enough storage in these avatars to hold the immensity of our full conscious lives," I conclude in an attempt to end this troubling debate.

"And that's why you go insane," Keoh says, still pleading his point. "Think about it. Say you have lived ten full lives in the SDS: those collected memories of those lives are incorporated into your Real Realm consciousness. You gain all that combined knowledge and experience to enrich yourself. It rewrites who you are and who you become in life. Who here can say that they are a carbon copy of what they were like during their First-Biological?" he asks in a rambling attempt to get us all scared.

Emily laughs out loud, and says, "Oh lord, I'm nothing like my First-Biological. I know that for sure. However, because I know that, I must have evolved my consciousness by all the time spent in the SDS. So, why can't I recall key moments from those SDS lives like I can in the Double R?" Emily poses again to the group, keeping this discussion alive.

"I know I'm Miranda Sage; I know that for sure," I say. "I also know that I'm close to 1,300 years old, and have spent close to 700 years of my life within SDS. Yet I can't recall any of my stasis avatars' names; it's a weird haze in my thoughts where those memories should be located. However, trying to explain what we clearly can't in our current state is simply pointless — let's change the subject," I tell everyone in hopes of shutting them up to focus on more uplifting topics.

"But you carry their experiences," Adayln says, making me wonder.

"I've lived in the real Penticton once —" I pause, before continuing, "I should know every inch of it, but as I look around, it's almost like —"

"That you're seeing this realm for the first time," Emily jumps in, finishing my sentence.

"It's so bizarre," I say, offering a slight smile towards the Cascadian sky.

"Best we keep an eye on one another in case Mr. Gloom is correct," Emily says, looking directly up at Keoh.

"You'll see there are reasons why you don't meddle with the SDS Systems," Keoh says, turning to face us as he walks backwards down the road. "I just hope to wake up from all this, uncorrupted — to point that fact out."

"We'll be fine, Keoh," Adayln says, puffing away. "We only have about another sixteen hours awake," she reminds him, still defiant that she hasn't jeopardized us.

"Ya," Keoh says dismissively. He turns back around and shakes his head. "We go to Okanagan Falls see that it is indeed a holowall, and then we head back home to go to sleep," he states aloud, pointing out ahead with his hand stretched out towards Okanagan Falls.

"It's not a holowall!" Adayln shouts, still lagging behind the group.

"We'll see soon enough," Keoh says. His slender frame marches forward with confidence.

"I hope it's soon; you look like you're fading, Adayln," Emily says, seeing Adayln struggling to keep up with the group.

"I thought it would be a quick walk," Adayln pants, trying to catch her breath.

"The information board at Skaha Beach says it's about thirteen kilometres, so it should be under a three-hour walk," I inform Adayln. This information makes her stagger.

"Another two hours," Adayln laments.

"Not part of your plan?" Keoh asks with another cackling laugh.

"Having this stasis avatar definitely wasn't," Adayln responds. She pulls in an extra breath of air to propel her body forward.

———⟿⟿⟿⟿———

"Miranda!" Emily interrupts my deep well of thought.

"Yes, Emily, what is the matter?" I ask, coming back to this reality.

"Do you think Torstein and Mikken are also awake?" Emily asks, looking up at me with those gorgeous sapphire eyes.

"More than likely," I tell her with an affirming head nod, still marching forward down the road.

"They should have shown up at the beach though," Emily says with her head down writing away in her notebook.

"Perhaps the message didn't play for them," Keoh insists, tilting his head to look at Emily walking right next to him.

"No, I'm pretty sure they would have received the message as well, if you both received it," Adayln says, letting out a great big sigh.

"Should we look for them?" Emily asks, lifting her head from her notebook to look us all in the eye.

"No, we don't have the time," I tell them, pointing with my extended finger down East Side Road. "We have a mission and limited time to do it. We march on forward, while Torstein and Mikken are resigned to their own fate."

"That message consistently repeating, though. Poor Torstein. Can't imagine what that may have done to his mind," Emily says with a shudder. "Does it stop playing after eleven o'clock, Adayln?" she asks turning to face Adayln while readying her pen for an answer.

"I don't know anymore, Emily," Adayln says in frustration while huffing and puffing. "You weren't even supposed to get the message, let alone wake up."

"Mikken for sure should have shown up if he had received the message," Emily points out, tilting her head to the side.

"Who cares if they got the message or didn't get the message? They are awake, or they are not awake. Who cares? They are not here," Keoh says resoundingly, looking straight ahead.

"My readers would want to know, that's why," Emily says, but everyone ignores her pleas for answers which none of us have to give.

"Speculation can be fun; however, with zero facts, there is no truth to be gained," I break the awkward silence. "We must save our thoughts to prepare for this new knowledge about a possible hidden realm. Torstein and Mikken, if awake, will be put back asleep like the rest of us with no damage done. Please, let's just focus on the task we do have control over," I tell the group in hopes of quieting the conflict.

"Wait, we need to stop — I'm tired," Adayln says. She bends over and collapses her hands on her knees.

"It's not much farther, Adayln; I can see the Okanagan Falls welcome sign ahead," I tell her, hoping to spur her forward.

"This stasis avatar isn't meant for this much physical endurance," Adayln says between massive intakes of air.

"Well, we are not carrying you," Keoh says, looking unimpressed in Adayln's direction.

"Maybe a ten-minute break is warranted," Emily suggests, walking back towards Adayln.

"Agreed, ten minutes," I say to them all, looking at my bare wrist.

"Are you sure that is the entrance sign?" Adayln moans, stretching her back and collapsing to the ground in one motion.

"Must be; we have walked almost the required distance, and there are no other billboards along this road so far to indicate it being just random advertising," I ramble.

"Okay, okay, I believe you," Adayln says, exhausted; clearly, there is no energy in her for verbal debate.

"What do you think will happen when we get there?" Emily asks gleefully. From her seat on the ground, she opens up her notebook and readies her pen to write again.

No one talks as Emily looks on, waiting to hear what everyone thinks. "C'mon, someone share what they think," Emily says, closing her notebook and retracting her pen. Adayln, you go first," Emily says, hoping to get the conversation started.

"Well, I'm not as old as any of you, and I may not have spent as many centuries toiling in here," Adayln begins slowly. "I also realize that I'm *One of the Last* to be a member of our species, but my lack of abundant wisdom shouldn't be overlooked or even dismissed. I'm bringing true facts over and above any vast wisdom that may have been spoken about this place. The Hidden Realms are true; they are not a myth," Adayln says feverishly.

"I'm not questioning your facts. Do you think that I have ever considered your wisdom or lack thereof?" Keoh says smugly.

"What facts are you disputing?" Adayln responds.

"What facts have you given me? No facts: just speculation on what you may or may not have seen when you were tampering with the SDS Systems," Keoh tells her, looking over at Emily to ensure she is documenting Adayln's words.

"Repaired — repaired the SDS System," Adayln attests, also looking over at Emily as the anointed barrier to document everyone's posterity. "Plus, I can't show you any facts while we are here as seventeen year olds," Adayln says, lifting her arms in the air.

"That is why we are going to Okanagan Falls, to get our facts," I tell them all. The conversation is once again heated. "Then we go back home and go to sleep."

"But you are not answering my question. What do you think we will find?" Emily presses Adayln again.

I think hard myself as Adayln seems to be ponder her next words. I would be lying to say that I haven't ever considered the existence of Hidden Realms. I imagine it is just more of the same, a never-ending valley. It's all so real in here that it's almost painful to believe that all of this wonder is manufactured by a species of an ancient biological form. We are the gods of this realm; LaPorte created it, every inch. If the Great Founder from many centuries ago constructed this world with hidden areas, it does beg the question of why? And why the firm stance of telling our entire species for centuries that these realms are merely holowalls on the edge of town? I know we will find something — the question is what? "The truth," Adayln says simply. "We will find the truth. That is what we will see."

Chapter 9

"C'mon, let's keep going. We still have to walk back home after we reach Okanagan Falls," I remind them all to pick up the pace. Adayln struggles to get up from the ground, but she eventually grunts her way onto her feet. It's 1:30 p.m., and I figure we have only another half an hour to go by the imprecise calculations in my head.

Off the side of the road, we file by two by two. I am up front next to Keoh, leading the way. I can feel the adrenaline rising in Josie's body with every step. I keep forgetting that I'm in her body; it is strange not having total control over your own body's emotions and functionality. It's almost like I have lost the remembrance of feeling what I was once like as a pure biological human. Perhaps Asia was right about this as well — not that I would ever give her any sound credit.

It's been over a thousand years since my First-Biological walked the Earth in the Real Realm. Even the sensation of the common cold has long dissipated from my mind. Perhaps it is the haze of being in Penticton awake that is clouding my thoughts of those specific feelings.

I've lived twenty-two full lives in Penticton, in the SDS, yet I can't remember any of the previous names of any of my former stasis avatars. There is definitely a limitation on my Real Realm thoughts while subjecting my consciousness to these extreme and dangerous conditions. I believe it's merely a storage concern, that a stasis avatar doesn't have the required memory capacity to uptake my full Double R conscious. Unnerving — that's how I can describe this current feeling. I wish I could just turn that sensation off.

"Ahh, look at this: it's a clear rendering of a holowall," Keoh says, pointing to a clear-cut line slicing through the trees up the East Valley Wall.

"Those are power poles, Keoh," Adayln says, shaking her head at her detractor directly in front of her. The large wooden sign welcoming us into *Okanagan Falls* now stands to the direct right. It is attached to a refreshing sugary beverage sign of a famous brand from that era in time.

"I could do with one of those Cokes," Adayln says, out of breath, while pointing with eyes wide at the sign. We stand side by side looking down the desolate road, knowing we are all one step away from entering a Hidden Realm.

"Okay, who is going first?" Emily asks with jubilant excitement.

"What does it matter?" Keoh remarks while looking down at Emily.

"This is history in the making, the first conscious mind to go beyond the realm of Penticton," Emily says with a scoff. "This is a milestone in the advancement of our species."

Sensing nervousness as none of us step forward, I reach my hand in front of me. I grasp around, feeling nothing, as the rest of the group looks on intently. I smile and step forward and turn to face the group. "Do I look okay? Do I appear whole?" I inquire fervidly as I pat down my body, feeling myself still there.

"You look normal; do you feel weird?" Adayln asks, peering at me with one eye closed.

"Wait, I should be writing all this down," Emily frets while reaching into her backpack for her notebook. "Miranda, could you do that walk again, this time more heroically? It would play better for my readers," she adds. I answer by ignoring her request.

"All is normal; all feels normal. I think it's safe," I say reassuringly as Keoh takes the next step forward to stand beside me. He then lifts both hands in the air.

"This proves nothing," Keoh states, distinctly unimpressed.

"Nothing? We are here, Keoh; look at the sign," Adayln says, pointing over to the *Welcome to Okanagan Falls* billboard. "We are right next to a Hidden Realm," she continues. She walks past Keoh who wears a look of disinterest etched on his face.

"Look over there; the town is clear and perfectly rendered," Adayln states empathically with bubbling glee. "Look at the details of that General Store with those rusty old wagon wheels outside the entrance. Why waste such detail and power consumption, if I couldn't visit it?" Adayln asks sassily, trying to get Keoh's attention. "Oh, and they have Coke in the window. C'mon, drinks are on —" Adayln begins, but she is immediately flung right past us at a jarring speed. Seemingly nothing threw her back forcefully ten feet. She tumbles violently along the road until her body flops suddenly to a full stop.

"Adayln!" Emily cries, tossing her backpack to the side of the road and running after her. Josie's body stands frozen, refusing to engage into action. I can only determine this immobility is from sheer fear, but I cannot be sure. Eventually, I gather myself and increase the required adrenaline to join Adayln and Emily.

We help Adayln up to a seated position. Her head struggles to stay up by bouncing from side to side. "Adayln, are you okay? Are you injured?" Emily asks frantically, grasping the back of Adayln's head to hold it still. Adayln's eyes blink rapidly. Her chest moves in and out, indicating that she is indeed alive. She slowly comes back to life.

"What hit me?" Adayln slurs while her face winces in apparent pain.

"You walked forward, and then you were violently tossed back," Emily tells her while checking all of Adayln's limbs for any damage. I remain silently crouched on the ground next to Adayln, my thoughts crippled of what to say. It's hard to explain. The fluidity of expressing my thoughts verbally is hampered by manufactured anxiety from my stasis avatar. My chest is pounding, my small hairs are standing on end; it's an exhilarating feeling, yet I wish only for it to end quickly.

"Holowall with a punch," Keoh says. He smiles, punching the air in front of him. "I told you so. There is no hidden realm; it is simply nothing."

"How far did Adayln go past the sign before she was thrown back?" I ask calmly. I stand up and walking back to where she last stood.

"Miranda, wait; that's dangerous," Emily calls out as I stand four paces in, past the border of the sign.

"What are you doing?" Keoh calls out. "We have proven it's a holowall; let's go home. Let's go back to sleep and forget this nonsense," he pleads with me to stop.

"Something just doesn't seem right," I say, looking forward down the road.

I reach my hand to stretch out past the point Adayln walked. Closing both of my eyes, I am expecting to get thrust back. I dangle and dance my fingers, spreading them out, feeling nothing but the air floating over them.

"You're reckless, Miranda Sage!" Keoh calls out as I look back briefly, seeing him stand there with his hands on his hips. I then take a deep breath and walk forward, wanting nothing more to prove him wrong. I am not sure why I am compelled to step forward while all this fear is crippling poor Josie's body. Think past it, push past it, you are Miranda Sage, you are stronger than these natural feelings. One step, two steps, three steps I go, well ahead of the spot where Adayln was thrust back.

"How is that possible?" Keoh remarks while walking towards me with a surprised look on his face. I twirl in a circle, allowing my dress to fly in the air with my arms stretched out wide. "It exists!" I cry out with a smile, looking up at the wondrous Cascadian sky.

"Let's not get too far ahead of ourselves," Keoh states precariously as he joins me. He stops me from twirling and looks me right in the eyes. "You're not acting normal," he then tells me.

"What do you mean?" I ask boldly as Keoh grabs my arms and starts dragging me back towards Adayln and Emily.

"How were you able to go farther than Adayln?" Emily calls out to us.

"I'm fine, Keoh, seriously," I tell him, yanking my arm from his grasp.

"There is an obvious obstruction in the way," Keoh says, looking menacingly towards Okanagan Falls.

"What happened?" Adayln asks in a daze, trying to be heard over the commotion.

"You hit the wall, Adayln, just like I said you would," Keoh says with a hearty chuckle.

"How is it that Miranda could walk farther into Okanagan Falls, though?" Emily asks, trying to help Adayln up from the pavement. Adayln quickly sits back down, pulling Emily down with her.

"*I need to sit back down,*" Adayln slurs. "*You made it in?*" she then asks in a shaky voice.

"About ten steps farther then you did. I'm going to see how far I can actually go," I tell them. My heart pounds loudly as I speak.

"Reckless, this is all reckless," Keoh says. "It's time to go back home."

"Maybe Keoh is right, Miranda; you may get hurt like Adayln," Emily says. She stands up from her crouched position.

"We have come this far, though; we may never have this chance for answers again," I say, standing but still not facing them.

"*Miranda, please wait* —" Adayln mumbles in discomfort.

"I want to know what this is all about!" I yell, looking directly down the road with Okanagan Falls in the near distance.

"Miranda, this is not you. This is not who you are," Emily says, coming up beside me.

"There is something here," I say to Emily, still not moving my gaze.

"Miranda, you are not this crazy. Think about what you are saying," Emily tells me, grabbing onto my left shoulder to sway me back. I feel Emily's slight tug, but without any care, I bolt forward down the road.

"Miranda, no!" Emily screams out in unison with Keoh as a feeling washes over me that I'm in no harm.

I'm twenty feet in, and nothing has pushed me back. I stop and turn to face the group.

"It's safe," I call back; however, none of them follow. They all look at me like I'm insane, but I feel no concerns for my wellbeing like they do.

"What about what happened to Adayln?" Emily calls out, pointing at Adayln who is still sitting down on the road.

"Whatever it was seems to have gone!" I yell back with my arms raised in a sign showing them that it is indeed safe. Emily walks forward, inching closer to me until she is standing right beside me.

"Adayln, are you coming?" Emily calls out to her.

"I don't — think so — I'm afraid," Adayln says with a sputtering stutter, dragging herself off to the side of the road.

"Maybe we should head back, Miranda," Emily says with an intense look of concern as two bright lights in the distance approach from the area of Okanagan Falls.

"Something is coming. It's a car," Keoh says, and we all move to the side of the road.

Our eyes are all glued to the passing vehicle. The driver notices us glaring and gives us a friendly wave of hello. "Seems to be occupied, at least by one person; odd that there isn't much traffic on this road," Emily remarks, watching the vehicle carry on down the road towards Penticton.

"Come on, let's keep going. Adayln, you stay there; we'll circle back for you," I call out to Adayln as she just sits there slumped over, giving back no response. We continue to approach the town. Keoh is on the left shoulder of the road while Emily and I walk on the right side.

"Emily, stay a step behind me just in case," I say, looking over at her. I am not sure where I am summoning the wherewithal to be so brave. Josie's body is screaming with anxiety and fear that is difficult for me to suppress.

"The detail is amazing, it's almost like—" Keoh starts to describe before collapsing to his knees, grabbing both sides of his head. He screams loudly in pain, tilting his head up to the sky. Emily and I run over to Keoh, but not before he is flung violently back down the road, just like Adayln. Keoh tumbles uncontrollably like a rag doll having to wait for its momentum to die down before his body can come to a complete stop.

"Keoh!" Emily calls out as we both run back to see if he is okay. "Keoh!" Emily cries out again. We kneel beside him, checking to see if he's alright.

"Experiment over," Keoh laments in pain, rolling over to sit up.

"What happened, Keoh?" I ask firmly of him. As he blinks, his eyes are out of sync with one another.

"The ringing in my head," Keoh says, grabbing onto the sides of his head to cover his ears. His elbows and knees are scraped and bloody from being thrust back along the hard pavement. "We are not welcomed!" he cries out in extreme pain, still covering his ears. Emily and I each grab underneath his shoulders and move him to the side of the road.

It takes a long minute for Keoh to slow his breathing down to a regular rate before he removes his hands from his ears. Another car approaches from the direction of Penticton and slows down when it sees us all crouched down at the side of the road.

"You girls okay?" asks the elderly man behind the wheel, rolling down his window to bring his car to a full stop.

"Yes, we are fine, thank you," Emily says sweetly. She stands up and approaches his window.

"Your friend looks hurt," the old man says, pointing his chin.

"She's fine, oh — she's just clumsy," Emily tells him with a lighthearted laugh. The old man looks puzzled and rolls up his window, proceeding again towards Okanagan Falls.

"Let's head back," Adayln mumbles. She is still laying on her back at the side of the road.

"Agreed," Keoh confirms soundly, standing up. "For once I agree with you."

Emily and Keoh begin walking back towards Adayln as she attempts to stand up to meet them. "Miranda, let's go," Emily says. Turning her head back, she sees that I am not moving. I don't answer her; I just continue staring down the road watching the old man's car disappear into the distance. My heart feels as though it wants to burst from my chest. I hear a voice, perhaps that of Josie, but I can't be sure. Every fibre of me is telling me to flee this area; my sense of flight is set to high. However, I'm conflicted. I want to know the full truth of what we are dealing with.

"Miranda!" Emily calls out again. I look behind me and see the three of them huddled in fear.

I tell them, "I'm pushing forward."

"Miranda, this is not worth it; you'll get hurt," Emily cries out.

"I'm not afraid," I say, turning my gaze back towards Okanagan Falls. I walk forward with a struggling shake as Josie's body shivers with a feeling of dread. I drown out the voices of my fellow shipmates as they continue their pleas for me to return.

I march on, oblivious to my recklessness yet knowing in my soul, deep down, that no harm will come to me. Those settling thoughts are not translatable to my stasis avatar as a trickle of urine now streams down my right leg. Keep it together, Josie; no harm will come to us. I must get these answers; I cannot turn back now.

Ten minutes of nervous sweats, goose-bumped skin, and urine-soaked undergarments later, I reach the middle of this small town's main street. "*Record grrr,*" I grumble. "What a bad habit — just think, and hopefully this mush will remember," I say, slapping my temple with my palm to mush my mush around.

Okanagan Falls is only about three blocks of small shops with a vast open area for a summer market. All of the shops are uniquely touristy in their appearance. However, all the businesses are closed shut except for the General Store at the far end of the street. I go to the sidewalk and peer into the window of the Okanagan Falls Tea Room only to see no lights on, just empty tables. I then look up and down the road to see no cars or people. I slip off my urine-soaked underwear and toss them in a nearby garbage bin next to the bus stop.

I take a deep breath and comb my hands through my curly crimson hair to help settle my body's nerves. This beautiful area is rendered in perfect detail just like Penticton, from every blade of grass to every buzzing fruit fly.

I make my way to the General Store, being that it is the only visible storefront open for business. It has a rusty ancient feel to its design; in fact, the whole town has the look of a forgotten era. The worn wooden steps creak and squeak as I ascend from the adjacent sidewalk. Pushing open the pale-lemon door, the ringing of a bell hanging from above drowns out the noise coming from its rusted hinges. An old woman, who appears to be at least in her eighties, stands behind the counter with a scowled look of contempt upon her face. I let out a nervous smile while her unwelcoming demeanour remains. The old woman's face remains still and unmoving, like it had petrified to stone over her long toil.

"Just grabbing some Cokes," I tell the old woman, pointing to the fridge near the back of her store. The blast of cold air circles around me and up my dress to make all my hairs stand on end. I quickly grab four cans, shut the fridge door, and taking the Cokes to the counter.

"Brrr, that's cold," I remark to the old woman as I zip up Emily's rusty-mango hoody.

"Four dollars," the old woman says with a rasp, placing the beverages into a plastic bag.

"I've never been here before; how many people live in Okanagan Falls?" I inquire of her as she counts out my change.

"Dollar change, have a good day," the old woman responds quickly, not answering my question.

"Okay then, thank you," I say with a smile. Not bothering to press her any further, I exit her store.

I take one more look around Okanagan Falls, now clearly seeing cars on the highway on the West Ridge heading south. This place is all too weird. LaPorte Industries maintains that there is nothing beyond Penticton; this is apparently not the case.

I sit down on a bench at the only bus stop. My eyes scan up and down, seeing nothing of note along this one desolate road. Every few minutes a single car drives down the street, yet I see no people walking about. The absence of people gives off an eerie feeling. I try to remember back to my days of living in the Real Realm of Penticton with just bits of flashing thoughts popping in and out of view. The overall narrative of my First-Biological has been somewhat fragmented over time to remain soundly in my past where it most likely belongs.

Visiting Okanagan Falls was never high on anyone's to-do list back in the day, not even for tourists — if I recall correctly. So, why render a town in near perfection only to limit its experience to those wanting to better themselves within the SDS? How far south of Penticton can I go before I hit a wall myself? Why are Keoh and Adayln denied entry into this hidden realm?

"*Record on,*" I say aloud again. "Damn it, Miranda; that doesn't work in here. "You'll have to rely on this brain to retain what you are seeing," I remind myself, feeling foolish about forgetting my limitations in here. I crack open one of the Cokes and take a big swig to quench my thirst. I spit it out immediately as the fizziness, without warning, tickles my throat. I gasp and cough, feeling that some of the beverage has exited through my nose during its extraction.

Coke? I haven't had one for a long time; I must remember to drink it slowly. Rising from the bench I take one last look at Okanagan Falls in its entire rusty splendour. I imagine the story I'll be able to tell our species about this new discovery — *or will I?* Do I risk being shunned by LaPorte Industries for part taking in the tampering of their precious equipment?

This world just seems as alive as I can remember it, but I'm not the owner of this world — none of us are. I kneel to the ground to hover over a colony of black ants. They scurry randomly in all directions, carrying about their ant-like existence, never wondering who or what they may be. They are programmed so perfectly that no one could ever tell them apart from their Real Realm counterparts.

I stroll off the main road and head north towards the southern beach of Skaha Lake. Penticton is basked in the distance by the ever-increasing crimson sun working its way slowly to the zenith of our upcoming summer. Everything about this realm feels and looks so real it boggles the mind that this is only a simulation created by the mind of a biological human.

How was LaPorte able to construct such a world down to the very minuscule detail of a fruit fly buzzing around my head or a drop of sweat forming on my brow? LaPorte was someone well beyond their own time in history to be such a builder of worlds in an ancient time of technology. I grant that not everything went smoothly with many of the Founder's firsts SDS devices, at the cost of many conscious lives. However, our species demanded that LaPorte may be allowed to proceed, despite the loss of countless souls.

I walk among the sharp reeds popping up close to the shore as I slowly meander back in the direction of the group. The blades of the plants dig small nicks and cuts into the soft, supple skin of my legs. Usually I would just ask myself to remove that painful sting, but no such commands have yet evolved. I yelp and cringe, hopping my way out of the forest of reeds to the soft marshy grounds of tall grass. My feet sink slowly into the soft ground and make a popping noise with every raised footstep. Again, I wonder at the attention to detail. No human could paint a picture like this in such vivid detail. LaPorte is by far the most celebrated artist of all humankind, but it nags at me more than ever before how LaPorte achieved this masterpiece.

Back on Eastside Road, I can see the group of misfits sitting patiently at the side of the road waiting for my return. They will most likely pose to me a barrage of questions about this strange journey I just undertook. What answers will I have for them? I am filled with more questions than solutions.

Keoh is lying on his back, propping his head up with his hands as a makeshift pillow. Adayln is sitting cross-legged, staring down at the ground; her body is slumped over like she just wants to fall asleep. Emily seems to be consoling Adayln by sitting next to her with her hand on Adayln's shoulder.

Nobody is looking at me as I approach, as they are all attending to their own business. I did leave them all abruptly. They may be upset with me for putting myself in harm's way. Perhaps these Cokes and the tale of my discovery will cheer then back up.

"I've returned bearing gifts," I say, handing Emily a cold can of Coke from the white shopping bag.

"Something is not right, Miranda," Emily quickly tells me, though I could read the worry depicted clearly on her face.

"What's happened?" I ask worriedly, placing a can in front of Adayln when she doesn't take it from my hand.

"Adayln has become less responsive to any verbal commands. She just sits there in a state of inaction," Emily explains frantically.

I crouch to one knee and lift Adayln's fallen chin so that I may look her in the eye. "Adayln, speak to me. It's Miranda," I tell her as her eyes struggle to stay locked onto mine.

"*We need — to leave — place,*" Adayln mumbles in an incoherent stutter. I rise up and look at Emily with a mutual concern that Adayln is not well. I immediately go to check Keoh, who is still laying flat on his back with his eyes staring up at the sky.

"Keoh, please tell me that you are okay," I plead, but he just rolls to his side. He then turns his head to face me and his serene look turns to a menacing scowl.

Chapter 10

I suddenly find myself flat on my back with Keoh straddling my abdomen. Keoh's stasis avatar has the frightened look of a little girl mixed with the aggression of a raving lunatic. Both of his hands are gripped tightly on my shoulders. His nails are digging into my skin, making me squirm. I let out yelping cries of pain as I continue to try to shift Keoh off of me.

His eyes are wide and crimson-shot accompanied by a continuous flowing of tears that stream down his wind-sailed cheeks. His mouth is wide open, allowing salvia to drool uncontrollably onto my face as Keoh wails in a feverish pitch. Keoh lifts my shoulders up with his nails embedded into my flesh, only to then thrust me back down to the ground, repeatedly shaking me with his more adaptive strength.

"Keoh, please," I cry out among his wails. Emily finally makes her way over to put Keoh in a chokehold. She then leans back to make Keoh release his grip on me. Emily and Keoh both roll back as I get to my knees quickly and crawl over to aid Emily. Keoh is out of control, lashing out in all directions and having a complete breakdown. Emily and I stand side by side. We watch him thrash around violently on the side of the road, succumbing to which I could only imagine being a fit of rage.

"Keoh, calm down!" Emily calls out to him as we remain at a safe distance. Adayln still remains frozen on the ground. She rests her hands on top of her knees and does not even bother to look behind her at all the commotion. "What is wrong with Keoh?" Emily asks me, confused.

"I don't know," I say in a sassy tone which I didn't mean to project. "Keoh was just lying there, and then in a flash, he was sitting on top of me, pinning me to the ground," I continue to explain. I am just as shocked as her.

Five minutes later, Keoh's dress is ripped and soiled from rolling around in the dirt. His stasis avatar's long greasy locks are matted and filthy as Keoh slowly begins to find a centre of peace to control his thoughts. The crying also stops, as does the uncontrollable screaming that voiced no understandable concerns. Keoh sits up quietly, sniffing repeatedly to clear his airways. His now mangled lemon strands are completely covering his face.

"Keoh, you okay?" I ask nervously as I approach him. He doesn't move. Instead, he just sits there with his hands in his lap with his legs straight and flared out, silently weeping and sniffling. I kneel beside Keoh, looking back at Emily for visual support in case Keoh attacks me again. I reach out and brush away his bangs to reveal the face of his stasis avatar calmly regaining her composure. Keoh's cheeks are rosy; his eyes and lips are increasingly puffy. The small dress Keoh has chosen to wear today is beyond repair, and he just sits there half naked.

"*What happened to her?*" Keoh mumbles slowly.

"What happened to whom, Keoh?" I ask, unsure of his question.

"Do you mean me, in the Hidden Realm?" I inquire, quickly glancing back at Emily. She shrugs her shoulders, just as confused as me.

"No, Madison," Keoh promptly corrects me.

"Madison? I don't know who you are speaking about, Keoh," I tell him, softly rubbing his bare back in an attempt to comfort him.

"My avatar is Madison; she is angry," Keoh remarks, glancing up from his lap to look me in the eyes.

"Oh, of course," I say, shaking my head. "Sorry, we never asked what her name is," I tell Keoh. His breathing becomes calmer after that menacing look from earlier.

"Are you okay, Keoh?" Emily asks cautiously. She comes closer, being careful not to startle him.

"*Anger* — pure anger!" Keoh says, wiping his eyes. "I have never felt that emotion so strongly before."

"Did you not have any control over this anger?" I inquire, trying to remove twigs and debris from his hair. Keoh just sits there, reflecting.

"No, I was there — I was just as angry and didn't know how to shut it off — Part of me didn't want to shut it off — Madison's mad," Keoh says with a nervous stutter, looking at both us with frightened eyes that are searching for answers.

"You are Madison, though, Keoh," I remind him, thinking that in his blind rage he may have forgotten that fact.

"I know that! I know where I am and that I'm awake in this infernal place," Keoh states, shaking his head in disapproval.

"Just making sure, Keoh. Can't be too sure given that the SDS sickness —" I begin.

"I'm not sick!" Keoh interrupts me resoundingly.

"Okay, okay," I reply, not wanting another blowback to occur.

"That was Madison, not me," Keoh says, standing up with a wobble in his step before finding sound footing. Emily doesn't question what Keoh has just said as it makes no sense and there is no point enraging the situation with more prodding.

Perhaps Madison is bleeding through, and there is a duality at play in Keoh's mind for control over Madison's body. The chances of that are entirely nil as a stasis avatar can only harbour one conscious mind, or at least that is what we know. Keoh shows clear signs of SDS sickness from what I understand of documented cases.

"Adayln, may Keoh have your hoody?" I turn to her, knowing we can't walk back into town with Keoh's dress in such a mangled state. Adayln doesn't respond and remains unmoving, still facing the direction of Okanagan Falls. I walk over and crouch down in front of Adayln. Her facial expressions are still, void of all emotions. Her eyes are unblinking and her jaw is slack and wide open with a trickle of drool cascading like a waterfall out of the side of her mouth.

I wave my hand in front of her eyes, yet get no response. I look over Adayln's shoulder to Emily and say, "This mission is over; we all need to get back home immediately." I tuck my hands under Adayln's shoulder, prodding her to stand up. Thankfully, she does.

"Where we going? Okanagan Falls — now?" Adayln slurs, bobbing her head from side to side.

"No, Adayln, it's time to go home," I say, removing Adayln's rusty blue hoody from her upper torso.

"Emily, takes this and hand it to Keoh," I tell Emily, tossing over the hoody. Keoh takes the hoody from Emily and puts it on. However, the hoody is too short to cover Madison's larger frame.

"It will cover your upper half," Emily says, touching her own breasts as Keoh stands there exposed with a look of bewilderment on his face. Emily helps Keoh squeeze into the tight top, zipping it up to his neck.

"*What about Okanagan Falls?*" Adayln mumbles, apparently not herself.

"I'll tell you all about it later," I say dismissively. I reach down and crack open that cold can of Coke. Adayln grasps the Coke with both hands, sniffing it curiously before taking a sip.

"Here, I bought a can for each of you," I tell them, handing Emily and Keoh their own refreshing fizzy beverages. I gather everyone in a tight circle as a sense of anxiety starts to wash over me. It is indeed time to head home.

The walk back from Okanagan Falls is exceptionally far and arduous. However, Skaha Beach grows increasingly more massive with every step we take towards it. Each member of our ragtag group of misfits is seemingly dragging their stasis avatar. The desire to continue on awake in this realm is far from anyone's mind.

Adayln is unresponsive with possibly a head injury as that constant stream of drool continues to pour out the corner of her mouth. She doesn't talk or complain about how tired her body is like she did when we first set out from Penticton. Adayln shuffles her feet along, aided by Emily next to her side to maintain momentum and pace. Keoh, who is in the lead, has not said a word since we started our walk back home.

"Miranda, could you give me a hand?" Emily yells and I slow my speed to match hers. Adayln falls to one knee, breathing heavily with sweat pouring out to coat her entire body. I grab hold of Adayln's slippery right arm and hoist her up to her feet as Emily does the same to her left side.

"This walk is too much for her," Emily says, looking over at me.

"We are almost there; a half hour more and we'll be back at the sundial," I tell her, pointing in the direction of the beach.

"What will we do once we get there?" Emily asks vigorously as we shove Adayln to start walking forward again.

"We'll cross that bridge when we come to it," I say exhaustedly. This day is not turning out like I had hoped it would.

"Okanagan Falls, when are we there?" Adayln moans, lazily tilting her head to look up at me.

"We are heading home, Adayln," I tell her, not knowing if she can comprehend anything.

"Did we enter?" Adayln asks slowly in a garble of words. I merely shake my head as I make my way up to Keoh to check on him again.

"Keoh — speak to me," I plead with him. "Are you alright?"

"*You've done it again,*" Keoh mumbles quietly; he is clearly struggling to remain calm. "*I knew you hadn't changed — what compels me to allow you passage onboard my ship?*" he continues to lament in a low rumbling mumble.

"Keoh, I swear to you," I say to him, grabbing onto his arm (I quickly release my grip on his arm when Madison stares at me), "you were never meant to be involved," I utter calmly.

"Not involved — Miss Sage, you're reckless; you have always been this way," Keoh says, shaking his head. "And here I am thinking this new incarnation of you with a stripped-down attributes table would bring forth someone with a more reasonable temperament! How could I have been so wrong?" Keoh continues to scold, his voice growing louder as he speaks.

"This will all be over soon," I plead, trying to stop his anger from rising.

"Tried not to involve me, you say," Keoh laughs. "LaPorte Industries will have my SDS License for this. How am I supposed to travel within the colonies with no license?" he asks as his laughing jest turns on a dime to pure rage again.

"No one will know of this, Keoh," I tell him calmly. "We can mask this excursion — no one will ever know."

"How?" Keoh asks, looking somewhat intrigued.

"You have to trust me — we have known of one another for centuries," I say while looking up into his eyes. "Adayln and I will hide these tracks so they will never appear," I affirm with a head nod.

"Trust — huh?" he says, exhaling loudly. "*Even if I did trust you and believe that you can magically hide all this treason from the powers that be — explain how you intend to keep Miss Stellar, a journalist, quiet!*" Keoh demands in a harsh whisper to me under his breath so that only I may hear.

I look behind me and see the raven-haired beauty that encapsulates Miss Stellar looking out towards the western horizon. That's a new wrinkle brought to light by Keoh which I haven't adequately considered. Emily's implication is well out of the scope of a solution that I can currently come to terms with.

"*I believe I can reason with her,*" I whisper to Keoh, although the bead of sweat trickling down the side of my face indicates otherwise.

"This won't end well for any of us," Keoh says, quickening his stride to get ahead of me. He no longer wishes to speak.

"We have been through worse!" I remind him, but his forward march with his head down low shows that this is clearly an unshared sentiment.

———✦———

We reach Skaha Beach and return to the spot where we had first set out from eight hours ago. "Okay," I begin as we all huddle in a small circle within the sundial, "everyone home to bed. We will all fall asleep, and when we awake this —"

"Nightmare," Keoh jumps in, not helping one bit.

"This will all be over soon," I say. I look at my bare wrist, expecting to see a watch which apparently has never been there.

"I believe Adayln's stasis avatar has a concussion," Emily says with her arm around Adayln's hulking frame.

"Where do you live, Adayln?" I ask her, looking into her eyes for a sign of coherence.

"*Riva Ridge number fifty-seven,*" Adayln says with a mumbling of drool.

"Can you make it home to bed?" I ask loudly as Adayln struggles to keep her gaze upon me.

"I can take her," Keoh says, walking up to Adayln. "I live in the trailer park beside hers."

"Thank you, Kaptin Keoh," I say, my tone full of respect.

"Emily, where do you live?" I turn to face her.

"Seacrest —" Emily says, looking amazed that she remembered, "can't remember the house number but it's a brick and creamy white coloured house," she says, scratching the back of her head. "I think? — I can find it again," she says with a confident stammer.

"I live on Pineview Road," I say to Emily. "We can walk together."

Keoh puts his arm around Adayln's shoulders and Emily steps aside.

"See you in seven decades," I tell them. Keoh and Adayln walk along the sunlit shore towards the West — towards the more poverty-stricken area of town. Emily and I head north up South Main Street. I look back one last time at Adayln and Keoh, feeling somewhat humbled by what happened to Keoh. He'll thank me later for this experience, I'm sure of it, even though he was never supposed to be involved.

"That Corey is going to have to get his head checked out tomorrow," Emily says, snapping my attention over to her. "He'll have one massive headache come morning."

"That will be the least of Adayln's worries — once she wakes up," I say, totally conflicted on what to do with our sensational new revelation about Okanagan Falls.

"Emily, can I ask you with the most certain of honesty a question?" I inquire with trepidation. I feel my facial expressions giving off uncontrollable nerves of anxiousness.

"Well — that's a big ask for a journalist," Emily says playfully with an adorable laugh.

"That is sort of what I would like to ask," I slowly drawl out. Josie's nerves are clearly slowing me down.

"Well, what is it then?" Emily asks sharply, seeing that I am obviously struggling to speak.

"This story about today's events which I assume that you wish to tell —" I begin with an explicit assumption.

"Oh, this story will be epic," Emily says, beaming with glee. "I sure hope I remember it distinctly after seven decades."

"Well, about all that —" I stutter, trying to wield Josie to gather some semblance. "You know I worked at LaPorte Industries once — many eons ago," I remind her.

"You mentioned it on the *Misfit* — or at least your dating video did," Emily says, showing off her impressive memory.

"Yes, SDS top salesperson many times from 2075 — 2273," I say, trumping up my meaningless achievements from a bygone era.

"Are you worried about how you will be portrayed?" Emily asks, emitting a wide, toothy smile. "You won't be seen in any villainous light," she enlightens me.

"No, that's not what I'm trying to ask," I say, shaking my head. "Although thank you for that. I just don't think you'll be able to tell this tale," I inform her, finally saying the words held back by my fickle biology.

"By heavens, what do you mean?" Emily asks, somewhat startled. "The Press is never silenced."

"Well, as someone who has worked at LaPorte Industries," I preface, "if a treasonous investigation happens to launch from this venture today — it will most likely be all classified."

"Classified?" Emily says with a gasp, sounding astonished. "They can do no such thing. I know my powers, and I know my rights as a journalist — there will be no stopping the publication of this story," she rambles with a dash of confidence.

"Alright — I'm just letting you know," I say with a lazy shoulder shrug. "Just didn't want you to be hit with a surprise, that's all."

"Well, that's ludicrous," she scoffs. "I have never heard of any journalist being silenced by writing insider stories about LaPorte Industries," Emily says slowly. I notice that her brow is now furrowed.

"You can't hear of any if they are silenced," I explain, using Emily's own unsound logic.

"What can they do?" Emily asks with a sneer, "demand I purge my memory of this event?"

"They could," I say, thinking that it is in the realm of possibility of an acceptable- ask. "Although LaPorte practices are harsher," I continue, attempting to shed some light on Emily's speculative mind.

"Harsher than a purge?" Emily asks alarmingly, looking taken aback. "Miranda Sage, how much harsher can they go?" she asks. Her mind is evidently closed to more awful scenarios.

"Denying you access to the SDS System — permanently," I state calmly.

"Oh, Miranda, don't scare me with your horror stories. Being awake in the Real Realm doesn't scare me," Emily says clearly with zero inflection, just like Torstein.

"Alright," I say. "You did ask," I warn her.

"Let's just go back to sleep with dreams, not nightmares," Emily says in a shivering shimmy.

"Agreed," I tell her, feeling a bit anxious myself to get under Josie's bed covers.

"That's Seacrest over there," Emily says, pointing down the street to a road running below the wealthy Wiltse Flats area of the East Valley Wall.

"Good dreams to you, Emily," I say as she moves in close to give me a hug.

"Good dreams to you too, Miranda," Emily says, pulling back her head to look me in the eyes. "And thank you for the most exhilarating day that I have had in a long while," she then utters with a playful wink.

We break our embrace and go our separate ways. A feeling of deep conflict still weighs heavily on my mind. I have no idea what to do with this information — I hope the full consciousness of Miranda Sage will know what to do once I'm awake. Josie's mush is just not cutting it.

Inside my house, Mother and Little Sister are sitting on the couch and watching TV. "Josie?" Mother asks with a slight scowl on her face. "You're late for dinner."

"Sorry, Mom," I tell her sheepishly, "I was just at the beach with friends."

"You have exams next week — you need to be at home studying," Mother scolds.

"Yes, I'm going right upstairs to study — right now," I tell Mother in a somewhat fearful state as I turn my body to go upstairs.

"Josie!" Mother says harshly, making me stop just as my foot hits the first step.

"Yes?" I say, turning to face her.

"Your dinner is getting cold on the table," she says with a point of her finger towards the kitchen.

"Oh right," I say nervously. I walk gingerly in the direction of the kitchen, not feeling even a little bit hungry. I pick up the plate of congealed macaroni and cheese and see a scattering of sausage meat mixed among the bright mango-coloured sauce.

When I make it up to my room, I place the untouched dinner on my desk and waste no time whipping off my clothes to my bare essentials. I quickly turn off my bedroom light and swiftly crawl into bed. I huddle in a ball under the covers, waiting patiently for sleep to overtake me.

Chapter 11

The alarm screams uncontrollably, making my eyes shoot open. The sun's rays hit me through the slits of my blinds. I sit up and blink to focus my gaze on that infernal clock. My hand methodically reaches down behind the bedside table to unplug the alarm from its wailing.

"This is not the *Misfit*," I snarl under my breath, looking about my room. I jump out of bed, run to my mirror, and see that familiar freckled face staring back at me. I feel my face with both hands, hoping for this not to be true. It didn't work. Adayln's protocol didn't work.

I'm still Josie Birch!

I'm still awake.

Collapsing suddenly to my knees is followed by an uncontrollable fit of crying.

What is this?

Why am I doing this?

Get your emotions under control, Miranda, I command myself, but that request is soundly ignored. My breathing is erratic like I'm being held under water. Josie is out of control; this avatar is refusing my commands.

Wait, I am Josie Birch though.

Keep it together, Miranda. You are stronger than any emotions emitted from any human or otherwise.

Stop this crying.

Stop the tears.

Slow your heart rate.

All these requests go unheard, and I am overwhelmed by the extreme anxiety crippling my body. I slump over to the floor. On my side, I raise my knees up to my chest, curl my body into a ball, and hold myself tightly for comfort. No clear thoughts are in my head, only worry and despair. Why can't I clear these unwanted thoughts from my mind? They are so loud; there is no way to fight it. There is no end to this — all is lost.

I attempt to break free my body from its locked fetal position, but all I end up doing is rolling over to my other side, with my arms still wrapped around my knees. Mucus streaming out of my nose mixes with the abundance of tears cascading from my eyes to smear my face with a sticky coating. The desire to wipe my face is a command that is clearly not available. Loud piercing wails start emanating from my mouth as my jaw quivers, allowing spittle and drool to spill out.

Where is the end to this?

When will it subside?

Miranda, you must understand this body's reasoning to help better gain control. This thought pops into my mind with no blueprint for how to take on such a task. The grip — this deliberating grip — is making me bend to its will. Thoughts of being forever trapped in Penticton cycle and circle my thoughts and I wail once again. The insanity that will inevitably follow enters my shattered mind, constricting my chest and making it hard to breathe. I gasp for breath, having to spit out an abundance of mucus to clear my mouth and throat. Loud coughs are followed by unexpected screams, allowing a large intake of air in the process.

"Josie!" a comforting voice calls out, running to my side.

"Mom!" I cry out instinctively as she cradles my body.

"Josie, what's the matter? What's wrong?" Mother asks desperately, wiping my face with a tissue.

"I don't know? *Just — severe — worry*," I stutter out with a quivering lip.

"Worry over what?" Mother asks gently, lifting my slumping chin to make eye contact with me. I can't tell her the truth about who I really am. This belt of insanity that rips through my avatar is my own creation. I inhibited my conscious mind to be awake, knowing full well of all past peril in doing so.

It has been documented for centuries that you will increasingly go insane after waking your conscious mind in the SDS. It damages you — the real you — the Double R you. This damage requires extensive repairs at an exorbitant cost that only can be performed by LaPorte Industries themselves.

The monopoly they have over our species has been unimaginably repressive. They control every aspect of the SDS technology, caught tampering with their sensitive equipment to be deemed to certain exile from our peoples. It is frowned upon because our people fear death as a result of being denied LaPorte's goods and services. We do rely on them, for we are all Longevists. That is what we strive to achieve in this life. It is our goal to become like God — to become immortal to stand next to such a deity. It is to be a god, which is what heaven must be indeed.

Asia is right. How did I not see this before? I've been so blind, so many centuries blind. Entertaining such thoughts in passing with other races giving an alternate perspective into my species was repeatedly deflected. How ignorant of me. Of all people, me. I'm one of the originals; I'm *One of the Firsts*. I've been there since LaPorte's creation; I saw the rise.

"Josie," Mother cries, followed by repetitions of "Calm down."

You won't understand. I can't tell you, Mother. I'm destined to go insane in your daughter's body. There is no way for you to understand the truth behind your own life —let alone your daughter's.

"What severe worry, Josie?" Mother asks again.

"I have no — control," I stutter.

"Have you taken your Draxten?" she asks serenely, looking over my shoulder to my bedside table.

"Draxten — no?" I tell her, also looking behind me at the table. Mother gets up from the floor and makes her way over to the table. Grabbing a yellow container, she twists the cap off. She then kneels down beside me, passes me two crimson pills, and tells me to "Swallow them right now." I do what Mother says. She passes me a cup of water and I drink, clearing my throat of blocking debris. "You need to remember to take your pills, Josie," Mother tells me with a worried smile.

"Let's get ready for school; you should be fine by then," Mother tells me, standing up.

"School?" I repeat, shooting my gaze up to her eyes.

"School starts in an hour; you will be fine in twenty minutes," Mother tells me as she walks towards the door. "You're not missing school today because of this episode. I want to see you downstairs in ten minutes," she says. She departs my room, leaving the bedroom door wide open.

"School today?" I say with a gasp, standing on my feet. I look over to my reflection in the mirror and see Josie stare right back.

"Shit." Although I haven't uttered this curse in ages, it certainly feels right in this era. "How am I going to get out of this shit?" I curse again, feeling better as I say it.

Okay, think Miranda, think.

"First, be Josie and act like Josie. There is to be no mention of Miranda from here on out. Second, get dressed. Third, take a shower — wait. That's the wrong order." I remove my boxer shorts and a t-shirt.

Naked, I run across the hallway into the bathroom and immediately turn on the shower. I leap under the falling water, yelping in shock at the frigid water that tingles my skin. Both shower knobs I hastily turn in opposite directions. This makes the pelting water even colder.

I jump out of the shower, slipping when my left heel makes contact with the smooth tile floor. I crash, falling backwards with both ass cheeks slapping hard to the ground. My head bangs against the wall. The floor tiles are cold as I sit wet and naked next to the tub, rubbing the back of my head.

Standing up, I grab the towel off the basin to rub the water from my ginger hair. Wrapping the towel around my torso, I quickly sprint over to my bedroom closet. I need to find something to wear.

I select a summer dress, dark blue with lemon sunflowers, accessorized with a short-top cream cardigan. Now presentable for the day, I make my way to the bedroom door, only to turn back. I forgot to put on underwear.

While descending the stairs, a feeling of calm washes over me. I breathe in gently through my nostrils. It must be the medication making everything seem so tranquil. My body is at peace with itself after warring to rip myself apart just moments earlier. I feel back in command; Josie is starting to listen to me again.

Remember you are Josie Birch, Miranda. Thinking of yourself as a split entity will only give way to more insanity. To be normal, you must act normal; to act normal, you must think normal. Thinking that there is a duality about you — is not thinking normal. Keep thinking of yourself as Josie Birch and not as Miranda Sage. The carnation of Miranda doesn't exist in 2005 — but Josie Birch does. The conscious mind of Miranda cannot survive here; you must transcend and be Josie Birch.

Adayln was wrong about putting us back to sleep after twenty-four hours. She was also wrong about only waking up me and her. Yesterday, I had a feeling deep down that she may have gotten this wrong as well. Maybe I'll enter the deep sleep again in forty-eight hours, maybe never — or forever!

Can I fight this insanity for that long?

If I could perform this act of living out the life of Josie Birch, I could possibly escape without much permanent conscious harm done. Suicide would put my consciousness in comatic shutdown; I could also wipe myself. No. Be strong, Miranda. No! Be strong, Josie! You are Josie Birch; be strong. I repeat this mantra over and over as I make my way into the kitchen.

"Wow, Josie. You look beautiful in that dress," Mother says, surprised.

"Thank you," I remark calmly. I smile, looking over at Little Sister.

"I have never seen you dress so formal just for school before," Mother says while filling up a plate of breakfast foods for me.

"Why are you dressed like that?" Little Sister asks through a mouthful again — this kid clearly lacks manners.

"What do you mean; isn't this how I usually dress?" I ask nervously as Mother places a plate of fruit and brown toast in front of me.

"Jeans and a t-shirt — not dresses," Little Sister struggles to say, swallowing her food as she continues to talk. Then why would Little Sister dress me like this yesterday?

"It's almost summer — isn't it? Why not get a head start?" I tell Little Sister with a slight shrug of my shoulders. My little sister is just a brat; they all suffer from that affliction. No reason to raise an alarm; you're in sound-mind, Miranda.

Mother kisses us customarily on the tops of our heads and then promptly exits out the front door. "Jeans and a t-shirt, huh," I say to Little Sister, grinning up and down. I promptly stand up from the table without touching any of my food and start walking confidently back upstairs. I tell Little Sister, "I'll be right back."

Back into my bedroom, I locate my jeans and slip them up under my dress. I then lift the dress over my head. As I try to clasp the front of my jeans, I have to suck in my breath. These jeans are tight and snug; however, they also show all my womanly features as I twist and twirl my reflection in the mirror.

"A bra! I need a bra," I call, grabbing both breasts and covering them with my hands. I locate a bright pink bra and secure it about my torso, jiggling each cup from its sides to make my breasts fit.

From the dresser, I select a well-worn white t-shirt imprinted with a faded decal of the word *Brazil* to add to the look. Heading back downstairs, I grab that rusty-mango hoody of Emily's that I wore yesterday to complete my ensemble. Now, I am feeling the part of being Josie.

We leave for school at the same time as yesterday and run into Ryan, again not by chance. "Morning, Josie. You look, look beaut — well, you look well," Ryan awkwardly compliments with a stutter.

"Smooth," Little Sister says mockingly, shaking her head.

"Thank you, Ryan. Sorry about yesterday; I just needed to be alone," I explain as Ryan walks beside me.

"It's okay; I was just worried. It's not like you to miss school," Ryan says.

"Missed school? You skipped Thursday?" Little Sister asks with a surprised grin.

"Walk ahead of us," I tell her, knowing that Little Sister would use such information against me down the road with Mother. Ryan and I slow down, so that Little Sister is outside of our vocal range yet still close enough to keep an eye on her.

"Ryan, I'm sorry to have barked at you yesterday," I tell him. "I just wasn't myself."

"That's okay," Ryan says, kicking a random rock with his foot. "I just care, that's all."

"I know you do," I tell him soundly, kicking myself for my rudeness.

We turn the corner onto South Main Street and right away I notice the raven-haired beauty of Emily Stellar nervously standing a block away — rustling her dress of amber marigolds from side to side in a fidgety manner.

"Ryan, can you do me a favour and see my little sister the rest of the way to school?" I ask hastily. I know that the conversation I'm about to have with Emily is not for his ears.

"Yes, of course — why?" Ryan inquires, looking confused.

"I just need to talk to that girl over there," I say with a point of my finger at Emily.

"Emma?" Ryan asks with a look of surprise. "You two are like enemies, have been since the sixth grade."

"Oh — well," I say with a stutter," we patched that all up — days ago," I continue to rift off my fluttering mind.

"Alright then, maybe see you at lunch?" Ryan says, but I have already taken my leave to dart across the street. I don't answer him and his request fleets quickly out my mush to a more pressing matter.

"Miranda!" Emily calls out. I lower my hands, signalling for her to quiet as I approach.

"*It's Josie, — remember?*" I whisper before harshly instinctively embracing her in a hug.

"It's been over twenty-four hours, and we are still awake," Emily says at a high register. I take her by the arm to lead her behind the school. We continue to walk in a fretful manner past the school and over to the large soccer pitch, clear out of view of anyone.

"Can we please stop walking, Miranda?" Emily cries out. She comes to a dead stop.

"I realize that we are still awake," I say as I keep my gaze set out to the Southwest corner of the soccer pitch.

"What are we going to do?" Emily cries out.

"We wait," I tell her, still not looking in her direction.

"What are you looking for?" Emily whines, coming up to stand beside me.

"The trailer park kids come to school through that chain link entrance," I tell her with a head nod. "I'm waiting for Adayln to arrive."

"You think she can get us out of here?" Emily asks, looking up at me with a glimmer of hope.

"No, I don't think she can do that," I tell Emily with a frown. "I just want to understand how Adayln stuck us here."

"Great, so there is no way out!" Emily laments. "We will be stasis bleeding in no time."

"There she is!" I tell Emily, pointing to Corey's hulking frame. Corey has jettisoned out of the chain link opening like a gazelle emerging from the high grass on a sunny plain. He is bent over, tired, out-of-breath, and un-gazelle-like to be sure. Then, in a flash, he is tackled violently to the ground by a stronger prey — the slender beauty, Madison.

Emily and I run at a sprinter's clip to reach them, but they are still tussling on the grass and grabbing each other by the hair. "Both of you — stand down!" I say in a commanding tone; however, they continue to scrap on the ground.

Emily and I finally pull them apart from each other; this is not an easy task as Keoh is immensely upset. "What have you done!" Keoh yells. He is enraged, most likely about our current predicament. We eventually get them up off the ground and walk them down a garbage alley behind a row of old townhouses.

Keoh marches with a mighty stride which reminds me of his centuries within the *Service*. He is a short-tempered Neanderthal of a conscious mind. The man doesn't even add any perks to his table — leaves it blank. There is no enlightenment coming from him — he's a Neanderthal.

Adayln, on the other hand, looks to be acting the weaker of the two, as she is clearly struggling for control over her avatar. Corey is apparently fighting his body for power. She just hasn't had enough experience in this place to have better control of herself. That consciousness battle must be playing a role in her stupefied demeanour — that lazy eye she is developing isn't helping matters.

This will be a train hitting a stern on its tracks — Keoh is going to rip Adayln in two.

And then that's when it happens — the nightmare within the daylight. Keoh, coming back to us from one of his outward pacing marches, unsheathes an ordinary kitchen knife and starts repeatedly stabbing Adayln — poor Corey's body.

The crimson is everywhere — it gets on all of us — Keoh the most. The scene explodes into sobbing, wailing, and lots of yelling to no one in particular. It feels like it goes on for days — can't tell how many minutes have passed. We are soundly surrounded by flashing strobes of lights and promptly strapped flat on our backs to gurneys which prevent us from moving.

That excessive clanking of metal against metal with my stretcher knocking back and forth in that ambulance — I'm not even hurt, but I scream, "Who are these butchers!" They are not making any sense when they speak. Just let me off this gurney! I scream out in silence, wiggling hard to break free my body. Let me go — you butchers!

That's when I devise a plan which makes me defy my knots. I break into calm with a game of possum and play slowly and sweetly into their hearts once we reach the hospital. Then, when their guards are down, I flush to the left and kick free down the most slippery of smooth floors with a woman in a blue jumpsuit on my tail.

I stop and stand my ground, throwing a hard-right-hand hook to the side of her face which makes her recoil to the floor. The stunned woman just kneels while holding her hand to her swollen face. She's got that look of one who has never been slapped or sucker-punched in all her life. With that notion in my troubled crazed mind, I bolt farther down the hallway away from her.

I turn sharply right at one of the corners of the building. This place is a maze of many locked doors and hardly any windows — I don't even know if I'm high above the ground or far below it. Frantically, I shake all these locked handles to no avail. My head pounds increasingly, thanks in part to the buzzing fluorescent incandescence above me.

"Emily!" I mutter, noticing her slumped over in a wheelchair. She is holding her head in her hands as she rests her elbows on her knees. "*Emily!*" I repeat in a harsh whisper, shaking her shoulders for her to look up at me.

"We are bleeding, Miranda!" Emily cries out. "We are defragging to a most certain corruption."

"*Emily,*" I mutter again, trying to keep my mind steady. "*We need to go,*" I then tell her, grabbing under her right arm to get her out of the chair.

"Where are we going, Miranda?" Emily says with an adorable squint under the flickering illuminations.

"We are getting out of here," I say. I grab her hand tightly and look into her eyes for support.

"Okay, I'll try," Emily says with a wincing half-smile. "My head mush is hurting so much though."

Hand in hand, we go through the labyrinth until we see a gentler glowing light down one of the halls, different than all the rest. We look at one another, both believing this mirage to be the answer as we follow suit down that path.

The opening to that bright light has a warming glow which reflects back at us, raising our spirits as we head towards it. When we enter, the doors to an elevator appear to show our way out. I glance to my left, for the first time seeing windows to the outside world. This tells me that we need to press down once in the elevator.

There is no one in our immediate frontal view. This looks to be a reception area, and I see three butchers to our right who haven't yet noticed us. "Let's go," I say, tugging on Emily's hand, my glare set straight towards the exit.

I check behind me as voices resonate down the hallway and I see three people in loose-fitting jumpsuits running towards us. I'm in slippery socks against their rubberized tread. We need to move now and fast — they surely will catch us if we don't.

"Miranda, stop," Emily says, stopping dead in her tracks with a longing stare at what — I cannot tell.

"What is it, Emily?" I ask fervidly, but Emily just points to her right, not speaking.

Across the room, a doctor and two nurses are talking among themselves. Emily continues to point as tears fill her gorgeous sullen eyes. "Who are you pointing at, Emily?" I ask calmly, putting my arm lovingly around her.

"I know her," Emily says softly.

"Who? The nurse? Which one?" I ask Emily quickly, still thinking we can make it to the exit.

"The one with the short auburn hair in the pixie cut — that's my wife — that is the love of my life!" Emily tells me with a slight stutter. We are indeed going insane.

Chapter 12

I look behind me to see the plunger of the needle being pressed down into my buttocks. I swing with the back of my right hand connecting with the face of a petite platinum-haired nurse. The nurse releases the needle to bring her hands up to her face, but the damage is done; the toxins have been released into me. I grab the needle sticking straight up out of my body and toss it, skipping it along the tile floor while grunting loudly in frustration.

My breathing, once pulsating on high and filled with adrenaline, now feels heavy and laboured. The energy to pull my legs towards my body and stand up is no longer there. I dig my fingernails into the edge of one of the floor tiles to drag my body forward to no avail. My cheek presses down firmly against the cold floor, calming my hot skin. My eyes close without a fight. I'll need a better plan for next time, I press into my mush before all goes black.

I awake sitting on the seven o'clock pillar at the back at Skaha Beach Sundial. It is late in the evening, as I can see the sun setting out of the corner of my right eye. The lake is calm, reflecting a perfect image of the sun setting beyond the West Valley Wall, behind me. Skaha Beach is vacant, yet the sand isn't smooth. It is imprinted with the footprints of many people that have trucked through it during the day.

I look behind me to the left and see that the concession stand is closed, sealed shut for the day. No runners or late evening dog walkers are on the Skaha promenade, in neither direction. I then turn my gaze back around towards the shimmering Skaha Lake as a person, unnoticed moments ago, now sits with me at the sundial.

I do not know which direction this individual has come from, nor whether they made a sound as they came to sit there unnoticed by me. Directly across from me at the two o'clock pillar the individual rests, body hunched over, face shadowed by the setting sun.

"Who are you?" I ask in a friendly tone. The individual sits straight up, lifting her head up from the slumping shadows to reveal Josie Birch sitting there, looking lonely and sad.

"What?" she asks, surprised. Startled, she quickly stands up. She walks closer to me; caution is shown with every dragged step within the sand.

"You are — me!" she lets out with a nervous stutter. "You are me?" I look down at my freckled hands before raising them up to my face to feel that I am indeed still Josie.

"How are you me?" Josie calls out, her anger rising with each spoken syllable.

"Josie Birch," I say to her calmly, making direct eye contact.

"That is my name; who are you?" she asks, growing increasingly angrier. "Why do you look like me?"

"We are one and the same, Josie," I tell her, hoping to settle her down.

"That makes no sense. What is happening to me?" she now asks wildly. She looks frightened, just like the real Josie Birch would be. This must be me; this is how I look muted. I sense the strength of her soul; her consciousness is well-defined after seventeen years of development. "Who are you?" Josie screams with a curdling series of yelps. She collapses to the sand and wells up with tears.

Oh wait, she has a struggle, a hampering that she must endure. I must not forget that, I tell myself, rushing to her side. I place my hand on Josie's shoulder, comforting her and soothing that erratic breathing.

"Why are you me?" Josie asks, lifting her head up and trembling as she speaks.

"All will become clear to you in time. We are one and the same, and you have no reason to fear me," I tell Josie, looking right at her — my own reflection.

"How is there two of us?" Josie asks, this time more calmly. She sniffs as she pulls back her tears.

"Because I am from a distant time, but still a part of you," I explain to Josie as confusion forms over her brow.

"Where are we?" Josie asks, moving her head to look around us.

"That I do not know; we shouldn't be able to see one another like this," I say honestly, not recalling any awakening cases of this type of interaction.

"Am I dead?" Josie asks, placing her right hand over her heart.

"No, you're very much alive; we both are," I tell Josie. I get up and sit down again at the seven o'clock pillar.

"How is it that you know more than me about what is going on?" Josie asks, standing up from the sand and brushing the grains from her legs.

"Because I am more than just you," I tell her, knowing that Josie will never understand.

"I'm smarter than I look," Josie says, joining me to sit at the eight o'clock pillar.

"Oh, I know you are," I tell her, confirming her statement with a slight smile.

"How?" Josie asks, reaching out her hand to touch my knee. I could tell her everything that I know, but it would take many lifetimes to bring her up to speed.

"This much I can tell you as I want this so much to happen — but I have gotten lost along the way," I say. "Our body is struggling; it is somewhat out of control. I'm at a loss of how to maintain clear thoughts so I may direct the corrective action I need to take to free us both from these restraints we are currently feeling," I continue. "I must find a way to gain an understanding of our body's failures," I finish. Josie sits up straight, taking in all that information.

"Our body?" Josie inquires, looking puzzled. "Are you talking about my depression?"

"Yes — I suppose I am," I say. I smile, wishing I had said that more clearly.

"Did something bad happen to my body?" Josie asks frantically, pinching her sides with her fingers.

"No, nothing serious; it's just in a profound sleep," I tell Josie, remembering the last actions that sent me to this place.

"How do I wake up?" Josie asks with an intense stare, tilting her head to the side.

"I'm working on that, but it's hard," I admit, turning my gaze to look away from her.

"How is it hard? Why can't I wake up?" Josie asks sternly, moving her body in front of me and forcing me to look at her freckled face.

"Because I need to wake up first before you can wake up," I speak logically, growing more tired of her persistent questions. Josie grabs my hands and places them in hers as she sits crouched in front of me.

"How can I help wake you up?" Josie asks slowly, yet with strength in her voice.

"Tell me how to control your emotions," I say, knowing that the wisdom I require is locked within the soul of this conscious mind.

———— ⁓⁓∽◦◖◉◗◦∽⁓⁓ ————

I wake up to the dry taste of a cottonmouth and look around for some water. With none there I sit up straight, hazily looking at the two other beds in this enormous mustard-painted room with many eastern-facing windows. Noticing a blue cup and pitcher on a table over by the far bed to my right, I hop out of bed, hoping to quench this foul thirst.

I walk to the far side of that bed, grip the blue pitcher with both hands, and bring my lips to the brim. It tastes like spring water from a hot summer place, and to my parched mouth it feels heavenly. I put the pitcher down, wiping my mouth with the starchy material of my sleeve. My heart is beating so fast; I must control my breathing. Yes, that will slow down the effects of stasis bleeding — I read that somewhere in an old user manual, I'm sure of it.

"That water had flowers in it," a voice says softly, and I slowly bring my gaze down to see Emily.

"Emily, are you okay?" I ask excitedly, wrapping my arms around her as Emily rises to sit up in her bed.

"We are alive," Emily says, "We are still functioning," she continues in a worrisome stutter, making me pause. I am unsure of how to respond. "We are in a hospital for the broken-minded," Emily informs me as we pull back from our embrace.

"How did we get here?" I ask baffled. Holding my hand to my head, I feel immense pressure from within.

"Keoh hurt Adayln and then it was all chaos after that," Emily says. "There was so much crimson. I asked one of the nurses if the boy we came upon was okay. She said Corey will live, but Adayln is also hospitalized."

"What of Keoh?" I ask flustered.

"I don't know where he is," Emily tells me. "I'm not wholly sure where we are."

"They drugged me," I say, just now realizing what caused that stinging feeling in my behind.

"I saw them inject you," Emily says. "I co-operated, but they forced me to intake a couple of pills that put me to sleep."

"Your wife!" I say somewhat loudly. I cover my mouth as I remember why our escape from this facility had failed. "You said that nurse by the exit was your wife?"

"Yes, I saw her," Emily says calmly. Her facial expression is blank.

"What do you mean, your wife? You're a seventeen-year-old girl. You live with your parents, remember?" I plead with her to keep her normality as being Emma.

"No, Miranda, not like that," Emily says. I gasp in shock.

"What are you talking about then? Emily, you are not making any sense," I tell her, grabbing her by the shoulders to sit down her down at the end of her bed.

"Miranda, that is my real wife in the Real Realm standing right over there," Emily says, pointing at her again. I quickly hold down that pointing hand in her lap.

"That nurse is a stasis avatar, Emily, nothing more," I explain, trying my best to make eye contact with Emily.

"Her name is Sydney — Sydney Dunnigan; I married her," Emily continues, not removing her gaze from the nurse.

"That's not possible, Emily," I say, turning her face with my hand to look upon me.

"You know I lived here as a biological human over a thousand years ago. I was in the real Penticton during this era of the early part of the twenty-first century," Emily rambles. She pauses to take a deep breath.

"That all happened in the Real Realm, Emily; this is not the Double R. Listen to me, believe me." I speak with intensity as I feel that I'm mentally losing her to stasis bleeding.

"I realize the difference. This isn't SDS sickness; that is my First-Biological wife who I haven't seen in a very long time," Emily says. She looks hard in my eyes, wanting me to believe her.

"That's impossible; this is not 2005," I say in frustration, shaking my head. "All of what we are seeing is manufactured. Emily, you must realize that."

Emily's skin starts turning from pale to crimson as she curls her lips in a grimace. "No!" Emily screams at the top of her lungs.

"*Emily, please calm down,*" I whisper, patting the tops of her hands in an effort to help her simmer down. The rage continues with uncontrollable constant repetitions of 'No!' and 'Please No!'

The two nurses quickly come over and hold Emily, making her lie back down on her bed. Emily begins lashing her arms out, spitting and drooling, and kicking her feet in the air. Both nurses grab an arm to hold Emily down as she struggles to break free. I get up from the chair and move to the side as the doctor quickly approaches, almost tripping on the slippery floor.

"Hold her steady," the doctor says as he taps a needle in her upper arm. Emily's breathing goes from a hot pant to a shallow exhale as the drug immediately brings calm to her whole body.

I watch the nurses release their grips of Emily's arms as the fight within her subsides. Emily's eyes grow heavy, and she passes silently into sleep. "What happened to her?" the doctor asks, placing his hand on my shoulder. I take my gaze off of Emily.

"Nothing, she just started screaming," I tell the doctor, not looking at him.

"You girls are going to have to start talking if I'm to able to properly treat you," he says as I affix my stare back at the sleeping Emily.

"There is nothing you can do for us," I tell him with a longing sigh, knowing that they would never understand and have no means to aid our sickness. I finally look over at the doctor as he removes his hand. I see that he is discouraged by what I had just told him.

"Can you tell me something?" I ask him.

"Depends, what it is?" the doctor says, folding his arms across his chest.

"Are you ever going to let us go?" I ask timidly, wanting nothing more than to go back home, even if it's Josie's home.

"When you are better, we will let you go. Something traumatic has happened to you girls. Without anyone giving us any solid answers, we won't be able to help," the doctor says. He taps me on the shoulder and turns to walk back out of the room.

"*This is not how it is supposed to be; we shouldn't have tampered with it,*" I mumble softly.

"Tampered with what?" one of the nurses asks discernibly. I had not realized she was standing behind me. I slowly look behind to see the same pixie-haired brunette Emily had been pointing at earlier.

"Sorry?" I stutter. I notice that her name badge says 'Sydney.'

"You said you tampered with something. What did you tamper with?" she asks me again.

"You're Sydney?" I inquire, still staring at her name badge.

"Yes, yes I am. And you are Josie Birch, right?" she asks in a friendly tone, probably already knowing the answer.

"Are you married?" I quickly inquire, panning up to her eyes.

"No," Sydney laughs. "No, I'm not married," she says again, flashing her left hand that is void of any ring.

"So, what did you tamper with?" Sydney presses me once again. Wondering what to tell her, I am struck by fear.

"I just want to go home," I say plainly. Sydney then brushes past me with nothing else to say. Poor Emily, she really is losing it. The SDS sickness is taking a hard hold on her; it won't be much longer until I'm next.

I bow my head low as a fleeting thought dangles off the edge of my soon-to-be-breaking-mind to call out, "Wait!" at the top of my voice. Sydney stops, startled by my jolting shout, and she turns back around to face me.

"What is your last name?" I ask Sydney. She peers at me, looking confused.

"My last name," she repeats. "What for?" Sydney asks like she is trying to test me.

"Please," I call out at her, but Sydney just stands there, tight-lipped.

"Please," I say again, welling up with tears.

"Dunnigan, I'm Sydney Dunnigan," Sydney tells me. She looks at me with eyes full of sorrow. I drop to my knees and look over at Emily, wondering if she had gotten the nurse's name beforehand.

How could Emily's wife be in the SDS as a stasis avatar?

It is finally here; the sickness is now taking hold of me. I'm now paranoid, just like Emily.

———— ∿◦◦⦿◦◦∿ ————

It's late at night, and I'm awoken by a strong spring shower. The rain pelts the windows at breakneck speeds, preventing from sleeping away this nightmare.

"*Miranda*," Emily whispers softly as she too rustles in her bed.

"I'm right here, Emily," I tell her, jumping out of my bed to lie in hers.

"What happened to me?" she asks dazedly, slowly blinking her eyes awake.

"They gave you something to help you sleep," I say, brushing the matted and tangled hair from covering her beautiful crimson-shot eyes.

"Before that, though?" Emily asks as I cradle her with a hug.

"You acted out, the stasis bleeding — it's getting worse for both of us," I tell her.

"I'm not sick," Emily says with a nervous ramble in her voice. "Whatever emotional problems that I am experiencing are those of my stasis avatar."

"Emily, you must realize that we are trapped awake in the SDS; the sickness is inevitable. Keoh and Adayln have both gone insane and are locked up — we are breaking down," I beg Emily to understand, grasping her hand lovingly.

"I'm not crazy, Miranda. I agree that Keoh and Adayln are inflicted; however, I am not. Please believe me," Emily says, making her eyes go wide to look deep into mine for a connection.

"You were just tranquillized last night for acting out —" I say to her.

"That was Emma, not me," Emily refutes quickly.

"You are Emma and I am Josie," I say, exhaling with a loud sigh. I'm trying to get Emily to understand.

"I get all that, Miranda, but our stasis avatars do carry Real Realm afflictions for authenticity. Emma has some mental trauma which I'm struggling to control. I told you I was crying when I was first awoken in the SDS. That crying was not manufactured by any thoughts or feelings I was expressing. Emma's stasis avatar is damaged by depression or at least something like it."

"You don't know that for sure. You are not a doctor," I tell her, shaking my head in disapproval.

"I know I have never been a doctor, but I experienced depression during my First-Biological," Emily tells me.

"You can remember that far back?" I ask Emily, feeling unconvinced.

"Like it was yesterday. That depression was crippling, from what I remember," Emily says with pondering eyes. "Yes — yes, I did for sure," she says, looking back at me.

"And you think Emma has this so-called depression?" I ask distinctly, trying my best to see her side of what Emily is telling me.

"Most certain of it; plus, I don't think it's been ever treated. That first day awake, I cried uncontrollably in front of Emma's family, and no one questioned it," Emily recalls.

"You said everyone was just busy and probably didn't notice," I remind her of what she had told me at the sundial.

"Perhaps they are all just used to Emma's crying. I have no medication bottle in my bedroom; I don't believe she has ever been treated," Emily repeats her claim.

"I wish I could believe you, Emily, but the absence of medication could also mean that there is nothing wrong with Emma," I say to her.

"You don't believe me," Emily says, visibly disappointed.

"Keoh and Adayln got increasingly worse; what makes us so special to think that it hasn't already happened to us?" I ask Emily, forcing to look at the facts rather than just speculate on her avatar's possible afflictions.

"They hit the wall at Okanagan Falls, they touched it, and it forcefully pushed them back. That didn't happen to us. Maybe that is which is causing their sickness," Emily surmises. I agree that neither Emily nor I were violently tossed back by the invisible wall the others encountered. "It's the only explanation; it's infected them somehow," Emily continues to ramble out her hypothesis minus any real facts.

"But we ourselves are infected, Emily — both of us," I tell her, clenching my lips together.

"You haven't shown any SDS sickness that I have seen," Emily says, giving off a nervous smile.

"Last evening I did, right after they put you to sleep," I tell her sorrowfully.

"What do you mean? What happened to you?" Emily asks overtly. She sits up in her bed, clutching my hand tighter for support.

"Paranoia came over me," I say to Emily, bowing my head low.

"Did you lash out? What type of paranoia?" Emily presses for more details.

"Do you remember why they tranquillized you?" I ask Emily.

"No. It's all a jumbled blur of extreme confusion and blind rage; I couldn't control what came over me," Emily says, straining hard to think about the previous evening's events.

"You said you saw your biological wife," I remind her.

"Oh my god, yes — I saw Sydney, that's right!" Emily cries out when I remind her. I put my hand over her mouth to calm her voice.

"*Yes, you remember now?*" I whisper while stroking her hair to maintain composure.

"I remember it threw me for a loop; it made no sense. Emma must have hallucinated. I'm telling you: Emma's mind is not a sound vehicle for my conscious," Emily says with a laugh as I remain silent. "But that paranoia had to do with me, not you; what makes you think that you have the sickness?" Emily asks me again with a puzzled demeanour.

"Well, one of the nurses is named Sydney," I slowly inform her, monitoring her reaction carefully.

"That's a common name. I must have read it off her badge," Emily relents, shaking her head. "She did remind me of my Sydney, but I'm obviously not thinking right," she continues to dismiss herself.

"That's what I was thinking as well; however, before your blind rage you mentioned Sydney's last name," I say cautiously, trying my best not to rattle her. "I asked that nurse Sydney for her last name, and it is Dunnigan. It is the name that you had mentioned," I tell Emily, now expecting an outburst to occur.

"*That's not possible*," Emily says quietly, placing her hands on her face and looking deep in thought. "How does that make you have the feelings of SDS sickness?" Emily asks, raising her gaze back up to me.

"It's impossible for your biological wife to be represented in a fictional landscape within the SDS," I say with a slight smile. "When you mentioned her last name and the nurse confirmed it, the impossible, which can't be true, only gives way to the fact that I'm sharing the same paranoia as you. It proves that we are both sick and that the stasis bleeding is taking hold of us — just like it has taken Keoh and Adayln," I explain to Emily, reaching up for a supportive hug.

Emily doesn't move her arms from her sides; instead, she just sits there seemingly frozen. I pull back from my embrace when I notice that it's not reciprocated. "*Her last name is Dunnigan?*" Emily whispers hauntingly with a blank, unblinking stare.

"That's what she claims," I say. Emily's face is emotionless.

"How can that be a coincidence, Miranda?" Emily asks, looking at me with worried eyes. "I lived in the Double R Penticton over a thousand years ago. Sydney and I lived out our lives and continued on once carnations into husks were possible. The Stasis Deep Sleep System was built long after that by LaPorte. How is my biological wife alive, just as she was back in 2005, if the SDS is supposedly only manufacturing fictional stasis avatars?" Emily rambles, her breathing becoming more and more erratic as she speaks.

"Calm down. Control your breathing, Emily," I say, placing my hand on Emily's shoulder to centre her thoughts.

"That's not — possible," Emily says with a slight stutter in her voice, audibly more unnerved.

"Exactly, because it is not possible; we are sick, Emily. You must face that fact," I remind her again.

"Okay. What if you're right and we are slowly losing our minds to give way to delusional thoughts. How can we both be having the same delusional thoughts?" Emily asks confusingly. I pause and tilt my head as I entertain her notion. The chances of both of us experiencing the same unusual coincidence would be somewhat rare.

"Perhaps LaPorte cloned Sydney's conscious experiences into a stasis avatar?" I guess.

"Stasis avatars are blank slates, though, so we may experience free will when we inhabit their form," Emily explains rationally.

"Limited free will. You are bound to remain in Penticton," I remind her.

"But you were able to move past Penticton to another realm," Emily says.

"Yes, but Keoh and Adayln could not," I point out.

"Are you saying LaPorte cloned every atom of this town, including the people, right down to their own individual thoughts and feelings? No technology like that exists," Emily says with a scowl.

"*No technology that we know of — what does anyone really know of the SDS device?*" I whisper. "*It is shrouded in so much mystery and tamper-proof protocols that no one other than LaPorte truly understands how this machine works.*"

"It's all a dream for our consciousness to stave off boredom in the Real Realm," Emily cries out defiantly.

"Feel these sheets; they feel real to me," I say, tugging Emily's top sheet tighter around us. "Everything looks like the Real Realm; you said as much yourself, Emily," I remind her of our walk yesterday.

"I grew up here and lived out my First-Biological here," Emily says with a sniffle. "The details have always impressed me. However, I've never been awake in the device to experience it firsthand. This scares me, Miranda. This is not our world. We need to get out of here. How are we going to get out?" she asks erratically as no answers form on my lips. I reach out to hold her again, and this time she embraces me back.

"We need to go back, Miranda. We need to go back to where we are from," Emily says calmly into my shoulder.

Chapter 13

"Just look at what they have done already to Adayln and Keoh," I ramble, dropping their files which spill out along the floor.

"We have nowhere to go, Miranda," Emily says, crouching to the ground to pick up the papers.

"This time period for biological medicine is considered obscene," I say heatedly, feeling a panic attack coming on. "You know how these butchers treated First-Biologicals back then. All those experiments by corporations who profited off the continued ailments of our former species; I don't wish to live this segment of history — *awake.*"

"Easy now — breathe, Miranda," Emily says in a calming tone. Emily puts the file folders back into the cabinet and locks the door.

The attending nurse is still nowhere in sight; most likely she's still in the washroom. We slink back towards our room with a playful slide along the smooth tiled floor and then hop back into our beds beneath the covers. We both turn our heads at the same time to look upon another.

"*We need to get out of here,*" I say again in a whisper.

"*Miranda, we have nowhere to go other than back home — with our stasis families,*" Emily whispers back, rolling her eyes. She does not sound confident.

"Families which we do not know," I remind her quickly, "to live out our lives as Josie and Emma! Adayln has been split in two with Corey in control and Adayln screaming in the background. I don't want to live like that," I continue.

"That might not even be our fate; maybe we'll grow to control these ailments so we can live in harmony with Emma and Josie," Emily ponders aloud, not making any sense whatsoever.

"Us, that much more evolved, cannot co-exist with an earlier form of what we once were," I ramble, raising my hand in the air to show Emily that I'm trembling.

"*It's going to be hard,*" Emily whispers calmly. "A struggle like we have never faced before, but one I believe we can overcome," she continues, reaching out her hand towards me. I extend my trembling hand to grasp hers. This makes the shaking dissipate.

"See, we can do this; we'll overcome this together. Overcoming our mental issues will be our fate in this realm," Emily says with a worried smile, trying hard to show confidence.

"I hate this period of time and everything about it," I say, shaking my head. "I admit that First-Biologicals had depression with symptoms I no longer thought I would care to remember. Not wanting to be among these people, back then — in the Real Realm — is how I feel now. I wanted to leave this place. I fought for years plotting to make my escape by doing everything in my power to avoid the easy way out. I can't do this path again, not this time around," I babble frantically, not knowing if I am making any sense.

Emily, sensing my growing anticipation of an upcoming panic attack, leaves her bed to embrace me under my covers. Emily has a sweet scent as her hair nestles under my nose. I lock my arms around her and feel her hot breath pant onto my chest, flowing warmth down the opening of my shirt. My breathing is becoming more erratic; the pain of Josie's worrisome ailment approaches with every passing second. Emily constricts her embrace even tighter to slow my breathing. With an unexpected release, Emily moves up to my face and kisses me on the lips. This makes all distraught emotions subside. Emily's eyes are closed as our lips tangle and stay locked in place. She is beautiful and so enticing that thoughts of desire that were not there a moment ago now appear.

Who wouldn't want to be kissed by a walking angel, no matter what form this deity may have partaken? I allow my thoughts to succumb to whimsy as I take firm grasps at her body with my fingers. My eyes are now firmly closed just like Emily's, and I allow these desires of human nature to take their rightful control.

———✦———

In the morning I awake to the clattering of trays from a rolling food cart — not so far away. Emily is beside me sleeping topless, as she did throughout most of the night. "*Emily,*" I say softly, shaking her gently on the shoulders, but she just groans, too tired to respond. "*Someone is coming,*" I whisper directly into her ear, making her eyes flare open wide. Without a second thought, Emily turns her head over to look at me for a long second before darting back to her own bed. I reach under my covers for my long pants as the rolling cart enters the room.

"Breakfast time," says a young man in his early twenties, rolling his cart of food to the foot of our beds. I reach out for my rolling table as he places my breakfast upon it. Emily, still shirtless with the sheets up to her chin, remains unmoving.

The young man, whose badge says Stewart, positions Emily's table in front of her before noticing Emily's panicky pose. Stewart acts normal, although we must seem like oddities to him. After placing Emily's tray of food in front of her, Stewart then moves between our beds. He extends both of his arms out and grabs each of our tray lids, lifting them up at the same time. With his bowing body below the raised tray lids, he says with a smile, "Bon Appetit, ladies." As Stewart leaves the room, he gives off a confirming head nod with zero context of what he may be confirming.

"How weird," I say, seeing Stewart roll his cart away down the hall to the next room.

"Can you toss me my shirt?" Emily says as she catches me staring at him, not moving my gaze.

"Of course," I let out a smirk and toss Emily's shirt into her waiting hands.

—⁓⁓⦿⦿⦿⦿⦿⦿⁓⁓—

That morning we do nothing but stare out the windows. We are still being denied access off this high floor. In complete silence, Emily and I sit opposite of one another with each of us staring at a different part of town. I start to imagine that perhaps the drugs being administered to us are now disabling our ability to speak. "Emily," I say, turning to her, hoping to break her gaze from out the window.

"Yes, Miranda!" she says in a jolting manner, turning to me in surprise.

"Sorry, did I startle you?" I ask her. "You've been so quiet this morning."

"I remember things — thoughts other than from this realm," Emily says in confusion.

"Are you remembering Sydney?" I ask, pointing over to Nurse Sydney sitting at the attending station.

"Sydney was the one who I was meant to be with — forever," Emily says with a reminiscing smile. "She would tell me such things."

"Where is Sydney now — in the Real Realm that is?" I ask, curious about why she didn't accompany Emily onto the *Misfit*.

"Oh, I haven't seen Sydney in ages; we grew apart," Emily tells me with a deep sigh. "Our love for each other was always there, but we drifted away from one another over time. I don't even know what name Sydney even goes by today. I'm guessing she's changed her husk a few times like I have. Humans weren't meant to be together for two hundred years or — even three hundred years," Emily continues, becoming more aggravated.

"That's a long time for two conscious souls to be together; can't expect love to last that long," I say with a gentle smile.

"You can smile about that, but our love was different," Emily says, looking at me intently. "I think about her a lot in the Real Realm. I don't hide from that emotion; I let it play out. I'll never stop loving her, wherever Sydney may be," Emily continues, looking over at Sydney.

"It sounds like it was special," I tell Emily. I feel lost inside, thinking that I may never have loved someone as much as she had loved Sydney — other than my sweet Cora. However, our encounter was quite brief.

"We used to enter SDS together at the same time —" Emily starts to say.

"Soul-Mating," I jump in, aware of the practice.

"Yes, we would go in as Soul Mates, seeing if fate would strike us again with love," Emily says, grinning with an adorable tilt of her head to the side.

"Did you ever end up together?" I lean in close, knowing that the odds of it happening are astronomical.

"No, our stasis avatars would never meet up, let alone bump into each other. Fate is a fickle bitch, they used to say; a bitch she truly was." Emily starts to laugh.

I'm amazed at how two souls can meet during this age of rampant depression. "So, what type of depression did your First-Biological have?" I ask Emily, prying if she even remembers.

"Depression — yes, I have to think hard to remember that ailment," Emily says with a chuff.

"You can't remember then?" I ask Emily. I struggle to recall the details of my depression which was segregated to the far regions of my consciousness centuries ago.

"I had so many different types of depression. I can't remember much; it's been too long. I know it was a daily struggle though," Emily says with a wince.

"We wiped out depression quite easily," I say, remember it fondly. "It felt like one-day depression was a thing, and then bang, it was gone."

"There was an immense uproar against eradicating depression, Miranda — don't forget that," Emily says bringing those old thoughts to the foreground.

"I didn't see what the issue was back then," I say to her in a matter-of-fact tone. "Depression was an ailment, and we cured it just like any other ailment."

"Society changed, people changed, our whole species changed, Miranda, with the abolishing of depression, and not necessarily for the better," Emily boldly challenges my claim.

"How so, Emily?" I ask politely, hoping to be enlightened yet feeling deep down that I won't.

"We all became more of the same; we all became more boring. Depression makes people think different and act differently. Many great stories and plays were written by humans suffering from depression, works that would never have seen the light of day otherwise," Emily explains in a long-winded ramble.

"Emily, that is a ridiculous argument," I say, shaking my head.

"It is true. Great artist and poets, their future great works never to be adorned," Emily surmises passionately. "Can you remember any details of your depression, Miranda, or was that way too far back in your ancient history to recall?" Emily asks with a playful laugh.

"For me, depression was a part of biology that did not need to come forward in the life of our species," I say with a confident smile. "It can stay in my past; that's where it belongs."

"Who were you — *Miranda Sage?*" Emily asks with curiosity in her voice and peering eyes that are trying to penetrate my soul.

"No one — I was simply no one," I tell Emily resoundingly, looking away to avoid eye contact.

"Oh my God!" Emily lets out. Shocked, she brings her hands up to cover her mouth. "What if we bump into ourselves?" she then asks worriedly.

"This has to be the SDS sickness — it's the only logical explanation," I tell her, trying hard not to entertain the thought of seeing my First-Biological.

"It is more profoundly probable given the current factors in play that we were both once here in this exact time and place —" Emily begins.

"Yes, but we were never stasis avatars to rinse, wash, and repeat life," I say emphatically. "Sydney Dunnigan is more likely a wife of one of your stasis avatars whose memory is slowly bleeding through," I explain. I'm trying to calm her sickness by staying rational.

"So, I can't remember any events of my SDS lives, yet I can magically recall Sydney from a single stasis event with such sharp clarity. How is that possible?" Emily heatedly rebuts my claim.

"Okay — calm down. I don't need you going into an uncontrolled fit," I say, moving my gaze to back out the window. "I have no desire to see myself back then if it is true that I walk in this realm manifested in some way — and neither should you," I tell her. I look straight into her eyes as my own breathing starts to feel hampered. "The mission of exploration which started all this mess ended when we awoke again past twenty-four hours. We are far below the depths of safety, and we are on limited life support," I explain to her with erratic breaths. "The goal is to now survive this place without causing too much harm to our true conscious minds," I finish, wiping the sweat from my brow.

"I agree, Miranda; I agree one hundred per cent," Emily says, now taking control of the mantle. "We have no plan though, as far as I can see," she continues while rolling her eyes. "Maybe it's the journalist in me that wants to know more about this place; I want the answers to the questions we have all pondered for centuries. Or perhaps I am resigned to my fate that I may never wake from here and that my conscious soul is destined to die. Regardless of which may be true, I must not die without finding these answers — if not for our own human race, then for my own living soul that has been shackled among this forever heaven," Emily says softly. She moves over to me, and we embrace. My erratic breathing begins to subside.

"You may have given up, but I never can," I tell her, grabbing both her shoulders tightly. "I'm *One of the Firsts* because I longed to be immortal. That is my goal in life. That is my religion as a Longevist. I have put my conscious life in harm's way so many times it would be too high to count. I was *One of the Firsts*, a pioneer in ensuring this SDS technology thrived for future generations as I experimented on myself while knowing that I may never wake," I continue in a tight-lipped ramble.

"That was well over a millennium ago, Miranda," Emily says, rubbing my extended arms.

"And it's been perfected after all those trials and multiple versions of SDS Systems that wiped out countless souls — so that we may have a device that works. It works so we can say that we lived in a point of time — a thousand years ago," I explain passionately.

"But we stopped evolving; we haven't been perfecting your goal of being immortal," Emily says, shaking her head.

"I feel we have been, bit by bit. Every new SDS life living in here adds to our overall collective soul. We are more enriched when we return to the Double R," I explain.

"But what is this enrichment without knowing how the Great Founder was able to create an exact replication of time and space in a sandbox for us to play in?" Emily asks fervidly, brushing my hands from her shoulders. "You said you wanted to be immortal and that you strive to be a god. Well, right now — LaPorte is God — and we all live in this God's realm. I want to know more about the God that we have served lovingly with our conscious souls for so many centuries," Emily says sternly. As I start to respond, that overwhelming feeling grips at my heart.

I roll off the chair and onto the hard-tiled floor, feeling my head bounce when it makes contact. I don't feel the pain, nor do I give it a second thought as the worrisome fear that clouds my mind reaps again.

Now, I curl up in a ball of fear without any halt mechanisms; I am embodying Josie's crippling depression more and more. Becoming Josie is to realize that I must embrace all aspects of her, especially the ailments of her mind. Emily huddles beside me on the floor, stroking my hair lovingly from my face. I'll find a way to get us out of here, I think while trying hard to focus my vision on Emily — I'll find us a way out.

Chapter 14

There is an immense beauty hidden away behind those thin and greasy strains of flaxen hair. I can see it in this girl's eyes; they have a shimmer of sultry mixed with depravity and despair. Her hands are shackled down on either side of her chair like she is some sort of rabid beast. I don't imagine that she could be more than five feet tall if given the privilege to stand upright.

How can someone so demure, so unintimidating, be such a danger to us that they would have the need to restrain this poor girl to a chair? A nurse with a portly affliction accompanied by a stiff leg limps around, periodically wheeling this frail soul from window to window so that she may gaze out to the freedom that is denied.

"Barbaric," I say, astonished, with my eyes still fixated on the poor girl in the chair.

"We are in a different time — this is what they used to do to us," Emily says, biting her nails on her left hand feverishly without reason. "I'm surprised you don't remember."

"I can remember, although whenever I think that far back everything seems to blur together as though it was a dream or in this case a nightmare," I tell Emily, still staring at the shackled girl.

"You're so right, Miranda," Emily says, raking the salvia off her left hand along the side of her pant leg. "That's why we need to get out of here. I have no wish to be experimented on by these butchers who have no means of fixing what ails us," she rambles, looking around the room aimlessly.

"What harm could that flaxen beauty locked down with clamps to a chair be to everyone in here?" I ask critically, turning my gaze back towards Emily.

"Perhaps they are trying to keep her safe from herself — suicide is prominent during this era," Emily remarks before turning to chomp down nervously on the raw fingertips of her right hand.

"Emily, let your nails grow out a bit," I say, using my hand to lower Emily's from her mouth. I then stand and brush the crimson strands away from cascading across my face. Next, I straighten my gown by stroking my fingers against the stiff and starchy material.

"Where you going?" Emily says, looking up at me startled with her right hand dangling off her bottom lip.

"I'm going to speak to her; that flaxen beauty looks lonely," I explain, looking over at that sad creature in the chair.

"What for? She is trapped in this facility just like us," Emily says, biting away on her fingertips. *Just seeing that girl restrained like that, is like reading a description of a character straight out of a Dixby novel,* Emily mumbles, shaking her head.

"I still don't understand what you all see in the written clutter of one Lord Devlin Dixby," I say again to Emily's rolling eyes. "He was a madman."

"Oh, he was no madman; Dixby was a pioneer," Emily quickly corrects me. "I remember him being an imaginative writer. He created stories built upon stories that you would have to read over many times to locate the true meanings behind the narrative. Maybe he was a madman — but not to me," Emily continues, tilting her head as she fondly recalls his works.

"Author — pioneer — even propaganda peddler. The list goes on and on to describe a man that in his infamy could not cement a sound vision to all that try to remember him," I scold her, feeling no love for his tales nor the man himself. "Why are we even talking about Devlin Dixby? Are you going to tell me a story from one of his great novels? I've read them all plus the history of him, which I recall solely being that of a madman," I ramble excessively, still building up the courage to approach this flaxen beauty in the wheelchair.

"A madman that produced great stories of fiction right when creativity started to wane among our peoples," Emily says sternly. "How come you can only see him as a madman?"

"I met the man once; our paths crossed — mine and Dixby's. He truly was a shallow man. It's a shame that history shows so little of who he truly was back when he was alive," I say, thinking unfondly of our first encounter.

"Well, proceed to enlighten me — what made him such a madman in your eyes?" Emily asks boldly, making me sit back down on her bed. "We have nothing but time in here to waste away," Emily continues, looking around in frustration at our confined surroundings.

"I came upon Devlin Dixby at a products expo for the SDS version 5.73 in the year 2651 I believe — or at least around that period of time. Do you remember that model?" I ask Emily to gauge her level of attention to that period of time.

"No, not really; there were so many iterations of the SDS back in those days," Emily says, straining to think that far back. "There were new releases every few months," she adds with disdainful boredom.

"There were," I say, giving off a slight smile.

"Most versions had no extra features or enhanced improvements on the experience itself," Emily recalls, shaking her head from side to side. "A new version usually meant that they had fixed an issue with a previous model. Wow, they were horrible devices back then — so unstable," she laments.

"Anyways, Emily, like I was saying, I bumped into Devlin Dixby rather randomly and immediately gushed at him like a rabid fangirl," I continue to recite, grinning from ear to ear.

"Oh my, you're Lord Dixby — I have read all of your works. Your writing is simply amazing —" I say in a playful pander.

"Hold that thought," Dixby interrupts promptly, holding his right index finger erect in front of my face. He then turns and grabs one of the overflowing glasses of Chardonnay from a waiter making his rounds among the busy expo room. Dixby guzzles it all in one gulp.

Wiping his mouth on his sleeve before placing the glass back on the tray from which it came, the man strains his head oddly from side to side as though he is working out a kink in his neck before bringing his attention back towards me.

"Who are you again?" Dixby asks sharply, looking at me like I had just appeared out of thin air.

"I'm Josie Sage, a fan of your fiction. Defy the Knot is wildly imaginative and by far my favourite —" I attempt to compliment him.

"Fiction? I suppose you have also read The Forever Love of Norran and Whenwig?" he asks curtly, somewhat derailed by his constant interruptions.

"Like I said, I've read all your works," I tell him as his eyes drift away from me to the stage about twenty feet in front of us.

"Look at that contraption. Safety protocols at a forty-eight per cent rating — Ha! They call that a selling feature," Dixby says sharply, pointing excessively at the revolving SDS 5.73.

"That is a vast improvement over the forty-seven per cent safety rating," I say, quite happy about the new improvement.

"They could have a one hundred per cent safety rating, yet I wouldn't trust them. LaPorte Industries doesn't understand the technology they are trying to peddle to us," Dixby says, a scowl starting to form on his brow.

"It is a dangerous delight — I'll give you that," I tell Dixby, agreeing that you can't deny that it is a reckless pastime.

"You have used one?" Dixby asks surprisingly, scanning me up and down.

"Just the once, at the Eckhardt Facility," I inform him. "I'm saving up to one day purchase an SDS of my own —"

"I personally own three models," he interrupts. "You know I can't make it past twenty-two years of age before being jolted back awake. Each time I emerge, I believe with a resounding bit of hope that after another two decades in the box an improved SDS would be available. I think that God would have brought forth a more stable unit, but every time I find LaPorte no more the wiser," Dixby says in a fast-paced blather still staring out at the stage.

"Twenty-two years, that's impressive," I jump in as his gaze falls back onto me.

"*LaPorte is a snake-oil charlatan, and we line up willingly to be duped by this imaginatarian,*" Dixby says with a scowl. "*Ten times, I've gone in on the long sleep. Ten times, never to live out a free will narrative, until something goes amiss,*" he continues to relent, looking around the expo room. *I assume he is looking for another waiter.*

"*Mine have only lasted until I was nineteen — I believe I kept drowning in a lake,*" I tell him. Dixby ignores me.

"*But I don't let LaPorte's inability to wield this marvel prevent me from getting my money's worth,*" Dixby says sharply.

"*They are rather expensive devices, however —*" I pause after seeing his mouth moving to interrupt me yet again.

"*You know what I do?*" Lord Dixby whispers, leaning in close.

"*What?*" I whisper back, tilting my ear towards his mouth.

"*I awake myself while inside that infernal box,*" Lord Dixby says, followed by a mischievous cackle. "*Two times in a row, awake; imagine that!*"

"*How?*" I ask firmly, but Dixby just places his hand on my shoulder and walks away, still laughing, towards the direction of a wandering waiter.

———⟊⟊⟊⟊⟊⟊———

"See, a firsthand account of a raving madman," I tell Emily with an affirming smile.

"Look deeper into what Dixby told you, Miranda," Emily says, her eyes squinting together like she is thinking hard. "Look very deep, like you are reading one of his imaginative novels for the fourth or fifth time," she continues. I recoil, thinking that I may have actually read that drivel so many times.

"Four or five times — oh please," I gasp, rolling my eyes, "there's nothing to glean from reading those tales repeatedly."

"But Dixby may have pioneered the limits of understanding the depths that you could submit a human consciousness to being awake in this realm," Emily continues to explain. I get the feeling that she didn't understand the point of my encounter with Dixby.

"And in the end, the great novelist of that time most probably died from this new enlightenment at his own reckless hands," I counter. "Dixby died, Emily, in one of his tinkered SDS pods — only confirming that he was a reckless madman," I say confidently.

"We don't know that for sure; it may have just been a malfunction of his SDS unit — LaPorte doesn't get off that easily," Emily says.

"I believe the history books written on the man are not accurate and require amendments of the man's intent — *regardless of any proof*," I say, crossing my arms tightly in disagreement of her claims.

"Anyways, the merits of Dixby's mind are not what I wish to highlight from your story, Miranda," Emily says passionately. "Look to the science of his actions in light of our current situational dilemma," she says with a look of exasperation. She does not want to debate me anymore.

"Okay — okay, explain," I say calmly tone, sensing Emily's tension.

"Dixby went in fully awake, willingly, two times out of ten lives," Emily says pointedly, recalling my story. "Dixby survived intact, but how?" Emily asks, holding up two fingers to make her point.

"Awake from babe to death — I can't imagine it," I tell Emily, looking down at my lap.

"He only wrote three great books, right around the time he said he entered the SDS system awake," Emily says gleefully. "Those three tales have to be from the telling of those lives while awake in the SDS. The themes and placing are all in Penticton — his other books are not," Emily says confidently. She is apparently riffing off of the top of her head with a wild developing theory.

"That means nothing," I tell her dismissively. "Many writers have written fiction based on the SDS's version of Penticton. The town became famous because it is the only available town rendered within the SDS. It is the most famous city in the history of our species. It was a popular narrative location back then during Dixby's era," I continue, throwing cold water on Emily's hot theory.

"Okay, I agree," she says with a jittery nodding of her head. "However, I now have a verbal account from the man's own lips that he did such experiments around the time when those three novels were created. So, Dixby had to go in three times awake. He never wrote a fourth after dying in that fiery SDS accident," Emily says, biting down nervously on her thumb.

"Good point," I say approvingly. I respect her analogy, however far-fetched it is. "So those novels, those tales, are not fiction?" I ask, trying to surmise my way to Emily's thinking.

"Yes, they are not stories; they are an observational account from someone who had survived many years — let alone hours — awake in the SDS," Emily says with a feverish smile.

"That's quite the theory," I say, not seeing how it helps us get back home.

"As a journalist, I'm compelled to let you know that this new information about Dixby will be shared among all, if we escape alive and unharmed," Emily says in a boorish dictating tone that journalists are known for.

"You can publish whatever; I'm well-documented by history," I say with a sneer. "Any new entries that mention me in the Double R won't change anyone's notion of me."

"As long as we are straight on my intent," Emily continues, nodding her head.

"First we need to get out of here before you can publish anything," I say bitterly, standing up to peek out the window for a possible escape. "The answer for how to survive this realm is in Dixby's novels, you say?" I ask, playing along with her theory.

"Perhaps — so maybe we just need to look to his stories to see if there are clues for how Dixby survived," Emily says. Her expectations sound terribly high.

"That is assuming if Dixby is portraying himself as the protagonist in his works," I say, rationalizing this unknown variable.

"True — but who else could he have been?" Emily asks with her eyes going wide. "He is writing the thoughts in first-person narrative. We only hear the thoughts of the protagonist and no one else. No, the protagonist must be Lord Dixby. No reason to speculate further on that fact," Emily tells me, batting away my claim with sound reasoning minus any proof.

"So, where are we going to get a copy of his books?" I say with a roll of my eyes. "It is 2005; his three key novels are not to be published until six hundred years later in the future," I continue, bringing up another valid point.

"That may be a problem," Emily says slowly, scratching her chin. "*Defy the Knot* is a long way from being on any bookshelves," she adds in a long, drawn-out whine, tilting her head back with a look of exhaustion. "Do you remember the stories in vivid detail?"

"I have read them at least three times each, but that was five hundred plus years ago — and I don't have access to my permanent neural bank," I tell her. I am struggling to remember those tales.

"I've read them many times," Emily says, pressing her palms to her temples, "yet being in here puts a strain on remembering many of the facts."

"Being on all this medication isn't helping matters," I say, letting out a smile to lighten our mood.

"*Dixby's books,*" Emily mumbles with a look of defeat written across her face, "*I haven't thought about reading one of those tales in more than a century.*"

"Well, focus on only his stories where the narration takes place in Penticton. What are the titles?" I ask Emily, jogging her memory. Emily then reaches over to the side table and grabs the sketch pad and crayons she had been drawing with earlier.

"Okay, so the second of his three great novels is *Defy the Knot*," Emily says, writing the title down in dark crimson crayon.

"The protagonist's name is Joseph Tompkins — and the story is about a firefighter, if I recall correctly," I say, trying my best to remember.

"He is a water-bombing pilot," Emily adds quickly, scribbling down that information. "Ugh, it's so hard to think in this realm," Emily laments. "So, what happens in the story?"

"It is a love story between Joseph Tompkins — and Ophelia — something," I remind her, feeling surprised I can remember that much.

"Not sure what survival intel we can glean from a condensed love story," Emily says dejectedly, dropping the crayon to the paper. "Maybe you're right, Miranda;

the idea is a bit of a reach," she says. I rub her back in support for at least trying to think of a theory of escape.

"Well, let's just call him up on the telephone and ask him for advice," I say cheekily with a laugh.

"I wish we could just call him up and pick his brain for help," Emily says, also laughing at that notion. She proceeds to scribble random doodles on her paper.

"Devlin Dixby, in person, was an unhinged conversationalist at best — can't imagine how he would be during a non-face-to-face conversation," I say with a slight chuckle.

Emily starts drawing a picture of our forever burning crimson sun in the corner of the paper. She allows her thoughts to calm with every stroke of the crayon. Looking back once again at our flaxen beauty restrained in her chair, I rise from sitting next to Emily and cautiously approach the girl.

Chapter 15

The sun is shining bright this day, coating this poor girl with blinding rays of light. She has no means to shield her eyes. I walk around her wheelchair and lower her blinds halfway to cast down a shadow to her upper lip. The flaxen-haired girl looks up at me, squinting painfully while trying to focus her vision upon me.

"Is that better?" I ask, presenting a non-threatening smile.

"Better than what?" the Flaxen Beauty says swiftly, quickly moving her gaze back out the window.

"Well, the sun was in your eyes; it looked uncomfortable. I'm Josie, by the way," I say as a formal introduction. I stick out my hand to customarily shake hers. The Flaxen Beauty looks back up at me and shakes her wrists which jingle due to the restrictive latches.

"Oh, I'm sorry," I blurt out, just now realizing my blunder. I force my hand into hers to accomplish the greeting. The girl's head twitches, I assume uncontrollably, and the greasy, blond strands of hair whip away from her face. A noticeable crescent scar from temple to chin shoots fresh down her face. Up close, her eyes look worn and her dry lips are cracked and severely chapped.

She looks older than Emily and I by at least ten years and carries the trials of living a hard life etched within her facial expressions. Even with all that the Flaxen Beauty has faced, and given her current plight, she still carries with her the beauty of a fallen angel.

"What are you looking at?" the Flaxen Beauty asks, sensing my stare.

"Oh sorry, you're just — so pretty," I say nervously to her, awkwardly placing both of my hands on my left hip bone.

"Looking for beauty tips?" the Flaxen Beauty asks, I assume jokingly. She shakes her head wildly again, making her greasy hair fall back down over her face.

"I was sitting there with my friend, and I wondered why you would be restrained to a chair," I say slowly and with caution in hopes of not unnerving her.

"I could tell that you both were looking at me; it's not polite to stare," the Flaxen Beauty says, blowing up her face to move those greasy bangs from covering her eyes.

"I apologize for that; it's just odd for us to see someone confined to a chair," I tell her honestly, trying to smile so she knows that I mean her no harm.

"First time in a place like this?" the Flaxen Beauty asks somberly, looking back up at me with her sullen eyes.

"This place is unimaginably horrific," I say, looking wildly around the room.

"I've been in this facility many times. Then I leave — but I always come back," the Flaxen Beauty says, shaking her head while biting down on her bottom lip.

"You have left this place before?" I inquire quickly, going down to one knee to match her at eye level. "They let us leave?"

"They used to let me leave; I'm not so sure about this time," the Flaxen Beauty says calmly. She pulls her right wrist to jingle her chains.

"How do you get out of here?" I ask calmly, looking at her intently.

"Medicine time, girls," Nurse Jody sings into the room holding out a metal tray littered with tiny white cups. I stand up from my one bended knee, adjusting my stiff gown as I rise.

"Josie, pill time," Nurse Jody says sternly, fanning her fingers towards herself to indicate that I should approach. I shuffle forward along the cold, smooth floor and take the small, white cup in my left hand once I am in range. The tablets are tiny. Two are crimson and diamond-shaped, and the other one is an oval, rusty-mango in colour.

I look up at Nurse Jody, sighing loudly so she may read the disdain written on my face. "C'mon Josie," she says, handing me a small paper cup of water. I do as I'm told and forcefully toss the pills to the back of my mouth. Then I drown them in lukewarm water.

"That's a good girl," Nurse Jody remarks with a smile as I place my empty paper cups back on her tray.

"Nice picture, Emma — beautiful sun," Nurse Jody says as I turn back towards the Flaxen Beauty to finish our conversation.

"It's a shame about Joseph Tompkins," I hear Nurse Jody state. This comment makes me turn back in her direction. "He was so young," Nurse Jody continues. Emily takes her pills.

"What do you mean about Joseph?" I ask Nurse Jody. Surprised, she looks my way.

"The man was so young, and to die in such a way — so tragic," Nurse Jody says, shaking her head as Emily and I gaze at one another in confusion.

"What Joseph?" I ask strongly. I peer cautiously at Nurse Jody with one eye closed, anticipating what she may say next.

"This Joseph — the Joseph that Emma has written on her drawing. Did you know him?" Nurse Jody asks peacefully, pointing to the name Joseph Tompkins written in block letters below the title of the fictional tale by Devlin Dixby.

"Joseph Tompkins is a fictional character from a book," I say to Nurse Jody.

"The newspaper printed a story recently about the upcoming one-year anniversary of the forest fire. Hold on, I'll fetch the article for you," Nurse Jody says, leaving our room. I join Emily and we collectively look down at Joseph Tompkin's name scribed out by Emily's hand on the paper in crimson crayon.

Nurse Jody promptly returns with a folded up local newspaper and turns to an article entitled "Local Hero Remembered." "Did you girls know Joseph Tompkins?" Nurse Jody inquires again, looking sad.

"Sort of," Emily says. With a squint of her eyes, she grips the article with both hands.

"Such a shame. Please return the newspaper to the nurse's station when you are done reading it," Nurse Jody says with a supportive smile as she exits our room to continue her rounds.

"Miranda, listen to this:

Joseph Tompkins, a resident of Penticton, died last summer at the young age of twenty-two. He perished battling the blaze along the East Valley Wall when his water-bomber unexpectedly crashed, killing all onboard. Joseph Tompkins was due to be married this summer after proposing to his girlfriend only one week before his death," Emily reads.

"Joseph Tompkins died at twenty-two. Didn't Dixby tell you that he never made it past twenty-two years old?" Emily asks slowly, holding out the article for me to take. "This account of his death mirrors the weird story of

Defy the Knot. What are the chances of that happening?" Emily asks unmistakably. I am stunned. I look at Joseph Tompkins picture in the newspaper.

"*The events in the SDS are all random with free will inhibitive. How is Devlin Dixby's story within the SDS?*" I mumble, feeling confused. "What if we have it all wrong?" I ask, looking blankly ahead at the pale lemony wall.

"Got what wrong, Miranda?" Emily asks firmly. My gaze remains fixed ahead of me; I am deep in thought.

"Your wife, Nurse Sydney; and now the protagonist from a novel not written until six hundred years later," I ramble. "What if the SDS is not what we think it may be?" I say wildly. My proposal sends shivers down my spine.

"Maybe Dixby is right, and everything we have been told is a lie," Emily says. "Sydney is my real wife, and that Joseph Tompkins was really just Dixby awake in Joseph Tompkins body," she babble. Her jaw goes slack in disbelief.

"*The events that are being played out in here in this SDS seem to be the same events that have been recorded through time in the Double R,*" I whisper, sitting close to Emily on the bed. "It doesn't explain how any of this is possible," I say, shaking my head.

"*Possible or not, the truth is that we have been sold a lie. The hidden realms are real, and you can enter them —*" Emily begins.

"Well, some of us can," I jump in to correct Emily, reminding her that Keoh and Adayln were denied entry.

"Granted. We don't have all the answers, but we have some unusual clues," Emily says. She sits back to rest her head against the headboard, and then tilts her head to look up at the ceiling. Her mind must be as exhausted as mine is from trying to process all of what's happening.

"You said we should just call Dixby on the telephone, maybe that's not such a bad idea," Emily says in a playful tone, making my thoughts go wild as she speaks. "If anyone knows more about this realm and the workings of being awake in it — it's Lord Devlin Dixby," Emily says slowly. She brings her gaze back towards me.

"Well, if Dixby was portraying Joseph Tompkins, then we are one year too late," I tell her with a snicker. "Can't call a dead man,"

"Not Joseph Tompkins, but perhaps the other protagonist he has portrayed," Emily says with her eyes going wide.

"Norran happens well after 2005; we can't call on him," I say assuredly with a nod of my head.

"Who did he represent in *Fallen Angel*?" Emily asks openly, scrunching her face and trying hard to remember.

"Hey!" a voice calls out from the corner of the room. "Come here." It is the Flaxen Beauty in the secured wheelchair looking over at us with that glazed stare.

"Yes?" I ask rapidly. I get off of the bed and approach the Flaxen Beauty as she blows her bangs out of her eyes.

"*I overheard you two talking,*" she whispers. "*Are you looking to escape?*"

"Do you know a way out of here?" I ask, not wholly convinced given that she is currently locked to a chair.

"I can get you out," she says in a calm, serene voice.

"Yes please — share it," I say with my hopes starting feel like they are falsely rising.

"You need to undo these straps," the Flaxen Beauty says, looking down at her left wrist and wiggling her fingers.

"Oh — you don't plan to hurt us?" I ask sheepishly. "Do you?"

"I'm harmless towards others," the Flaxen Beauty says with a smile. "Look at my arms — I only do harm to myself," she says, laying both her palms up to show the crimson marks crisscrossing up and down each arm.

"Did you do that?" I gasp, extending my hand. I trace one of her puffy scars from wrist to elbow.

"Yes, so see — I'm no harm to you," she says, looking at me kind of sweetly.

"You are not going to do any more of that?" I say with a mild point of my finger at her arm.

"No, I want out of here," the Flaxen Beauty says calmly and with a bit of confidence which I am having a hard time sharing. Without any more thoughts to sway me otherwise, I unfasten each wrist strap. I hear Emily gasping in disapproval.

"*Josie, what are you doing?*" Emily calls over to me in a scolding whisper.

"It's not right just leaving her strapped barbarically to this chair," I say appallingly. Also, I see no other available option to escape this prison.

With her hands freed, the Flaxen Beauty reaches down to undo her leg shackles. She then stands up slowly, evidently stiff from being confined to that chair. A mighty yawn follows as she stretches her arms far above her head. She is limbering up before (hopefully) showing us a way out.

"So, what's the plan?" I ask intensely of her. The Flaxen Beauty continues to stretch other parts of her body like she's preparing for an Olympic race.

"Well —" the Flaxen Beauty starts to say.

"*Someone is coming,*" Emily calls out in a whisper as the Flaxen Beauty sits back down in her chair, loosely draping her latches over each wrist. I slowly slide across the floor back into my bed, hitting the sheets right when that odd male orderly enters with a rolling cart of lunch foods.

"Afternoon, ladies," Stewart says aloud in a cheerful tone. "Beef and broccoli soup," he announces, licking his lips weirdly. "I'll hand you yours first," he says, placing a steaming hot bowl in front of Emily before handing me mine. "*She'll need to be spoon-fed,*" Stewart then remarks quietly, pointing over at the Flaxen Beauty in the corner.

"Morning, Madame," Stewart says, holding the bowl of soup cautiously with both hands. He sets the bowl down on the tray in front of the Flaxen Beauty and then hunches over to see her eye to eye. In a flash, the Flaxen Beauty raises up her left knee while simultaneously grabbing the back of Stewart's head with both hands.

Stewart's face crashes violently into her thrusting knee — blood gushes immediately. The Flaxen Beauty then gets out of her chair, straddles the boy, and pummels him with a series of punches. The orderly is knocked unconscious.

I jump out of my bed and slide across the floor to be by Stewart's side; the Flaxen Beauty still straddles his chest. "Oh my God," I say, looking up at her calm demeanour. "Your knee is bleeding," I tell her, noticing that her bare knee is bloodied.

"That's not my blood," she says proudly. As she stands up to tower over him, her five-foot-one stance looks imposing. I also stand up and look down at the face of Stewart; his nose seems broken, as do his front teeth. He'll live, but it is clear that the Flaxen Beauty was restrained for other reasons besides the one she mentioned to me.

"Now what?" I ask wildly, looking at the Flaxen Beauty.

"We escape this place," the Flaxen Beauty says confidently. She pushes her bangs away. "None of us belong in here," she says. The Flaxen Beauty makes her way to our door and looks both ways before heading left.

We follow close behind her, but not too close. I look over at Emily with a face of worry, unaware of what's been unleashed. The Flaxen Beauty is heading towards the exit at the end of the hall. I wonder if she knows that it is locked; if not, then this venture will sadly come to an end.

Our weapon walks with a strange confidence down the shiny hall; there is no trying to be sneaky — the Flaxen Beauty acts fearlessly. "What!" a nurse named Sandra hollers out after exiting one of the rooms and noticing our loose missile. The Flaxen Beauty strikes Sandra so hard with a quick overhand right that Sandra's jaw goes immediately slack; obviously, she is out for the count. Emily kneels next to Sandra's slumped-over body to check her pulse before we pass by her.

The Flaxen Beauty's stride never quickens. Her posture is straight and her composure is focused on her one and only goal. I pity anyone in her path — she is one formidable foe. She eventually reaches the double doors at the end of the hall. She reams on the handles, but they are indeed locked. I know somewhere deep down that this plan may fail.

"So much for that," I say to Emily, as we both stop ten feet behind the Flaxen Beauty. She then unlocks the doors, thrusting them both open.

"How did she do that?" Emily asks, looking over at me in astonishment. Hearing Emily's comment, the Flaxen Beauty twirls the orderly's keys in the air for us to see. The Flaxen Beauty then turns to give us a beaming smile. She says, "Good luck, girls; may you both find your way out."

The Flaxen Beauty then dashes down the hall at a neck-breaking speed, indicating that she would rather not have anyone tag along. Emily and I stand unmoving at the threshold of the double doors. The Flaxen Beauty is about hundred feet down the hall from us when she sharply darts right, out of view.

"Ready?" I ask Emily as she reaches over and grabs my hand.

"Ready," Emily says, exhaling loudly. We step forward in unison out of this house of horrors.

Suddenly, a piercing alarm shoots a stream of echoing down the hall and we unclasp our hands to cover our ears. This place is on high alert with this debilitating ringing that makes us collapse to our knees. "What is this?" I yell, but she's not even looking my way to read my lips.

Then, as quickly as it had started, the alarming noise ceases to bring much-needed relief to my ringing head. I get up from my knees and then help Emily who is still crouched on the ground. Orderlies, doctors, and nurses spill out of every room to run and roam the halls haphazardly. We stand innocently up with our backs to the walls as a rush of people pass us by in a panic to stabilize the events I may have put in play.

Right now, during all of this commotion, would be the perfect time to make our escape. However, what then? We are still trapped in yet another prison with no clear lines of flight. Emily has a plan. It's far-fetched to say the least, but it's more than what I have.

"*Do we go?*" Emily whispers, looking over at me. We both then look over at the threshold of the open double-doors. I suppose we could go, but Emily's plan isn't one that can be acted on in an instant. It may take many months to locate the stasis avatar of Devlin Dixby — we surely won't find him while we're being chased around town by these medical butchers.

"*I don't know, I'm thinking,*" I whisper as extreme hesitation rushes over my mind. Our choice gets cemented to us when the double doors are soundly closed shut by a passing orderly. A loud click follows, and I roll my eyes at our missed opportunity at freedom.

"You girls go back to your rooms," the orderly says after locking the doors. "We are on lockdown," he explains, pointing at us to go. We both unstick ourselves from our flattened stance up against the wall and sheepishly march back towards our room. We pass Nurse Sandra dizzily coming back to awareness, aided by her fellow nurses.

"Over here!" a doctor calls out, passing our room door. "Someone is hurt," he continues. He goes into our room, I assume to help that poor Stewart. When Emily and I reach the entrance to our room, we are quickly pushed aside by another doctor and two nurses coming to the poor boy's aid.

———— ᨒᨆᨆᨆ ————

It takes all of twenty minutes to get this place back to its normality. Emily and I are back staring out the eastern-facing windows, wondering if we squandered our one and only chance at freedom.

"Okay girls, you are free to go," Nurse Sydney says, walking into our room with her hands placed firmly on her hips.

"What do you mean?" I ask Nurse Sydney, thinking that this must be some sort of trick.

"It means your families are waiting for you downstairs," Nurse Sydney says, pointing down the hall. "Your forty-eight-hour observational period is up."

"Observational period?" I ask earnestly, querying what she means.

"You both witnessed a traumatic event — a psych evaluation is mandatory by Health Canada."

"We passed?" I ask, surprised.

"Yes, for the most part — enough to satisfy Health Canada's requirements, even if the bar is somewhat low," Sydney says with a roll of her eyes. "You have ten minutes to get dressed," she says, unlocking our wardrobes, "and then I'll escort you to your families."

Sydney leaves the room and we both walk cautiously to our clothes hanging freely in view. "Is this a trick?" Emily asks as we reach in to grab our garments.

"I don't think by law that they can detain us here," I say to Emily while whipping my gown off over my head.

"Thank God for that," Emily says, "although I'm still rattled by what Keoh did to Adayln."

"Well, keep those thoughts to yourself — Emma," I say with an emphasis on her name in this realm. "We stick to our story that we just came upon them — let's not give these people any reason to keep us here longer."

——————⟿⟾——————

Faithful to her word, Nurse Sydney leads us downstairs to where Mother is there waiting with a worried smile. A man and woman stand next to Mother — presumably Emma's parents, as Emma looks to be a mixture of both of them.

Mother embraces my head firmly between her breasts. Emma's dad places his hand coldly on Emily's shoulder with a look of embarrassment written up and down his face.

"Mom," I say, looking into her eyes before looking back at Emily. "Emma!" I call out, making her stop to turn. Her dad's hand is still latched to her shoulder. "See you at school tomorrow?" I ask, bringing a smile to her face.

"We'll walk together," Emily says.

"1404 Pineview," I blurt out. Emily's dad turns his body, clearly wanting to go. "Meet me at my house," I say. After she leaves, I turn back to give Mother a smothering, much-needed hug.

Chapter 16

"Miranda, do you remember his last novel before his death — *Fallen Angel?*" Emily asks with a puzzled smile.

"Vaguely; it was just another love story," I say with a groan, getting myself ready for my first day back at school.

"Yes, but the protagonist, Wade Jennings, falls in love with a girl with fiery crimson hair. Shame that she was never named; however, they are both seventeen years old in the story," Emily rambles. She is starting to get excited.

"What are you getting at, Emily?" I growl from within my shirt which I have flung over my head.

"What if that story is about you cuz we actually, like, find him?" Emily asks with glee, jumping to her knees on my bed.

"Don't be ridiculous — I'm not the only one with crimson hair in town that is also seventeen," I sassily reject her ponderous speculation.

"Anything is possible from what I have seen in here," Emily says, her beautiful eyes shining brightly at me. "Open your mind, Miranda: this is our best chance for survival," she continues in a heartfelt plea.

"Okay — okay, we'll seek the boy out," I say coyly, if only to stop Emily from beaming, "but this won't work."

After seeing Little Sister to her school, we part ways to not only go to school but to also complete an impossible task. Emily and I look at our school in unison, surmising how we are going to locate the fictional character of Wade Jennings.

"We don't even know if he went to Princess Margaret High. He could have gone to McNicol or Pen High," I tell Emily to lower her expectations.

"Wade lived on Railway Avenue. He was also poor. Because he resided on the west side of town, and given those demographics, they would have sent him to this school," Emily says with a confirming head nod. I wish I knew where she was gathering all her facts.

"Let's just ask the main office," I say, tapping Emily on the shoulder as we enter the school's main doors.

"What do I ask them?" Emily asks as I force her through the office doors.

"*Just tell them who you are looking for,*" I whisper to Emily as the office secretary looks at us squarely with an unpleasant sneer on her face.

"Yes, girls," the office secretary says in a bored yawn.

"Umm, yes — I'm looking for someone, umm —" Emily mumbles. It's rare to see her lost for words.

"Wade Jennings," I say, speaking up over Emily's shoulder. "Does he go to this school?" I ask the secretary, getting right to the point.

"Let me check," the secretary says in a slow drawl while typing away into her computer. "Yes, he attends here. Why are you inquiring?" the secretary asks in curiosity, tilting her glasses to the end of her slender nose.

"Oh, Josie has a huge crush on him!" Emily says, followed by a loud laugh. She bolts out of the office.

"I do not!" I yell as the bustle of the office comes to a standstill with everyone looking at me. I'm embarrassed;

my skin must be blushing to a high pitch as I saunter out of the office doors with a smile on my face. The doors close as I turn to see Emily still giggling away from her antics.

"*Geez, that was embarrassing, Emily,*" I whisper, punching her harshly in the shoulder. "I'm not his love interest," I tell her emphatically.

"I had to do it; I'm sorry," Emily quips, giving me a hug.

"Hey Josie!" a familiar voice calls out from the gym door a few metres away.

"Who's that?" Emily asks quickly.

"Oh, that's just Ryan," I tell her, followed by a sigh. "Oh hey, Ryan!" I yell, followed by a wave.

"*He's cute,*" Emily whispers into my ear.

"*Take him; the boy follows me around like a lapdog,*" I whisper as we approach the gym door. Ryan is all decked out in the school's crimson athletic attire; he seems to be attending a morning basketball practice.

"You feeling any better? I heard you were sick," Ryan sheepishly asks, juggling a ball from hand to hand.

"Ya — I'm fine now," I say humbly. "I'm alright."

"Okay, good — Umm," Ryan says, lost for words as usual.

"Hello, I'm Emma," Emily says assertively. Happy to butt in, she walks in front of me to shake Ryan's hand.

"Emma, ya, — we have, like, English class together. I, like, already know you," Ryan says. He is confused, but he shakes Emily's hand nevertheless.

"Well, we have to go find someone. Maybe see you later," I tell Ryan in a chipper voice. I am trying to act friendly. Emily just continues to stand there ogling poor Ryan up and down.

"Let's go, Emma," I moan, grabbing her by the arm to pull her down the hall.

"How can you or even Josie for that matter not be attracted to that?" Emily says, still looking in the direction of Ryan as I continue to drag her away.

"Seriously, Emily, there must be at least three hundred students here — how are we going to find this guy?" I ask exhaustively as we get swallowed up in a tight stairwell of students.

"Does anyone know Wade Jennings?" Emily starts shouting out to students going down the stairs as we ascend.

"Since when have you two been friends?" a tall girl with short sandy hair calls out from the top of the landing.

"We go way back," Emily says cautiously while we approach.

"You haven't called in days; thought we were friends, Emma," the tall girl says with a sneer.

"I was in the mental hospital this weekend," Emily tells the tall girl, who doesn't look all that impressed with Emily's answer.

"The weird deserve the weird — you're a good pair," the tall girl says to Emily in a huff, brushing past her with a shoulder bump.

"What happened there?" I ask Emily, confused by the interaction.

"I think I just got defriended," Emily says with a blank stare, apparently thinking about the encounter.

"Come on, let's keep going," I tell her with a head nod to continue up the stairs.

At the top of the landing, I call out, "Wade Jennings! Anyone know Wade Jennings?" I continue to holler as we walk down the hall of the second floor.

"*I know Wade Jennings,*" a voice mumbles out from behind a thin locker door just ahead of us.

"You do?" Emily says in excitement, quickly walking up to the boy as he closes his locker door. He has a slender build and lightly toned muscles, most likely from hockey. Lemony hair, clean complexion, and an adorable dimple is just now coming into view.

"Do you know where we can find him?" Emily pleads passionately, her adrenaline clearly pumping.

"I am Wade Jennings. You've found me — although I'm not quite sure why?" Wade says with a devious smile. Wade then looks from Emily to me, and scans me up and down. Emily turns to me in a panic about how we should proceed. We shrug our shoulders in unison about what to do next.

"Are you Devlin Dixby?" I blurt out, looking sharply into his stunning indigo eyes.

"Oh shit!" Wade lets out as those eyes go wide in fear. In a flash, he then drops his books and starts running away in the opposite direction with panic written all over his face.

We run after him, shouting at him to stop, but he acts as if his life is on the line. It takes a while for my feeble mush of a mind to process why he would be running away. "We don't work for LaPorte!" I yell out, making him finally slow down and bend over in exhaustion.

"How can I tell?" Wade asks, ambling away from us as we continue to step closer.

"Well, if we do, you've just confessed your guilt," I say. He finally halts on the spot, wincing at my truth.

"Okay, you got me," Wade turns and walks back towards us like he wants to be handcuffed. I quickly push his arms down, doing my best not to gather any attention.

"Put your arms down; we are not here to arrest you," I tell him. "We are here for answers only."

"We are awake, and certainly not LaPortan agents," Emily tells him. "We are from the year 3272."

"The future?" Wade asks, looking puzzled by the year. "You are not from 2673?"

"Actually, we are from 3289 — now," I jump in, accounting for these seventeen years that we have spent in the box.

"I knew something with time played a part in the simulation," Wade laments, scratching the back of his head. "But this is beyond what I have ever pondered," he continues, looking up to the ceiling in a deep well of thought.

"Wade," I say, grabbing him by the upper arm. A shot of electricity tingles through my body.

"We need your help," Emily says exasperated. I let go of his arm to stare at my hand. It was like touching a pure spark of exhilaration. I look back up at him, and a throbbing passion washes over me. I smile uncontrollably. I bet I'm even blushing with this fair skin of mine.

"So, you don't work for LaPorte?" Wade asks, looking at both of us.

"*No, not even LaPorte agents are permitted inside the SDS awake; it's way too dangerous,*" I inform him in a hushed whisper.

"We are from the Double R," Emily says, making him give off a look of befuddlement.

"The Double what?" Wade asks, still looking at Emily strangely.

"The Real Realm," I say distinctly. Wade shakes his head.

"We are awake in our SDS pods!" Emily calls out, her voice echoing down the long hallway for all to hear.

"How do you know about me?" Wade inquires with a villainous rasp in his voice, grabbing each of our shoulders to bring us in close.

"From your books," Emily says with a head nod. "Are you the Devlin Dixby who authored *Defy the Knot*, *The Forever Love of Norran and Whenwig*, and *Fallen Angel*?" she inquires to make sure that this is indeed the true Devlin Dixby.

"From my books?" Wade asks, sounding surprised.

"We figured out that you were talking about Penticton while awake — in here," I explain to him. "That's what you wrote about."

"What was that last book — called?" Wade asks with a coy smile. "Didn't quite catch the title," he says, continuing to smirk.

"We need your help," Emily says, grabbing him by the wrist.

"Help with what? Who are you guys, anyway?" Wade asks with his playful demeanour changing rapidly to a peering look of distrust towards us.

"We need help getting out of here," I say to him frantically. "It's dangerous to be in here while consciously awake."

"Says who — LaPorte?" Wade says in jest. "Naw; you can't trust them," he continues. Shaking his head, he starts walking back to pick up his books.

"Are you saying it's safe to be awake in the Penticton realm?" Emily asks fervidly, making a few passing students laugh.

"*Keep it — down*," Wade says in a slow hush, "*they will lock you up in the Carmi Looney Bin for making comments like that.*"

"Is that a different place then the Carmi Mental Health Centre?" I ask out of curiosity.

"No, it's the same," Wade says with a roll of his eyes.

"Oh, we were there all weekend; they just released us," Emily enlightens him with a massive grin.

"I'm not surprised," Wade says, followed by a long sigh. *"You girls need to act normal in this period of time,"* he warns us in a scolding whisper.

"How do you know it's safe to be awake in this realm?" I whisper, sensing something suspicious about him.

"Look, girls," Wade says, huddling closer to us, "this is not the time nor place to be discussing these matters. There could be LaPorte agents spying on us as we speak," he continues, swiveling his head to look down both ends of the long second-floor hallway.

"LaPorte agents wouldn't enter awake; that is just crazy," I tell him with a laugh that was meant to be serious but somehow came out playful.

"I have math class on the other side of the building — " Wade says, interrupted by the first block bell, "and now I'm going to be late!" Flustered, Wade starts to walk in haste down the hall.

"When can we talk — again?" I ask Wade with my voice breaking awkwardly.

"Green Beans Café around seven o'clock tonight; I have a four-hour shift at Canadian Tire after school," Wade says before his fast walk morphs into a sprint.

"Green Beans Café?" Emily repeats, as her head tilts in thought. "That's downtown, I believe," she continues. I collect my dizzy emotions after that exchange with Wade.

"Miranda?" Emily asks intently. My mind seems to be elsewhere as I stare down the hall, watching Wade leave.

"What? Yes?" I stutter, coming back from my brief daydream.

"You okay?" Emily asks, placing her hand on my shoulder.

"I'm fine — why?" I ask like nothing is wrong.

"You look lost in thought, that's all," Emily notes.

"Can we trust him?" I ask Emily, sighing deeply.

"Really?" Emily asks with her devious grin. "Is that really what's on your mind?"

"Yes, he's very umm —" I begin to convey.

"Good looking," Emily jumps in to finish my sentence.

"That has nothing to do with it," I tell Emily soundly as she starts laughing.

"C'mon, let's get to class," Emily says. She looks at her wristwatch, still grinning away.

"What class do you have for A block?" I ask acutely. Checking Josie's schedule, I see that I have Consumer Education.

"I have French?" Emily says with a surprised look. "That's going to be hard without a linguistic translator," she continues as the second warning bell chimes.

"Okay, I'll see you at lunch," I tell Emily, knowing that I still need to go to the third floor.

"Lunch at your locker then," Emily says as we part in opposite directions.

———— ∞∞∞∞∞∞ ————

When the lunch bell rings, I realize that I'm starving from not partaking in morning breakfast with Little Sister since Emily showed up to change Josie's routine. I hustle to my locker and quickly open the door to grab the brown paper bag lunch that Mother has packed for me. A white bread sandwich, an apple, and a bag of Old Dutch salt and vinegar potato chips comprise the contents of the bag.

I close my locker, pressing my back flat against the door as I slide down the smooth metal surface to sit on the floor. The sandwich is creamy butter with some soft fruit jelly that I inhale at a fever pitch. Emily soon meets up to sit beside me, her lunch bag only including a folded over piece of white bread and a well-bruised banana.

"That's all you got?" I ask Emily, looking over at her sad lunch.

"That's what was left for me on the counter. Everyone in my family is in such a rush," Emily says, looking sorrowfully into her lunch bag for more food that surely isn't there.

"I'll share my chips," I tell Emily, handing her the bag.

"How were classes this morning?" Emily asks, taking a bite of a chip, cringing when the alkali flavour hits her taste buds. "Ugh — what is that?" Emily spits out, looking at the front of the bag, "*Salt and Vinegar*? I wasn't expecting that combination," she continues with a snicker. Then she reaches into the bag for another chip.

"Classes were fine; it was hard to concentrate though," I tell her with an overwhelmed moan.

"Thinking of that cute boy?" Emily asks with a beaming smile, still acting the tease.

"Well ya —" I say, just realizing her words in more detail, "but not like that!" I correct myself quickly.

"It's okay, Miranda. You're seventeen years old; it's hard to fight your urges of lust," Emily says with a cringe before biting down on another chip.

"I have no urges for him," I tell her sassily. "All I want is information about how to get out of here."

"How can you not find him attractive?" Emily asks keenly. "You're not a first-generation AI — you are embodying a human, remember?"

"We don't have time for any of that," I tell Emily. I am frazzled. "We need to rein in all human emotions and desires if we are to escape," I say with a bit more vigour in my voice. Emily's attention wanders away from me to stare gawkingly at Ryan coming our way.

"Are you listening to me?" I ask, feeling ignored.

"Yes — ya," Emily responds, not looking at me at all.

"Seriously," I say sternly, pushing Emily gently on the shoulder to knock her off-balance.

"I got it, Jo — sie," Emily says mockingly, looking my way, putting an extra emphasis on speaking my name correctly in this realm.

"Hey girls," Ryan says, stopping to hover above us.

"Hello Ryan, what are you up to?" I ask him plainly with my emotions towards him set at low.

"Just going to the vending machine for lunch," Ryan tells us with a point of his finger down the hall. "Can I get you something?" he asks, looking at me with his puppy dog eyes.

"I'll have a bag of chips," Emily says, leaning in front of me, "if you're offering."

"Oh — ya, for sure, Emma," Ryan says, finally taking his eyes off of me. "What flavour?"

"Not this type," Emily says, holding up my now empty bag of salt and vinegar chips.

"Okay, ya — got it," Ryan says, giving a weird two finger point in our direction before walking down the hall.

"Geez — he's odd," I say, biting into my apple.

"It's because he likes you, Miranda," Emily tells me like I haven't picked that up.

"I've given him no reason to have affection towards me, and neither has Josie, according to what Little Sister has told me," I explain to Emily.

"The heart doesn't listen to reason," Emily says with a giggle. "If it did, the human race would have gone extinct eons ago."

"Regardless, we have a task at hand that we must focus on," I tell her in a commanding tone to deflect all this teenage nonsense.

"Oh — ya, the dreamy Wade Jennings," Emily banters, playfully bumping my shoulder with hers.

"Okay, let's get a few things straight," I tell her, still trying to act seriously which I find extremely hard to do in this body. "We need to use the names that we have here; no more Miranda or Emily," I say with conviction, staring intensely into her eyes.

"Agreed. Got it; no more mentioning the names of Keoh and Adayln, as well," Emily adds, as I strain my mush to eliminate our true names from my mind. "I will not utter a word," she continues to merrily say, shaking her head with a smirk.

"I'm serious," I press, "this element of space and perhaps even the fabric of our own timeline are unexpected."

"I agree," Emily says. "That is a complex variable we must somehow navigate to avoid annihilation."

"Are you talking about a time paradox?" I ask, shocked, as that scary thought just now enters into my mind.

"Well — ya, it's like totally possible," Emily says, calm as can be. My heart starts to pound.

"*What if we cause a time paradox?*" I mumble in a panic; my lips start to quiver.

"Miran-Josie," Emily says, correcting herself. "Calm down," she continues, noticing that I'm starting to shake. "*Breathe, Josie — just breathe,*" Emily says slowly, looking directly into my eyes.

I begin to think more serene thoughts, but this muddle is hard to navigate and I'm way out of practice. It is like the sub-directory is missing — the design is truly awful. I ramble in my mind for many fast-ticking seconds until I come to a place, that time this morning with Emily in my bedroom. Emily was so full of glee going on about that fate-driven ballad that she believes I'm on a destined path to partake.

I don't see how that is possible. I haven't loved anyone for a very long time, not since my own raven-haired angel left me so long ago; however, that thought is not fighting with its normal intensity. So, I smile, thinking about Emily when she jumped to her knees on my bed. She was happy and excited. That feeling was infectious, and it did make me ponder the idea of love — that powerful emotion. Emily has that tenderness in her; she doesn't hide it away.

So why do I deflect the fluttering of my heart to the prospect of maybe fondness towards another to happen — even if the chances are fictional? Just that look of glee on Emily's face encapsulates the whole meaning of the word love. This is the thought I bring forward on command to lower my worrisome trepidation over the idea of a possible time paradox.

"*That's it, breathe,*" Emily continues to say softly as I start inhaling through my nose to signify that I'm now okay.

"I got you a drink, too," Ryan says, coming out of nowhere to tower over us again. Emily takes the drink and chips from his lowered grasp, grinning seductively from ear to ear.

"Sit here, Ryan," Emily commands; he is helpless not to follow. Ryan does what he is told and sits next to Emily, squeezing his knees up to his chest so as not to have people trip over his long, gangly legs. Ryan gives me a worried smile, although I see him glance at Emily's bustline before his eyes dart straight ahead. Perhaps Emily could help me shake this lost little dog from his constant following. "Oh, we have English class together next block," Emily says, blinking at Ryan.

"Yup — E block, umm —" Ryan says nervously. "E is for English," he continues to mutter, awkwardly throwing his words around. Luckily for him, Emily is never lost for words, and she continues to talk his ear off for the rest of our lunch hour. I can tell by the passing minutes that his vision has started to shift more towards Emily than me, but that could be because she's talking all the damn time.

How hard can it be? Emily should have no problem taking this boy's heart from wanting mine. It's not that I don't like Ryan; I just don't like him in that profound way. Wade is who I'm focusing on; he is the new mission that I must keep clear thoughts towards. The goal is to meet with Wade tonight and extract what useful intel we can about this realm in hopes of finding a way to escape.

That's it; that's all.

Nope — there is nothing else to ponder.

Well, maybe his indigo eyes for just a fleeting second; they are so — Miranda, stop! Keep your thoughts focused on the mission; resist this teenage urge of infatuation. You are letting it boil over; control your biology, Josie!

"Josie!" Emily shouts, looming above me. "The bell rang, you coming?" she asks, probably wondering why I'm still sitting on the ground.

"E Block, yes," I say aloud, frantically standing up. "*First-floor room 'B' History class,*" I mumble, prepping my body on where it needs to go next.

"See you after school," Emily says. Her hand grasps Ryan's upper arm, making him wait to take her to class.

"After school," I repeat, ensuring to myself that I'm awake before we head off in opposite directions down the third-floor hallway.

The stairwell is always hellishly packed right after the first bell; I've got to remember to leave early instead of all this running to class. I encounter nothing but squeaking sneakers and snickering impatience while getting swallowed up by this melting pot of sweat and anarchy. We bump back and forth, elbow to elbow, as I ping-pong my way to the first floor. I enter flushed-out of a cannon into the classroom; my hair flies uncontrollably forward, covering my face.

Instinctively, I raise my right hand to caress my face. I dance my fingers through my tangled crimson hair, gently flying the locks away. I sway my head from side to side to settle my hair. Then I quickly adjust my shirt before turning to find a chair.

The back corner by the window is open, and I dart in that direction in haste. The students spill in quickly like a river flowing at high tilt. I grab the back of the chair in the corner, the one I was aiming for from the start. I am relieved to have gotten it, as the desks all around me fill up with students mere seconds later.

With a smile of pure glee shining sunnily across my face, I take a seat in my rightful victorious chair; only to slip and miss it when I notice Wade Jennings sitting at the desk next to me. I hit the ground with an embarrassing thud followed by a chorus of laughter from a few classmates.

However, I am back on my feet after two muscular arms tuck under mine to lift me up into the air. My back slides along his apparently toned chest. He is tall, whoever this is, as he picks me straight up off the floor before

I land back on my two feet. I turn slowly, still in his arms, and look up to his face.

"*Thank you,*" I mutter in shock. My vision goes straight to his stunning indigo eyes — yet again.

"No problem – Josie?" Wade asks with a squint in his eyes. "It is Josie, right?" he inquires again, this time with a somewhat flirtatious wink.

"Yes, I go by Josie," I tell him. "Wade, right?" I ask nervously, already knowing this name on the edge of my lips. We smile enticingly at one another as we take our seats. Our eyes dance back and forth followed by an uncontrollable toothy smile, for one of us. Keep it together, Miranda; the goal is to escape this realm. Wade Jennings is Devlin Dixby, remember? The same Devlin Dixby that would foolishly enter this dangerous realm awake against all laws forbidding it.

The nerve of breaking the rules of our species for only the trivial, selfish pursuits of pleasure — he chose not to believe. People like this have been a danger in our society over the centuries. All of his kind have been routed out of the million of us who are still left. Everyone now plays by the rules governed by their signed user agreements.

I slink down lower into my chair as haunting thoughts enter my mind. These same user agreements which I have witnessed with my own two eyes contain false statements. This realm is more extensive than just the town of Penticton.

Why was I never told?

I'm *One of the Firsts.*

Number One Hundred and Forty-One.

I, of all people, should have been made aware of this ability to navigate past these holowalls. What other errors and lies might there be written within our holy scripture? It must be a mistake; don't give thoughts to those hindered by human emotion. If I could only turn these commands off. That programming, of course, doesn't exist in this heaven.

I have spent 760 years collectively in Penticton spanning twenty-two different lives in a realm as perfect as God intended it. Now, after all this time, can I shelf this new wrinkle of concern until I'm given a legitimate answer? But then there is the element of time that gives me pause. How could LaPorte have created such a place with those un-probabilistic laws? With my eyes and consciousness awake, I see with certainty that this realm is more than a mere simulation.

I look over at Wade; our eyes lock and my heart skips a beat. Get your gaze back to the front board, I bellow in my mind. I look ahead, and my anxiety is brought down.

He's just a boy, Miranda, relax. He's also a man who I have met before and who made a harsh impression on me. I felt nothing but sorrow and disgust for Dixby during our brief encounters back in that era of time.

Wade picked me up, though; that is an act of such a different soul. I could feel his embrace and warmth; I could even feel his heart beat within that muscular chest. I can feel my teeth dig into my bottom lip as mischievous, unwarranted reflections of Wade start to dance through my mind.

Could I be his love interest from the book?

Emily may be correct as I do kind of look like the character. Well, that is going off of Emily's wayward description. It's impossible, though; Dixby and I have such different ideals. He is only an ancient soul. Chronologically speaking, though, I was biologically born in 1976, and Devlin was born in 1980, so we are only four years apart if we are thinking of the Law of Ages.

I suppose there is some whimsy in reading his novels if this is the human melancholy they transmit. That robust emotion of being held in his arms, cradled so gently by his strength, has allowed intense speculations to enter my mind.

Keep it together, Josie.

Keep strong, I remind myself over and over until the afternoon bell rings to end this eventful class.

"Seven o'clock, Green Beans — see you there," Wade says with a confident smile while grabbing his stuff. I just nod my head. Lost for words, I feel embarrassed about not uttering anything. I need to collect myself and prepare for what I need to do tonight.

Be strong and resist.

Don't let him challenge your beliefs; he will try to sway you.

I have one block left today. "Art class, Shatford Building — basement," I tell myself to plan out the route I need to take.

Art class. Oh God, I hope they don't expect me to paint!

Chapter 17

We make our way downtown via the public bus system and then set out on foot to find to this Green Beans Café.

"Canadian – Tire," Emily says with a slow giggle, looking up at its massive triangular sign. "Do you remember when British Columbia used to be part of Canada?" Emily asks, showing her true ancient age.

"Yes, as I recall they rebranded this store as Cascadia Tire after we annexed ourselves to become a new nation of ideals," I tell Emily. "Such a knee-jerk marketing blunder if I say so," I continue to lament as we take a detour into the massive parking lot.

"This was once one of my favourite biological survival stores," Emily says with fondness as we go inside to quickly check this museum out.

"What does Wade do here?" Emily asks overtly. She looks around, dazzled, while I strain to think.

"Oh, Wade probably sells tires — actually, I honestly can't tell you what he would do here," I say with a shrug. I'm looking an odd display of fishing rods next to bags of grass fertilizer. We promptly walk back out and continue on our way down the street to find the Green Beans Café with its signature peach-coloured awning.

"Why do you think Wade does it?" I ask with a jarring uncertainty. What does Dixby get out of being so reckless by coming into this realm awake?

"Well, he is a poor student and needs the money, and Canadian Tire looks to be a good job —" Emily begins to ramble.

"No, not that," I interrupt. "Why does he enter the SDS awake?" I ask explicitly this time.

"I think he wants nothing more than to live a long life within the SDS," Emily says passionately in regards to Wade.

"That's as much as I can understand, but why does he want that?" I continue to inquire, shaking my head. I know that we just may find out the answers if we ask him the right questions.

We enter the Green Beans Café and find ourselves a private booth near the back. "Now, remember, Josie, you need to fall in love with him," Emily teases. "You are both teenagers," she continues, reminding me painfully of the obvious.

"There is still a 600 year old consciousness in that teenage boy's body," I point out. I sit down at the booth with a head nod to Emily to sit right next to me.

"That is a child even to us; they are allowed to still dream," Emily says, looking dizzily up at the high ceiling.

"*Oh, there he is!*" I whisper in a state of shock to Emily as Wade enters the café. "*No, you would never form a union with someone that young, even in our time. They would have the smell of PHR rejection stamped all over them,*" I continue to whisper scornfully. "*However, he is awfully cute.*"

"*Do we tell him that he is long dead in our period of time?*" Emily asks with a sudden look of worry on her face.

"*Do we tell him about his future, that he dies as a foot-note writer from our golden age of transcendence?*" I repeat sassily while rolling my eyes to that idea.

"*Okay, so — how does this work?*" Emily asks. "*We are in the past, about to have coffee with someone else in the past, in a device that is supposedly a simulation,*" she says feverishly. "*No software code can create time, especially not during the era when LaPorte first created this world.*"

"Ladies!" Wade says loudly, full of boyish charm as he notices us. He swaggers over to our booth, his confidence spilling over, and sits down right across from us.

"So, how did you do it?" Wade asks right away with a wide, toothy grin.

"How did we do what?" Emily responds as we look at one another, confused by what he is asking.

"How did you hack your SDS pods?" Wade asks, this time with more context, drawing out the details of his request.

"Oh, it's a long story," I tell him nervously, rolling my eyes, "and one that I wish not to relive even in spoken form."

"Nevertheless, you are here as am I," Wade says, pointing to his chest with both thumbs.

"Why are you smiling?" I ask him. Wade apparently isn't well and not of a sound-mind, I begin to surmise.

"No reason," Wade remarks, looking taken aback by my question. "What's wrong with being happy?" he asks sharply.

"Well, we are dangerously awake within the SDS," Emily says anxiously, making Wade sit up straight like he just now understanding our concerns.

"I told ya: there is nothing to fear about being con-sciously awake within the SDS — it's perfectly fine," Wade tells us yet again, although I'm still not convinced.

I may need to observe him some more. A very close examination might be in order. My mind goes to thoughts of pure pleasure, seriously unravelling my train of thought.

"Josie, seriously!" I say out loud. Emily and Wade look at me for obvious reasons. "Sorry," I say awkwardly after interrupting Wade in mid-sentence.

"It's okay — so like I was saying, it is purely safe," Wade finishes his thought. "Now, more importantly — *what year did you both say that you were from? 3272?*" Wade asks in a low voice, squinting out of one eye.

"Yes, that's correct," I say, releasing a massive sigh, "and that's not important. The concern is that we should not be awake in here."

"It's safe," Wade says again bluntly, tight-lipped while nodding assuredly.

"You say it's safe, but how can we be sure of that?" Emily retorts quickly; she apparently isn't convinced either.

"Look, sweet angels, this ain't my first time doing this; it's my third — so quit fretting," Wade attests, holding his hands up in the air like he is swearing an oath. "Now, do you have any real names, or will I not have the privilege of knowing them?" Wade asks openly, scanning both of us with his endearing eyes.

"Josie and Emma," Emily says, pointing to me with her thumb when she mentions my name.

"No, your real names — *Ahh never mind,*" he says, shaking his head and quickly giving up. "Tell me about my next book, the one about this life," Wade asks with a cringe on his face showing that he may not want to know.

"I don't think that it is a good idea," Emily remarks slowly, "that is — from a journalistic point of view — to release such information."

"Oh, you're a journalist. Good to know that the written word hasn't been abolished in the future," Wade says in a mocking banter towards Emily.

"I agree with Emma," I tell him, still feeling that we all may be playing with fire. "We wish not to reveal information that may cause a time paradox," I explain. This is why we are cold to his questions.

"Well, as far as you know, maybe I get the idea for my next book from you two angels," Wade tells us coyly with one eye open while he slurps his iced tea. "*You may cause a paradox by not telling me,*" he follows up while his mouth is full.

"We're alright with that risk," I reply confidently for both of us.

"So, no more questions about that topic," Emily says distressingly, obviously annoyed that Wade would ask about his future. "If we have lived out this path before, I can tell you with certainty that I would never give another writer a chance to plagiarize his own work," she berates blisteringly, looking at me and then back over at Wade.

"Plagiarism on something that I have written myself?" Wade says with a snort. "Now that is one crazy paradox theory."

"Maybe the paradox of time is why our minds fracture if we ever attempt suicide on ourselves," I say, knowing that path would surely cure us all away from this realm.

"Look, I've scoured every inch of this Eden," Wade says in unabated excitement, leaning in close. "I have been able to do that in these combined sixty years awake within the SDS. Now, I can't get past Okanagan Falls, Summerland, or even Naramata due to an invisible wall. However, I've slowly been writing a handbook, trying to map out what I have discovered. For example, I've witnessed a weird dilation of time along Green Mountain

Road. I've experienced firsthand the whip-cracking consequences of straying far from your path. Oh, I've also
documented the flora and fauna which doesn't belong
in this area," he babbles relentlessly, speaking nothing of
worth.

"That's all fascinating, Wade, but it doesn't help us
get our consciousness back to sleep," I plead, hoping that
Wade may know something that could help.

"Just live out your lives. There is no harm here, as
LaPorte claims," Wade says calmly, not realizing that we
cannot wait the decades it may take to play out our narra-
tives. "You don't go mad from being awake in this infernal contraption. It's not like drowning," he continues, but
we need exit now; our friends are in trouble. I'm not convinced that Wade would understand or even care about
that notion. I must remember that Wade is an ancient
ancestor from a bygone time.

"So, you can't help us?" Emily says with a loud
defeated sigh.

"I didn't say that. I can tell you how to survive, but
that does come with a cost. Nothing in life is free — *that
even applies in this realm*," Wade says with a devilish grin.

"We just want to escape," I implore him.

"You can't change anything. The world plays out,
and you die when you are supposed to die. It's constructed with limited free will in mind," Wade explains
plainly. "The problem is that I can never get past twenty-two years old. Say — have they fixed the fan in the Six
Series? That's the SDS model I want to buy next when it's
released," Wade inquires. "I need to know if there is any
vast improvement before I lay down any credits."

"Wade, please — stop asking us any questions about
the future. That is a clear rule that we must obey," I tell
Wade sternly, not caring at all about what he wants.

"Oh, Josie, give him something; Wade looks so sweet," Emily tells me with a beaming gush.

"Okay, fine: they fixed the fan in the Six Series," I tell him with a frustrated exhalation. "Version six point two if I remember correctly."

"Oh wait, I don't want to waste my question on that," Wade howls wildly while patting my hand playfully. "So c'mon, what are your real names then, or is that still to be held against me?" he asks, shaking his head while leaning back against the booth.

"In your period of time, I went by the name of Josie Sage," I tell him, seeing no harm in revealing my name.

"Josie Sage — that sounds familiar. Have we met before by chance?" Wade asks intensely, peering at me with that one eye closed again, as if that would aid him in seeing the truth.

"Oh, we have met. Doubt you would remember, though," I inform him, feeling safe that he most likely won't recall our brief encounters.

"And what about you?" Wade asks, looking over at Emily. "What's your name?"

"Well, my close friends call me —" Emily begins, but I grab her wrist to stop her from speaking.

"No more questions until we get some answers," I state in a sharpened tone, tired of this endless game.

"A question for a question, I propose," he then says with a smirk. He rests both of his palms up on the table in a sign of openness.

"That can be dangerous for us," I stammer, glancing over at Emily uncertainty. "We still don't understand how time plays out in this realm, and we don't know how being here can affect our present timeline," I explain. I am hiding a question within a concern.

"Like I said, you cannot change the narrative structure of this timeline," Wade reminds. "You can visit. You can move around freely — *for the most part.* However, if you deviate far from your chosen path, life then converges on you to put you back in line. I have tried to re-write this past — this will be my third and last time," he says with a sad shrug of his shoulders.

"Why stop? Why is this your last time?" Emily inquires with her full journalist intent on high alert.

"I can feel LaPorte closing in on me. They don't let anybody deviate from their user agreement. Right when my books are starting to take off," Wade says with a tremor, giving us a glimpse of the fear LaPorte generated in our ancestors. "Now that was two questions. It's my turn," Wade says coyly. Emily and I sit back, waiting for his wish.

"Does the revolution happen — do we topple LaPorte?" Wade asks. He leans in and drapes his upper body over the table, looking at us fervidly for an affirmative answer.

"No," I tell him soundly. Wade recoils.

"No?" Wade says as his head jerks forward. "No to which part?" he asks sharply, looking for clarity where there is none to give.

"No to both," I say mystified. I look over at Emily, puzzled about what Wade had hoped to hear.

"Now that was three questions," Emily says with a raised eyebrow, showing us that she is also tallying in her head.

"No, that was only two," Wade retorts quickly, counting digits with his fingers. "Did it happen? Did it topple? No, to which parts? That was three questions," Emily says gleefully with a cheeky smile.

"Fine, ask your next three," Wade says, resigned to defeat.

"How did you try to change the timeline?" Emily inquires. Her question is wasted as it offers no help to our current situation.

"I wanted to extinguish the Great Forest Fire of 2004 to then live out a life with Ophelia, a life that I have never been granted in the world outside of this simulation," Wade tells us, giving a better understanding of his famous fable.

"Why awake, though? You get all these experiences once you emerge from the SDS," Emily asks foolishly, wasting all our valuable questions at will.

"When you are asleep in the Deep Sleep, and then rise again, if you're lucky," Wade begins, "then yes, you get the experiences added to your table. You gain extra attributes from living an extra lifetime within that box. However, it feels like a lifetime that I never lived. It is like someone gave me their dreams. It's just a story of someone's life, but not mine — I require free will," Wade tells us vigorously.

"Do you seek out to look upon Ophelia?" Emily asks profoundly, looking for a heart in the story and not for the heart of an initial answer that may get us out of here.

"I can't — *it's too painful,*" he says with a shudder. "Locked in this box in a tiny touristy town, I can't avoid Ophelia — she is everywhere, haunting me like a ghost," Wade continues. "Yes, this is definitely my last time."

"Well, we need to leave Penticton too, but we need to leave now," I say directly to Wade after Emily detour. "Now, what advice do you have about that?"

"No — that was three — I'm counting," Wade says with his boyish smile. "It's my turn now."

237

"Ask away," I slur in frustration while exhaling loudly through my nostrils.

"*The revolution doesn't happen, LaPorte doesn't fall, which means our society has surely perished,*" he mumbles to himself. "Do I make it past twenty-two in this life?" Wade asks passionately. Emily and I wince.

"A man should not know too much about his own future," Emily warns him, shaking her head again to his request.

"This is pointless!" I say, looking over at Emily, "We just need to find some tech in this realm; there must be something there next to the walls."

"What type of tech?" Emily asks wildly, taken aback by my bold statement. "This is 2005!"

"I remember reading about a piece of tech in an old user manual once," I explain. "However, the manual was never published — it may not be true," I continue as my gaze drops down.

"I found a box or contraption one day when I was thirteen," Wade offers up for free. "I spent the better part of one Sunday afternoon mapping the wall on the Northeast side of town. It goes under the lake. I can't tell you how deep, but it does indeed connect to the other side."

"So, that's why you can't leave Penticton through the northwest exit," Emily says, following along.

"Yes, one of the six main road exits out of Penticton," Wade adds, counting on his fingers again.

"Six? I thought there were only four," Emily retorts quickly, challenging his high number.

"Northwest Highway, Southwest Highway," Wade says, leaning over the table.

"That's one and two," Emily responds quickly, counting.

"Eastside Road and through Lower Bench Road," Wade says, listing off the other two obvious exits.

"Those are the third and fourth ways," Emily says, proudly holding up just four fingers.

"Ahh — but you have forgotten about Carmi Road and Green Mountain Road," Wade says with a wide grin, nodding his head up and down to add weight to his high number.

"Those are dirt roads, not main roads," Emily dismisses his claim.

"They are exits, nevertheless," Wade quips.

"But you need four-wheel drive machines," Emily says sassily.

"Both of you!" I interrupt loudly. "Shut up about stupid exits," I tell them, not understanding myself how we all got so far off track. "You said you found a box," I say, reminding them of the topic which should be at hand.

"Yes, a box. It is cloaked, but it is most definitely there," Wade says, sitting back confidently.

"I would like to know more about that," I tell him in a tone that I swear is meant to be harsh but somehow comes out sounding sweet and sincere.

"So, anyway, like I was saying," Wade says, adjusting his posture, "I was mapping out the North East Wall, being careful not to touch it. That bastard has a donkey kick to it if you set yourself within a hair's breadth of it," he tells us, slapping his hand against the table in a demonstration of his extraordinary force, which we have already witnessed.

"We are quite aware of the wall's jolting power," Emily says, looking over at me.

"You are — but how?" Wade leans in to ask.

"Two other members of our party were soundly rejected when we attempted to enter Okanagan Falls via

Eastside Road," I say, cringing as I relive the memory of Adayln's body skipping down that asphalt.

"Two other members?" Wade asks, surprised. "How many are there?"

"Four of us for sure —" Emily says, followed by a long pause.

"Possibly six," I finish Emily's sentence.

"Six of you, all awake at the same time," Wade says, his eyes big. "Golly, that's impressive; how did you link all your SDS pods together to consciously awake at the same time?" Wade asks with his jaw still slack with amazement.

"We are six hundred years further into the future, remember?" I say confidently. "We have advanced quite a bit from your period of time."

"Of course," Wade says, embarrassed. "I'm still wrapping my head around that," he says, scratching the back of his head. "It's a damn shame to know that even in your time we haven't discovered any answers to this godforsaken place," Wade complains.

"We haven't had a reason to look," I tell him somberly. "Until — we noticed something weird when we decided to go in awake."

"After another six hundred years of this technology being wielded, why hasn't anybody had a desire to see how this box works?" Wade implores, peering at us almost like he is losing his trust of us.

"It was an accident," Emily tells him, jumping in quickly.

"Now about that piece of tech," I again attempt to steer the conversation back to our original topic.

"An accident?" Wade says, looking over to Emily and disregarding my attempt to stop us from meandering between topics.

"Wade, the tech?" I press again, this time reaching out to grab his hand. I can feel his pulse as an uncontrollable tingle overwhelms my body. Wade doesn't retract his hand from my grasp. My heart beats fast, matching his racing pulse.

"I need to know more," Wade says sternly, finally pulling his hand back. My heart drops a beat and my mind goes blank.

"More?" Emily says, sitting up straight in our booth. "We have told you plenty," she continues with a bit of sharp sass. I remain silent, still looking at my outstretched, empty hand on the table.

"Are you telling me that our human society has regressed to just accepting this devious delight at face value?" Wade asks distressingly. I slowly let my hand slip back off the table to drop into my lap.

"Human society?" Emily says with a laugh, turning to me. She slaps my shoulder lightly with the back of her hand when she notices that I'm unresponsive.

"We have no time for this," I utter out of nowhere, making zero eye contact with anyone.

"No time?" Wade questions. "I have plenty of time," he continues to say, resting back and interlocking his fingers comfortably behind his head. "Plus, that tech is hard to access; I bet part of it extends to the other side of the Northeast Wall. You probably couldn't access it even if you wanted to," Wade continues as Emily and I look at one another.

"Josie can do it," Emily says, looking straight at Wade with her face still as stone.

"Sure, she can," Wade says with a nervous chuckle, looking over at me, not entirely convinced by Emily claim.

"It's true," I say softly, looking down at my lap. "I was able to enter the wall via Eastside Road," I continue, still feeling conflicted by my embattled emotions towards Wade.

"That's impossible. How?" Wade asks acutely, leaning in again as my eyes glance back up to look upon his indigo eyes.

"We don't know why," Emily says. "It rejected our two other friends but allowed Josie to enter," she continues to enlighten in hopes of getting him to trust us.

"Look, you girls have told me some fantastical stuff," Wade says in a pander. He grabs his knapsack, stands up, and prepares to leave. "Even if I could help, there is no way of knowing if there are even the means to escape. So why don't you girls just sit back and enjoy life in this wondrous forever land? Fate will awaken you, once it is done with you," Wade tells us. He puts on his hat and throws his knapsack over his shoulder.

"Wait! Where are you going?" Emily says in shock, seeing him about to leave.

"I'm in here for myself, girls," Wade says with a charming yet selfish smile. "I'm going to push back and live a long and healthy life. Good day to you both," he says, placing money on the table before walking away.

"Your avatar dies — young!" I call out, not turning back to see his reaction. I can hear his footsteps come to a halt. A few long seconds pass; I can hear the loud ticks coming from Emily's wristwatch.

The sound of approaching footsteps is heard next as I keep looking straight ahead at the empty booth seat across from me. "*Well, he does,*" I whisper harshly to Emily's burning gaze.

A thrown knapsack crosses my field of view, followed by a slumping Wade sitting back down. He sighs loudly.

His hands are placed out of sight in his lap and he just sits there, breathing in and out through his nose. His mouth is tight-lipped as though he is trying to gain some composure before he speaks.

"What was that again?" Wade asks calmly, looking directly at me.

"You die young," I tell him again as his face turns rosy.

"I know that; I heard you the first time!" Wade retorts, shaking his head. "When? How young?" he quickly follows up.

"We don't know for sure on—" Emily begins.

"Oh, you don't know — you just said you did," Wade says, obviously losing his patience. "Do I make it past twenty-two?" he asks, baffled as he looks up at the ceiling. "Do you at least know that much?"

"You don't make it past twenty-two," I tell him mixed-in with Emily's loud gasp.

"Josie —" Emily gasps, somewhat appalled by my revelation.

"In your book, the book you will write about this life — you don't make it to twenty-two," I continue to tell him chillingly.

"Josie, we agreed not to talk about —" Emily scolds.

"Emma, we have no choice," I interrupt. "We don't belong in here awake and we can't navigate this realm without his help — without your help," I turn from Emily to face Wade, making a heartfelt plea.

"*Goddamn it*," Wade mutters, not looking upon either one of us.

"Will you help us?" I ask again in the sincerest tone that I can manufacture in this sass-ridden teenage body. However, Wade just sits there; I see a tear forming in the corner of his eye that he swiftly wipes away, hoping that we don't notice.

"I've had enough of living in this lie that I'm in," Wade tells us coldly.

"We are not lying to you, Wade," I say to him sweetly. "We just want help."

"*Help?*" Wade murmurs, shaking his head. "I don't have all the answers, just piles upon piles of questions."

"By working together we may solve some of those questions," Emily says calmly, offering her appeal for Wade to help us.

"I thought to be in here awake was the next best thing to being back as a human, until I realized that I had no control over my fate. My narrative is pre-written. What type of life is that?" Wade says in a bluster. "Fuck it, I'm in," he says. Emily and I look at one another in collective surprise.

"You will help us?" I ask, just to be sure.

"I would rather wake up by my own hands of fate rather than wait for this shitty simulation to do its deed," Wade says with chagrin, slapping his hands together.

"Where do we begin?" Emily asks with excitement, leaning in to hang on his next revealing words.

Chapter 18

"So, why you?" Wade asks, looking over at me calmly.

"I don't know," I tell him, shrugging it off.

"Not good enough," Wade says, looking dissatisfied. "What is so special about you?" he then asks with a sharpness in his tone.

"Nothing," I say again. "I'm just as puzzled about it as you."

"Think — what is so special about you?" he asks again with an interrogating gaze.

"She is *One of the Firsts*," Emily says, sensing his thin patience.

"*One of the Firsts?*" Wade repeats, looking somewhat puzzled.

"I am the one hundred and forty-first conscious mind to have transcended," I tell him again. I am slightly offended by his ignorance even after my explanation.

"Well, la-de-da and I must have been number one millionth to have transcended," Wade says in frustration, still not understanding.

"Josie," Emily says, grasping onto my shoulder, "he's well before the Law of Ages."

"No," I scoff. "We've had the Law of Ages since Most South Eastern Cascadia came into existence."

"Law of Ages — Most South Eastern Cascadia?" Wade calls out over Emily and me. "I don't know about anything you two are talking about," he then says in a fluster.

"I'm trying to explain why Josie can enter the hidden realms," Emily says.

"Hidden realms?" Wade queries quickly; this is another term that is unknown to him.

"The areas past the invisible walls," Emily says, correcting herself.

"I still don't follow why Josie being *One of the Firsts* grants her special access," Wade asks with a mocking emphasis on my title.

"Hierarchy has always played an important role within our species," I tell him. "All societies of a species need their rules; these are ours."

"So, because you are higher up on this so-called hierarchy — you're more special?" Wade asks more politely while still giving off a mannerism of being unconvinced.

"Oh, he'll never understand," I say, shaking my head and looking over at Emily. "Doubt he knows anything about this weird time loop we are in, if this truly is the past, or maybe the Anthropic Principle has a part in all of this —" I continue to ramble.

"Anthropic — what, no way!" Wade blurts out.

"It's a possible reality," I tell him.

"No more than this being just a simulation of the past, a vast computer program," Wade says adherently.

"I thought the same as you when I first awoke," I tell Wade. "How could I tell if this is a simulation? Everything looks so real; there is so much detail. But what else could it be? All I've ever known of this world is a simulation of an ancient town called Penticton."

"So, what changed your mind?" Wade asks after a long pause of Emily and I looking at one another.

"We saw my wife," Emily says softly, making it sound weird coming from the lips of a seventeen-year-old girl.

"Your wife?" Wade repeats, looking obviously confused. "I don't understand."

"I was alive in Penticton during this period of time," Emily says sheepishly, "when I was a biologic."

"And you saw what?" Wade asks, looking over at me for clarity. "Your wife?"

"It's true," I tell Wade, nodding my head.

"*I bumped into my First-Biological wife,*" Emily reflects, looking sorrowfully down at her lap.

"Where?" Wade asks overtly, still shaking his head.

"While in the hospital," Emily says calmly, looking up. "Her name is Sydney."

"Sydney?" Wade gasps, sitting up straight. "While you were in the mental hospital — the same hospital where they most probably drugged you girls up," he says as he arrives at a possible conclusion for us seeing Sydney.

"It wasn't the drugs," Emily says, turning to me and looking annoyed. "Tell him that we saw her, Josie."

"It was her, but —" I say, turning to face Emily, "*but I've never before met Sydney,*" I finish with a wince.

"Oh, so you believe him, now?" Emily says shockingly, standing up, apparently offended by my honesty. "I know what I saw," Emily attests, looking at both Wade and me.

"Sit down," I tell her, patting the seat with my hand.

"No, I'm annoyed, now. I'm going home," Emily says, giving off a heavy sigh.

"Oh, come on, please," I beg Emily, grabbing her wrist so she won't leave.

"I need to study, anyways. I have two exams tomorrow, unlike you," Emily remarks, quickly glancing at her wristwatch. She then grabs her bag off the floor as I just sit there stunned about what to do.

Do I go with Emily? Of course, but I would kind of like to stay with Wade.

No, I should go. My emotions are taking over.

"You both have a nice evening," Emily says with a sly wink at me.

"No, I'm coming —" I start to say.

"No, stay," Emily says, putting her hand on my shoulder. "Wade, tell Josie to stay; have a cup of coffee with her," she says, looking over at him.

"I'd love that," Wade says as my eyes dance back and forth from Emily to Wade and then back to Emily.

"Okay, I'll stay," I relent, taking a deep breath.

"Good, I'll see you tomorrow at half-past four," Emily says, beginning to head to the door.

"Okay, four-thirty," I say, looking back at her. Then, I nervously turn my head around towards Wade.

"So," I say, feeling bashful being left in his presence all by myself, "thank you for helping me up in History class today."

"Oh, my pleasure," Wade says. "I was clumsy myself when I first came into this place awake."

"It's a lot to take in," I say with a nervous head nod. "Feeling every biological and chemical emotion — is daunting, especially when you haven't been biological for an awfully long time."

"Is it rude to ask how old you are?" Wade asks timidly, cringing like he may have just offended me.

"Well, Emma and I are the same age. We are 1,296 years old, not counting this SDS life. However, I have her beat on longevity in the Real Realm while being consciously awake," I ramble quickly to him in a nervous flutter. "I'm sorry; I'm talking too much."

"No, no, that's all fascinating stuff," Wade says, looking surprised. "So, being out of the SDS pod is seen as essential in the future?" he asks leaning in.

"It shows a guiding hand to travel both realms — sound of mind above everyone else," I inform him proudly. "Plus, I have loads of people I'm ahead of in transcendence age," I continue to gush at him about my accolades in longevity.

"So, you were around even before SDS pods?" Wade asks, looking at me somewhat impressed.

"Oh, ya —" I say to him, breathing heavily, "and I still remember *The Winter Purge* — Yes, I'm that old. I even used to sell those SDS pods when they first went on the market — hideous things back then," I ramble excessively.

"*The Winter Purge*, sorry — I don't recall that," he says with a laugh. I immediately roll my eyes as I realize my mental blunder. "However, I do remember when the SDS was first advertised," Wade says fondly, thankfully not pressing me on the topic of the purge. "SDS looked like the ultimate cure," he adds.

"It still is for many," I say, wondering where Dixby went wrong with his own sound-mind. Wade doesn't seem anything like the raving madman I met at the sales expo. This boy has my heart beating a song of endearment — how is that possible? I smile at him again sweetly as he catches me silently pondering.

"*I must say* —" Wade utters softly, looking somewhat bashful as he runs his hand nervously through his lemony locks, "I find you rather attractive, Josie."

"Oh, my God — I find you attractive, too!" I say in full amazement. "Oh — I mean you do?" I stutter, just realizing the gravity of our inner revelations.

"Since I first saw you — yes," Wade tells me, stretching his hand across the table to meet up with mine. Our hands touch delicately in a soft embrace as we quickly interlock our fingers. "Over a thousand years old," Wade says with an endearing smile. "You sure don't look it."

"I definitely don't feel it," I say with an affectionate giggle. "I was born in the year 1976."

"In '76," Wade says looking surprised, "I was born in '80. Well, what do you know; we are practically the same age," he continues, though I already knew.

"We are definitely old regardless of outer appearance," I say coyly, looking deep into his indigo eyes.

"We are survivors to be sitting here across from one another; I feel lucky that an SDS box hasn't devoured me yet," Wade states, giving off a funny grin.

"Oh, I know — so many people died in those boxes back the day," I confess, as there is no denying the history. "When I used to move that merchandise, it was such a struggle to sell the units at first. They took so much energy to run that your pod could glow crimson hot. LaPorte had given our people something that would change our world; we just couldn't figure out how to make those pods work properly," I ramble quickly, reminiscing. I am still somewhat jittery about being left in his presence all alone.

"When I was a human, I once believed in a god greater than me," Wade says, tilting his head to the side. "As time went by, I grew away from that fairytale as I grew to worship a new deity," he continues, searching far into his own past.

"I have never carried a belief in any time period, ever," I inform him. "We were just biological muck in a rocky blender whipping around a hot heat source for energy. I see no beauty in calling that a creation of God. People tried. They would dress God up, but I wasn't a fool; I know a made-up tale when I hear it. When I transcended into a husk, for the first time I felt clean. That disgusting feeble shell that we were forced to start our life inside is just unimaginable today. I still can't believe the human race still exists today as a choice — those damn cultists. I don't even like the smell of them anymore," I babble continuously to Wade, not thinking fondly of our shared past humanity.

"If you sold them, then you must have some inner knowledge of the workings of the SDS System," Wade notes as I bow my head down.

"Unfortunately, no. A separate division handled development," I say despairingly. Then my eyes light up; I can feel them going wide. "Describe that weird box you believe you found at the North East Wall," I ask, looking deeply into his eyes.

"Can't tell you much; it's half submerged with part of it extending onto the other side of the impassable wall," Wade tells me, matter-of-fact.

"Submerged," I repeat, my mush thinking hard about transcending time within my vast memories. "Dimensions?" I ask fervidly, grabbing a pen out Wade's top pocket and prompting him to draw what he saw on a napkin.

"Draw it?" Wade asks. "I could only feel it. Like I said, it was masked or cloaked."

"How big?" I inquire, still holding his pen.

"It's like a half-submerged basketball with a weird indent," Wade says in a frenzy, finally taking the pen to draw out what he had found.

"Any inscriptions?" I ask excitedly, looking at the spherical drawing Wade is making. "Any letters or numbers?" I continue to press.

"I don't know, Josie," Wade says heatedly, laying the pen on the napkin. "It was five years ago — plus it is invisible," he laments with a big sigh.

"Sorry, it's just that…" I say. I look at his drawing, trying hard to piece the parts of my memories together.

"I couldn't get it out of the ground — it is buried," Wade says disparagingly. He leans in over the table and grabs both my hands again in an embrace.

"I think I may know what it is —" I say, biting my bottom lip coyly and looking into his stunning, hypnotic eyes.

"Well, what is it?" Wade asks after a long pause.

"I think it's our way home," I say as a beaming smile overtakes me. "Can you take me there?" I ask him boldly.

"Where?" Wade asks, surprised. "Munsen Mountain — right now?"

"Yes," I tell him, grabbing Emily's rusty-mango hoody. I stand up as Wade just sits there, looking down at his drawing.

"This?" Wade says, pointing to the napkin.

"Just maybe — c'mon," I plead with him.

"Oh, alright," he says with a puerile smile. "Hope I remember where I found it."

———— ～◦◯✺◯◦～ ————

Wade and I drive to Munsen Mountain from the Green Beans Café, a mere five-minute drive. Munsen Mountain is a tourist lookout spot which offers an expanded view of all of Penticton to the South and far up Okanagan Lake to the north. The name of our fair city is carved into this extinct volcanic mountainside, similar to what one might see in Hollywood — just on a much smaller scale.

Wade parks at the top of the lookout. I bolt out of his truck and walk around impatiently, not knowing where to go.

"C'mon, Wade!" I call out to him as he slowly gets out of his truck.

"Hold, your horses, Josie," he calls back. "I'm coming," Wade says, running up to me. Wade comes to my side as a cold spring's night wind blows from our high vantage point.

"Brrr, that wind off the lake is freezing," I say aloud with a shiver. "I was so excited to get out here that I have forgot to bring my hoody."

"Here, let me warm you up," Wade says softly, putting his warm arm around my shoulder. He then pulls me in tightly to his body.

"Where is it?" I mumble, looking up from his chest, although being this close to him is creating a flutter of amorous feelings in my head.

"It's rather dark out, Josie," Wade says worriedly, squinting over the edge of Munsen Mountain. "I don't think it's best to be fumbling in the dark next to a donkey-kicking wall."

I reach my hand up to his caress his face as he brings his gaze down to me. "We are going to need a flashlight," Wade says and then pauses as his eyes lock into mine. Our mouths move closer together as I stand on the tips of my toes to meet his lips.

The anomaly Wade may have found along with the possibility of it getting us home gets soundly shelved as we stroll hand in hand back to his truck. Wade unhinges the tailgate to his vehicle and hops into the back before reaching out his hand to hoist me up.

I stand there, still shivering as I look over at the gorgeous view. Wade unrolls a sleeping bag to line the bed of his truck. Standing there with my arms wrapped around my chest for warmth, Wade rises up to take me in his arms.

Our lips lock as our bodies frantically tussle and fondle; clothes are quickly coming off. I've never breathed so hard; my heart is beating with such a vigorous intensity. I want to feel every inch of Wade. My mind goes blank from any concern about the Anthropic Principle or any time paradox as we make love in the back of his truck under the moonlight on top of Munsen Mountain.

―――――

"*Record on. It's early in the morning on Tuesday, May 6, 2005 at sunrise on Munsen Mountain,*" I dictate quietly to myself while strolling the edge of Munsen Mountain and looking down to the placid lake below. Wade is still asleep in the back of his truck where we both spent the night after making passionate biological love.

I'm not sure what came over me; it's just not like me to couple again with another so rapidly. I apparently don't have a good handle on the emotions of being Josie Birch. I was promiscuous in my incarnation as Lena Sage; however, that was four hundred years ago. I believed I had shed that attributes table in becoming Miranda Sage. Perhaps it's in those memories from that time of exploits which may have gravitated my risqué venture last night with Wade.

"You're awake early," Wade says suddenly, jumping out of his truck to make his way up beside me.

"I haven't seen an Earth sunrise like this in over two centuries," I say, squinting at him with the sun rising brightly over his shoulder. Wade reaches both arms around me and pulls me in close, pressing my head against his pounding chest.

I pull back almost immediately as a clearer mind moves my gaze to look out over the edge of Munsen Mountain again. Back to the task at hand and the reason we came to this spot. "So, where is this wall?" I ask forcefully. I walk away from him to ponder while looking over the edge.

"You want to look for it now?" Wade asks, sounding surprised.

"Well, it's not dark anymore," I tell him raising my hands up in the air.

"That's true, but I have an exam this morning," Wade cries out. "Damn it, it's seven o'clock already!" he continues to lament, looking at his wristwatch. "Can we do this later in the afternoon?" Wade asks hastily, making his way back to his truck. "You have an exam yourself this afternoon — History, remember?"

"*History?*" I utter with a sneer. "But there might be something here that may get me home," I say, shrugging my shoulders at the thought to have to care about any History exam.

"Please — later today?" Wade asks again, opening the passenger door to his truck. "We'll come out here again, I promise," he says emphatically.

"Okay," I say, followed a copious sigh. Maybe there is no harm in playing this role of Josie Birch a little bit longer.

Chapter 19

Wade drops me off at home and I slink silently inside. I tactfully close the entry and then slowly engage the bolt lock. I peer around me to check if anyone is awake.

"Oh, there you are!" Mother shouts, stunning me. She fluffs her locks as she descends the staircase. "I didn't see you in your bedroom when I came to wake you," she then enlightens me.

"Yes!" I tell her, still startled, with a fleeting feeling that she has just caught me after being out all night. "Yes, I'm up studying early for my History — I have an exam I mean," I stutter with high hopes that I sound convincing.

"Good for you, Josie," Mother tells me, squeezing my shoulder gently as she walks by me in the front foyer. "So, you'll have to make your own breakfast this morning," Mother says as she walks into the kitchen. "I'm taking your little sister to the dentist at eight o'clock."

"No problem, Mom," I tell her with my eyes looking to dart away, up the stairs. "*Oh wait,*" I mumble to myself, "*eight o'clock?*" The idea that I need to talk to Emily right away fires blazingly into my head.

"I'm heading to school, Mom!" I holler, unlocking the door and quickly dashing back outside. I slam the front door shut while Mother wishes me something of probably no importance.

I sprint down Pineview Road. Looking at my bare wrist, I believe I am timing myself correctly to run into Emily heading for her early morning exam. Just as I hoped, I notice Emily coming off Seacrest Avenue. We arrive on South Main Street at the same time.

"*Oh — record on,*" I mumble aloud to myself in a jumble of nerves as I approach her. "*Emily, we were out all night,*" I then tell her in a whispery voice once we are within range.

"*Are you serious?*" Emily whispers back, slapping my shoulder. "*Did you kiss him?*"

"Oh, we did more than just that," I say with a tight-lipped smile.

"Sex?" Emily gasps, sounding surprised.

"Yes, sex!" I answer with a roar. "It felt amazing."

"Miranda, you are seventeen years old, and you just met him," Emily gasps. "You're not a husk," she then scolds.

"Thank God for that!" I say, my eyes wide in amazement. "This is a way better task performed as a biologic, no doubt about it," I affirm.

"Miranda, you need to show some self-control — this is 2005, remember," Emily relents disappointingly; however, I believe that she is just jealous.

"You're the one who pushed me to have a relationship with Wade," I recite back honestly to her. "Do you deny that?"

"Well ya, but in essence behind the theme of the story," Emily utters, scratching her chin. "There was no chapter I recall of the love interest having sex with the protagonist after just one day of meeting one another," she then tells me, squinting her eyes while trying to think.

"I didn't expect sex — it just happened," I tell Emily, matter-of-fact. "Both of our bodies desired the act — so I suppose Wade and I saw no harm in that."

"Well, I suppose when you put it like that," Emily says in an emphatic tone of spite. Yet I know deep down that she understands. "I see your point, and it is well-taken, but how can explain coupling with a man that you hold in such low regard in the Real Realm?" Emily asks boldly, making me blow out hot air.

"Oh, please," I moan, covering my ears. "That is not Devlin Dixby. It is Wade Jennings that I had sex on — *or is it with?* I forget the proper vernacular," I continue, rolling my eyes.

"Well, if Wade wasn't going to help us before, he most definitely will now," Emily boldly surmises, and she finally laughs.

"How so?" I inquire.

"Geez, has it been that long? Do you not remember yourself as Lena Sage?" Emily reminds me with a bit of sass bringing up my past days of exploits.

"Oh, I assure you that Lena's entire perk table was shelved when I transcended into Miranda," I explain to her. "I've been living like a bohemian monk since my last carnation."

"Ouch, it's been that long?" Emily says with a shiver. "Seriously, no suitors?" she asks, looking surprised. My husk is rather beautiful.

"If only beauty could solve my problem of reinvention," I say with a sigh. "Everyone remembers everyone's past; it is utterly hard to rewrite that which has already been carved into granite."

"Munsen Mountain of all places," Emily says with a giggle. "What made him choose that romantic location?"

"Oh my God," I say with an unbelievable gush, "I haven't told you the best part; I think I may have found a way to get us home."

"What!" she says with a massive grin from ear to ear. "How are we getting home?"

"That box Wade was telling us about last night," I remind her. "I believe it may be an ancient Failsafe."

"A Failsafe?" Emily repeats, looking dumbfounded. "When can we use this so-called Failsafe?" Emily asks, obviously still puzzled by the term.

"Wade took me to Munsen Mountain last night to locate it, but it was too dark," I say, somewhat embarrassed that we didn't even look that hard.

"When are you going to see him again so we can check out this Failsafe?" Emily asks excitedly as we reach Green Ave, where we will go our separate ways.

"I have an exam with Wade this afternoon," I say calmly. "It's History — I think Josie will be safe getting an A on this test."

"Well, that's a big load of confidence," Emily says, laughing. "So I take it that you're not going to study?"

"We are leaving this place!" I yell aloud with my arms stretched up high, looking the fool to passers-by. "None of it matters; we'll be gone!" I shout, eliciting a dirty look from Emily.

"And in your place will be Josie Birch," Emily says, placing her arms on my shoulders to lower my arms back down. "Let's not ruin her life."

"What life – this?" I ask wildly. Confused, I pause to think about Josie Birch.

Is she alive?

Does she even get a life?

Before entering the SDS, I would have said no. Now, seeing anomalies that transcend space and time, my thinking has started to change.

"This is a nightmare situation," I confess angrily. "This simulation warps all meaning behind it just being a form of reality. How did LaPorte create a simulation portal within our timeline?" I ask, feeling betrayed yet again since we first entered awake.

I grab onto Emily's outstretched out arms and hold her in a loving embrace. "If we get back, do we pursue this — act of treason?" Emily asks, looking conflicted.

"Let's just focus on the task at hand of escaping this realm — all thoughts of a revolution can wait." I confirm with a head nod that we are more or less in the same sound-mind.

———— ∾∿◦⌒⊙◦⊱⊰◦⊙⌒◦∿∾ ————

"Record on. I enter the large gymnasium sharply at two-thirty for Josie's — I mean — my History exam," I mutter under my breath while taking in the grandeur of the room. There must be at least fifty desks and chairs placed out at equal lengths apart from one another to thwart any cheaters. I choose a position along the edge by the door so that I can look out for Wade when he enters.

I put my Math book with the curious sunflower on the desk ahead of me to save that spot for Wade. I can't locate Josie's History book anywhere.

"Is this seat taken?" a cute boy asks me with a coy look on his face.

"Yes, it's taken!" I tell him promptly, pointing to the book I placed on that desk.

"Math?" he says with a sight giggle that quickly morphs into jolting worry. "Shit! I'm at the wrong exam," the boy stutters frantically. "I thought I was in History," he then babbles, bolting out of the gymnasium like a fool.

"Josie," my name is called from behind me and an immense smile fills my face.

"Wade," I turn to say, seeing him walking my way. "I saved a spot for you," I tell him, my heart fluttering. Why am I so encapsulated by him?

"Aww — that's sweet of ya," Wade says before affectionately kissing me on the cheek. We look around us to see if anyone notices us being amorous with one another, but no one seems to care.

"Did you study?" Wade asks foolishly. He sits down at the spot I saved for him.

"Study?" I reply with a quick head shake. "I was with you last night," I tell him with a coy smile.

"Oh, I meant this morning," Wade clarifies. "Emma said you had no exams."

"That's true, but I didn't study," I tell him, shrugging my shoulders. "I couldn't find my History book," I explain, pointing beyond his shoulder at the curious sunflower. "Anyway, is it okay if Emma comes with us back to Munsen Mountain this afternoon?" I inquire plainly. I am excited by the prospect of heading home.

"Ya, I suppose," Wade says as a dejected look is drawn upon his face.

"What's the matter? You look sad," I say worriedly.

"I like you, Josie," Wade says, biting gently down on his bottom lip, "and you may be leaving."

"Oh, I'm sorry, I haven't thought —" At that moment the school bell rings, bringing the exam in session. Wade turns his body promptly around as our History teacher reads off his boorish rules for this examination.

The teacher aides quickly run up and down each row placing a stapled paper exam facedown on each desk. I look down at that blank back page in front of me, not caring one bit about performing this menial task. However, when our teacher yells 'Begin!', my competitive nature spikes me in the spine to grab the corner of the exam and flip it over.

I finish that test with ease. Looking over my right shoulder, I see the rest of the class struggling away. Wade himself is still writing; his side shoulder and moving elbow indicate that to me. Poor Wade; he looked so distressed earlier. I never considered his feelings about me leaving. Josie will still be here; however, I won't be embodying her. Josie may well fancy some other boy. I have a feeling that our tastes are not the same.

I need to think of the bigger picture though. As safe as Wade claims this place to be while awake, there is still some peril in regards to my friends Keoh, Adayln, and perhaps even Torstein and Mikken — wherever they may have landed themselves. I must think of them. As *One of the Firsts*, it's my duty not to be selfish to my comrades in their times of need.

So, I must be strong.

So, I must be vigilant.

So, I must not give in to the intoxicating scent Wade is giving off as I lean forward on my desk to breathe him in.

How could I give this up — this feeling that I haven't felt in so very long?

Wade's toned physique stretches within the fabric of his shirt, and I shake my head from allowing lustful thoughts to manifest. Where is the off switch to these amorous emotions? I am genuinely conflicted. I need to find that Failsafe quickly.

I think I may be falling in love!

The school bell rings. I bolt to the front of the gymnasium to hand in my exam, quickly b-lining towards the exit doors outside. I can hear Wade yell after me, but I need more time to think. I have mixed feelings of what is right and wrong, I need more time to process my emotions from my duties as a citizen of our species.

I go out in the direction of the soccer pitch as I find it quieter than the hustle and bustle of that noisy school. Wade is walking fast behind me. Why won't he let me think?

"Josie, why are you fighting with me?" Wade pleads, throwing a pine cone affectionately at my head. "I know you like me."

"No, that is not possible —" I say with a lasting pause as I contemplate my scattered thoughts.

"You're blushing," Wade points, making me grab my fickle-skin cheeks.

"Stop teasing me. Seriously, we need to keep the focus on finding that Failsafe. Members of our species are in peril!" I say to him in all seriousness, but it comes out sounding whiny.

"You talk like we have transcended even further when you speak of us as a species," Wade says calmly, holding me tight in his arms.

"I don't mean to offend," I say softly, reaching my hand up to caress his face.

"That's the end of the line for evolution?" Wade ponders aloud, looking up to the sky. He has chosen the worst possible time to start a theological debate.

"Evolution is about survival," I say sharply, never one to back down from such a topic. "We can still transcend further — evolve ourselves as we are still not invincible!" I postulate thunderously back at him. I am somewhat emotional.

"So, what becomes of humankind in your era?" Wade asks, starting to caress me in his arms again. "The ones who couldn't afford to transcend?" he continues to ask as my mush turns to butter.

"Oh, the Pure Human Race, or PHR as we refer to them, is still thriving — if you can call it that," I say with a scoff. "It's more a religion of a species wanting to hold onto their biological ideals," I explain with obvious low regard. "I don't even understand them anymore. Their dialect is so unusual — I refused to learn it. I think that's why most have left Northwest Cascadia," I babble on excessively while my heart beats mightily fast.

"Northwest Cascadia?" Wade says, shocked. "How many Cascadias do we have?" he asks with a snort.

"Many where I'm from. The Yukon straight through to the Okanagan Valley is Northwest Cascadia," I inform him, slowly kissing up his neck as he lowers his body. "*We have grown so big that we had no choice to make ourselves into a province,*" I mumble. His scent is enrapturing. "Not too many LaPortans live there, though; they were overrun by humans after *The Winter Purge,*" I say. It's curious that we are out in the middle of the soccer pitch.

"*Well — golly,*" Wade utters softly. "I sure like the way you speak," he says. He cups my chin to bring me in close to his lips.

"I'm babbling again," I tell him feverishly. Wade must know I'm nervous again. "Sorry, I'll try to stop —" I attempt to say, but I'm halted by his lips pressing against mine.

We pull back slowly, looking calmly at each other. My mouth still vibrates as it tingles with exhilarating electricity. I quickly look down to the ground. "*No — I can't do this,*" I stutter.

"You sure are one stubborn girl," Wade laments as I turn my back to him. "One day you like me, the next day the cold shoulder — make up your mind, Josie Birch," he cries out.

"I'm leaving this place," I say to him nervously, pacing around the big open grass pitch. The sky looks like glass, reflecting the image of my fair Cascadia. Anybody not wanting to live here forever among this wonder of realism would be seen as mad. "My friends are in peril," I explain, stopping in my tracks to look at him. "We need to wake them up from their current nightmare."

"Can't Emma do that by herself?" Wade asks, making me seriously ponder the notion of staying a bit longer in this realm. I do have feelings for Wade, but these feelings could just be because I'm in Josie's body. It may be Josie's hormones and pheromones that are kindling this coupling toward Wade. However, I haven't felt this strong of a coupling towards another for many a long century, maybe even four. Perhaps this experience can be extended a little longer, at least until Wade dies.

Oh my God; I forgot Wade dies five years from now!

"But you die, Wade," I remind him, making his brow thicken. He grimaces at that thought.

"Goddamn it!" Wade shouts, looking sombre. "I understand; why would anyone want to be an around a dead man walking?"

"Sorry," I tell Wade, running back into his arms. "Perhaps if I stay, we can change this fateful narrative."

"Impossible," Wade says softly before kissing me on the cheek. "If you deviate too far from your main path, the universe snaps you back in line," he reminds me.

"But I'm here. I can walk through the almighty walls into realms no one else can," I say with a strong conviction. "Maybe all these rules to living life in Penticton can be bent."

"That's sweet and all, Josie, but we still don't know why you can pass through the walls," Wade counters my bold claim.

"I'm *One of the Firsts*," I tell him soundly, kissing him on the lips.

"Yes, I know that," Wade moans, "but how is that relevant to me staying alive past twenty-two?"

"I just feel it — I'm willing to try," I say confidently. This brings an immense smile to his face.

"You are —" Wade pauses. "An angel," he says affectionately, squeezing me tight.

Chapter 20

"Memories are what life is — you are just made up of memories," I stammer, but Emily turns stubborn when I tell her that I may want to stay.

"No matter how we look at it, we need to leave," Emily says emphatically, looking at me straight on, "no matter what your feelings are towards Wade."

"Are you jealous — Emily?" I ask strongly, knowing all too well her flirty mannerisms.

"No, I'm not jealous," Emily pleads, crouching to her knees in disbelief, "I just want to go home. No, I need to go," she says with a stern look upon her face.

"Then go," I tell her coldly, "you don't need my permission."

"It's just not right," Emily scolds slowly. "This world is perverse," she continues, lifting her hands in the air with a sneer upon her face.

"It is what we have been missing, though," I tell Emily, "another way to transcend via the past."

"That's what I mean," Emily emphasizes every syllable, acting as if I'm deaf.

"It makes us better," I say firmly.

"But at what expense?" Emily asks with exasperation in her voice. "These lives we are hijacking do not belong to us — we are to them a parasite," she interjects nonsensically.

"Well, that's a bit harsh," I say sassily, turning my gaze away from her.

"You can feel her — can't you?" Emily asks vehemently. I attempt to maintain composure without revealing my bluffing skin. "I feel Emma," she tells me. "We are suppressing them."

"Oh no, not another plea from the old *Book of Humanity* to treat all as equals," I groan.

"Miranda, I'm a realist," Emily says senselessly, "and what I see is real — so much so that right now everything we do in here is appalling."

"Then go, Emily," I tell her. "Wake everyone else up. And when you do, I will wait and die naturally."

"Wade dies at twenty-two if you are planning on staying for his sake —" Emily stammers followed by a long pause. The nerve of her to speak to me like a fickle human child! "You are wasting your time," she continues, brushing those raven-haired locks off her shoulders.

"If I can transverse the walls of this realm," I say confidently with a raised eyebrow, "who is to say that I can't chart a different path for whoever passes mine?" I ask profoundly, minus any real facts.

"You're speculating!" Emily shouts aloud. "Wade told us that you can't stray from your correct chosen path. If Wade dies at twenty-two, then he must die at age twenty-two!" she continues to drill at me.

"That's my choice, so go," I tell her once again. "Stop trying to convince me to leave. Who knows if we can even go?" I continue to lament. "We still need that old Failsafe to work, if I remember correctly."

"You sounded confident earlier," Emily says, taking a step back.

"I'm still in that mindset that it will," I say charmingly, like any good salesperson.

Wade drives down Seacrest Avenue, stops in front of Emily's house, and rolls down his window. "Are we ready to go?" Wade asks coldly while opening the passenger door to his amber-coloured pick-up truck. I push Emily to the back-seat cab; she won't mind. Wade still has a sad look upon his face. I don't believe he likes going to Munsen Mountain, given the prospect of him looking for a device next to a wall that can hurl a punch at him.

An odd awkward silence hits us as Wade drives methodically north up Main Street towards the direction of Naramata. I can tell that Emily is not a fan of quiet air as she poses between our two front seats, readying herself to talk.

"Wade, as a writer myself, I was wondering if you could explain how you craft your stories," Emily asks passionately. "They are so imaginative," she continues to purr, making me roll my eyes. However, I note that Emily has finally brought a much-needed smile to Wade's face.

"Well, you just let the story grow organically through you," Wade starts off saying, scratching his chin. "When I need to write a chapter to fill in a certain plot point, such as two people falling in love. I never sit there pondering how these two people fall in love. I open my notebook. If nothing hits the page, then the story is just not ripe — it's still a hard peach. So, sometimes you need to pine all week or all month, even on trivial things like a nagging plot point. Your body and mind will stew a solution for you, if you just give it some time. It's like when you are baking a cake. If the story hasn't solidified yet, leave it in the oven longer. When the story is baked and is ready for the page, you'll smell it. Your pen will glow hot crimson from the friction and speed at which you rub that nub against the paper. At first it may be incoherent, but pay no mind to that. When the story is spilling out of you with complete visual descriptions; *mmmm* — the smell of burning paper cooled gently by a splattering ink topping. It's beautiful to look at when flipping through those many pages just ready to be typed out. Understanding the organism is the key to survival. I have learned this while being awake in Penticton. I couldn't write that well in a husk body, void of all real human emotions," Wade continues to ramble on as I stare out the window, bored.

"Hold on, we do have emotions in a husk body though," I remind Wade, turning my gaze towards him.

"Yes, but emotions that are manufactured and tightly controlled, not freewheeling and unabashed," Wade quickly replies. "That's why nobody liked my old books: they were boring," he says with a laugh, "just like our society we have evolved into."

"Hey, we are still around and flourishing, even in my time," I interject to enlighten him.

"I don't see how we can be with LaPorte still in control and all of God's rules and protocols," Wade says, tilting his head to the side.

"Why do you hate LaPorte so much, Wade?" I ask passionately, caressing his cheek.

"There is something weird going on in this place," he says, shaking his head. "If LaPorte has the power to create time, that's dangerous," Wade says disturbingly. I pause before answering.

"Perhaps the safeguards are there so nobody can do any harm to our timeline," I say, trying to be positive while giving Wade a comforting hug. That moment fails awkwardly when he does not embrace me back.

"Josie, you don't understand," Wade tells me, sitting up straight with a burning stare through the windshield.

"Help me understand," I say, smiling playfully in a vain attempt to break this tension.

"We need to destroy this device," Wade tells us. I slump down, confused about what he is trying to convey to us. "It is a poison to the human consciousness," he continues. I sit silently to ponder deeply whether there is validity in pursuing the truths that Wade has repeatedly spouted.

Wade pulls into the same spot on Munsen Mountain where we spent the night, and we all exit to find this beacon of hope.

"*Record on,*" I mutter under my breath, knowing that today will be of great importance. If Wade has indeed found something that we could use to wake ourselves up from this realm — perhaps maybe we should use it. I feel so conflicted.

"So this Failsafe, what exactly is that?" Emily asks wearily, still looking puzzled by that term.

"It's a Failsafe — like a portal in case you get stuck awake," I tell them as both their jaws drop. "It's not mentioned in the official user manual, amended after the all-out ban on going in awake. However, the Failsafe most likely hasn't been used in ages," I say cautiously. It may have rusted out.

"How do you know so much?" Wade asks shockingly, looking impressed.

"It's because she is *One of the Firsts*," Emily jumps in with a mocking laugh.

"That has nothing to do with it," I say back sassily. "It's because I sold these boxes. I've read all the user manuals, even some of the unpublished versions," I then enlighten her.

"Is the Failsafe going to send us back to wake in our realm?" Emily asks with clenched teeth.

"In theory," I say, shrugging my shoulders.

"In theory?" Emily gasps in shock with her mouth wide open.

"Yes, in theory," I confirm. "I've never used one, plus it's old tech. Old tech from that age was volatile. It most definitely hurt sales," I continue, affirming my statement with a head nod.

"What happens if it doesn't work?" Emily asks rashly as she watches me snuggle up against Wade.

"It could work," I say, looking sweetly into Wade's eyes, "or explode — it could be volatile, remember?" I look calmly back at Emily.

"Let's start over here," Wade says, pulling away from me. He then continues to walk by the crest of Munsen Mountain descending over the name of our city carved into the mountainside.

"Well, where is it, Wade?" Emily asks. We both look at him on his hands and knees trying to locate the Failsafe.

"It's around here somewhere," Wade says, cautiously feeling around.

"Be mindful of that wall," I tell him, fearful of him getting hurt.

"The wall may be invisible, but I remember that it is in a direct line with the long shaft that makes up the 'P' in Penticton," Wade says, pointing to the large white letter affixed above. "I just need to keep that letter in my line of vision."

"Yes, we see it," I say as Emily and I walk closer to him.

"It is so easy to forget —" Wade says before being suddenly tossed back towards us.

"Wade!" I cry out, running to his side.

"Damn it!" he cries out immediately. "See — my hand touched the wall. Damn donkey-kicking wall!"

Wade continues to lament, standing up from the ground. "Believe me when I say this: I hate visiting these invisible walls!"

"Where were you digging?" I ask ponderously, noticing that Wade is feeling better. "Is that where it's buried?" I say with a firm point of my finger to the ground.

"Yes, right there," Wade says, pointing. He stays far back. "Along the shaft of the 'P' is the wall," he continues to say as I walk confidently over, closer to the wall.

"Carefully, Josie," Wade says worryingly, reaching out with both hands towards me.

"I'll be fine," I tell him, with a quick glance over my shoulder.

"What if you can't pass through this wall?" Emily calls out with a theory I too have considered.

"We'll know that answer soon enough," I tell her as I walk gingerly forward.

As that imaginary line I drew down from the 'P' gets closer and closer to me, I stretch out my hands to be safe. However, my caution is not needed as I go far past the area that vaulted poor Wade.

"That's amazing," Wade gasps, seeing me twirl in a circle beyond where no one else has ever been.

"She's special, for some reason," Emily says sassily. I can see her biting the inside of her cheek. Emily shouldn't have waited so long to transcend, I suppose.

"Okay, well, let's get to work!" I call out, feeling a bit dizzy from all that twirling.

"Dig right there," Wade says with a long point of his finger to a spot on the ground; he still keeps his distance.

I get to my knees and start grasping at loose wheat grass which quickly gives way to pebbly dirt. "How do you know this is the correct spot from five years ago?" I ask him, looking up momentarily. Wade is peering at his co-ordinates with one eye open and stretched-out arms.

"Yup, that's the spot," he says confidently while standing in a weird pose. "The y-axis is the letter P, and the x-axis is the Marina lighthouse. It intersects there on the ground where you are digging," Wade confirms.

I dig for only a minute longer when a hard voidance of space hampers my path. "I found it," I say, pushing the dirt away from all around it.

"See! All your life you said you had no purpose being *One of the Firsts* — that you had no extra knowledge. You are walking past walls, right here, to prove otherwise," Emily says with her hands resting commandingly on her hips. "Miss Sage, your knowledge as *One of the Firsts* is why we will be able to leave this place," she continues. For the first time, I feel worthy of my title.

"So, what does it look like?" Emily asks intensely, running over to take a look. Emily doesn't realize that she's behind the wall; maybe there is something special about you too. I'm not going to bother to ask. My head is pounding from pondering today!

"Looks like nothing," I say bluntly, pointing down the hole that I just made.

"That's just weird," Emily says. She goes to her knees. "Can I touch it?"

"Go ahead; it shouldn't hurt ya," I say, shrugging my shoulders as I'm not all that sure.

"Feels hard, oh, and there's a groove," Emily says, all excited.

"How do you use it?" Wade calls out, still staying back about ten feet from us.

"All you do is run your finger along the groove, from top to bottom," I say. I place my finger on the masked spherical object and then strike my finger swiftly along the groove in one motion. A loud mechanical clicking noise is heard followed by a moaning echo as a flap suddenly pops open, out of the mysterious hole.

"A door — we can't fit through that!" Emily shouts out, rather stupidly.

"It's for your arm to fit through, silly," I tell her with a roll of my eyes. I stick my arm through the hole.

"What do you feel?" Wade asks gloomily, cringing to see my arm disappear into the ground.

"Yup — yes, there it is," I say joyfully after a few long seconds of feeling around with my hand. "There are many knobs and switches in here — I located the Failsafe, though," I confirm with a smile.

"It's a switch?" Emily asks as I take my arm out the hole.

"Yes, in the shape of a snake. You will just need to turn it counterclockwise until it clicks, to activate," I tell Emily, placing my hand reassuringly on her shoulder while looking over at a smiling Wade in the background.

"I need to?" Emily loudly rejects my instructions. "I don't know how to use a Failsafe — switch — device," she gasps repeatedly. "Josie, you know!" Emily says intently, staring directly into my eyes.

"I've never used one before," I tell her. "I've never claimed to be an expert. I've only read about the theory of them in an unpublished user manual."

"Well, that knowledge alone trumps mine," Emily says, looking away in disgust.

"I can tell you what to do — it's quite straightforward," I say, straining to think. "*If I remember correctly,*" I then mumble, looking out in the distance.

"Great — that's reassuring," Emily says, pulling on her raven-haired locks in apparent stress.

"What if the Failsafe doesn't work?" Wade asks lightly, making me roll my eyes.

"Guys, it should work," I say, feeling them losing faith. "Why would the LaPorte technicians install them if they didn't work?" I argue to bring them some confidence.

"Their track record is not the greatest, if you want to discuss successful installation," Wade says with a laugh. "How many SDS installations have you had in your long life? I'm on my fourth, and the improvements are laughable," he points out, reminding me of his triad at the Sales Expo many centuries ago.

"It's a gamble to use them, especially in your time, Wade," Emily says sorrowfully. She is probably thinking about Dixby's eventual Double R death by the hands of this device.

"Can we lighten the discussion a bit?" I ask wearily. I am feeling the topic of faulty tech bringing us down. "Like a flick of a switch — the Failsafe should wake you up," I say calmly and precise to Emily.

"Or?" Emily asks sternly, staring me down like a hunter aiming at its prey.

"Something might — overload," I admit, looking up to the sky. I try to remember the actual wordage from the manual. "Ugh, it's just so long ago to process — something to do with power," I say dismissively.

"How could you not remember?" Emily laments, visibly disappointed.

"Emma, it was something I read a thousand years ago about a piece of tech never implemented in any official user manuals," I say to Emily in complete honesty. "As a salesperson, that is hearsay-knowledge that you don't dare pitch. You can't promise a customer something which is not gospel within the official user manual," I explain to her with a bit of sass.

"It had better be like flicking a light switch," Emily says, rolling her eyes. Back then people trusted me, back then with the best of success statistics, yet these two have no faith in the technology. How appalling.

"Josie, do you mind if I speak to you in private?" Wade says with a tilt of his head to come toward him. I leave Emily to hover over the Failsafe, scratching her chin while pondering her task, and make my way closer to Wade.

"We may need a backup plan," Wade says, pulling me to the side out of earshot range of Emily.

"What do you mean?" I ask him, shrugging my shoulders.

"If that Failsafe goes awry —" he starts to say.

"It won't — it shouldn't," I stutter, quickly correcting myself from being too overconfident.

"Let's make a pact to seek each other out in the Real Realm," Wade says blissfully. I sigh, knowing full well that he is consciously dead in my period of time. "I will disavow fate with a promise never to step inside an SDS again, and I will meet you in 3289 to continue this love of ours," he tells me, holding me in his arms.

Wade's promise gives my heart a stabbing pain, for what he says will never be true. Even if it were possible, a conscious mind goes insane in the Real Realm without the aid of deep sleep. "That's a long time in the Double R to be awake," I say, knowing that what he says can never be right. Wade believes we can't change the fate of our lives in the realm; perhaps the same rules and laws apply back home.

"Are you saying that life is so boring in your period of time?" Wade asks with a raised eyebrow.

"Yes, especially during space travel. It's a good way to kill a century-long journey," I tell him with a laugh. "I'm not saying that people don't go long stretches without the SDS; many have done so. However, those people are not rational; they are not like the rest of us. Two hundred years is the ceiling: you either go into the box or you go insane. The human consciousness is not structured to live a path that long," I continue to babble at him.

"You angels have transcended to become something rather different," Wade says softly, stroking my cheek with the back of his hand.

We are an ancient biological conscious construct of neurons and receptors. That's the software which our consciousness hubris manifests among its artificial circuits — by an antique design. Yet it's a design with faults not given the evolutionary merits of an upgrade to a species never wanting to die. Those insane people, those half a million souls that chose not use the SDS, are so bored, they ought to be dead. Why bother existing? Just turn yourself off — permanently.

And now my love is willing to battle against those odds for our hearts to beat in unison. This is the grandest of gestures from such a sweet mind, still too young to have ripened, lacking any great wisdom. He hasn't even reached one thousand years old with his Double R and SDS lives combined. Wade has no idea of that which cannot be done.

It is romantic, though; who wouldn't want to be enraptured by this love the two of us have manifested here. It's powerful; so powerful that I am surprised that I could have dismissed this whimsy for so long.

"I can do it," he tells me, squeezing me tightly in his arms. Wade speaks, but his fate is cemented in stone. I don't know how I will ever reconcile these events once I return to the Real Realm. He's the one — the one soul to help me relive the meaning of true love. Can there be some other way?

"*Wade,*" I mumble into his chest. He pulls back slowly, looking lovingly at me. "Please, why can't we just change the fate here in this realm, for us to just stay here forever?" I plead with him passionately.

"It can't be done here, in this realm," Wade tells me. "I've told you: I tried twice before and failed. We are not in power of our fate here, as much as I want to believe that you are special."

"We have to try," I say again to him, looking deep into his indigo eyes.

"What are the chances that Josie and Wade even make it together in this timeline?" Wade postulates. "If we are wrong, and that is not our true path, then fate will snap us back in line," he continues to explain in a defeated tone.

Why would he be so remissive to even want to try to make a life here with me? Why can't we change the fate here? It is just as foolish for Wade to attempt to change the outcome in the Double R. I have no nugget of information to relay to him now that could prevent him from eventually dying in the Real Realm.

"What if I seek you out back in my Real Realm time, and not wait for you to emerge back in your era?" Wade suggest with yet another failed theory, destined to not work. Josie Sage was a hard person back then in 2673. It doesn't help that I didn't think fondly of the man or his works of fiction, although I felt that way before I met Wade.

However, he dies so quickly in The Double R, right after this short life here in the SDS. Dixby comes out and immediately begins writing *Fallen Angel* for two months straight, and then he dies. Dixby locks himself in his house for those two months, only leaving from time to time to get food and supplies.

What message could I give him to give to me in the past that would soften my heart? Two months is not a lot of time, especially when he is on a self-anointed lockdown. I wish I had a neural map of my brain from that period of time. Trying to remember anything in this biological shell is near impossible.

"How would you do it?" I ask deeply, so badly wanting to hear a reason for us to extend this union.

"Where were you living around the year 2673?" Wade asks acutely. I don't have to think long before reaching an answer. "San Francisco, Central Cascadia," I answer him, tight-lipped and nervous to hear what he plans to do.

"San Francisco?" Wade says in shock. "I live there too. I will seek out Josie Sage; this will be easy," he says with his confident, boyish smile.

"How will you remember me?" I ask, puzzled. "When we wake from the deep sleep, this life is all but a dream to be added to our collective consciousness. Wade Jennings will not one-hundred per cent embody you as Devlin Dixby in the Double R," I continue to tell him, not sure how I will feel myself once I return home.

"When you go in awake, you awake the same person," Wade says with a smirk. "You remember everything; you embody one-hundred per cent of what you just lived in Penticton," he continues. He firmly grasps my shoulders to look upon me at arm's length.

"Then when you go back, if we happen to cross paths again, say this one word to me," I instruct him. I move in close to whisper into his ear, giving him the key to make my heart skip a beat — the beat of love.

"But what does it mean?" Wade asks profoundly. He looks confused, as I expected he would. "I'm a hard individual back then during your era," I explain to him, hanging my head low. "I'm hard as a rock with a wall around me as thick as granite so that none shall enter. However, this one word is the key to crumble that wall down," I explain to him.

"How do you know that will work?" Wade asks, still looking befuddled.

"Seek me out, right away — right after you emerge from deep sleep. Don't wait or hesitate," I plead quickly with Wade, looking penetratingly into his eyes.

"I will, I promise," Wade says assuredly, kissing me hard on the lips. This venture will have a slim chance at working; I have travelled this path in life before — unsuccessfully.

"You must say it quickly, as soon as you see me," I say emphatically to him again.

"Yes, right away," Wade repeats with a smile.

"I'm serious; you've got to use it quickly," I repeat. "Don't hesitate."

"As soon as I awake," Wade tells me again, kissing me on the lips. I peer over to Emily still standing over the Failsafe, looking perturbed.

"Okay then, I'd better to talk to Emma before we trigger this Failsafe," I tell Wade. I push him back, keeping my mind steady on this task. *"She doesn't look too happy,"* I whisper to him.

Emily stands with her hands on her hips and a scowl on her face as I approach. "Well, if you are hell-bent on staying, so be it; I won't wake you when I get back," Emily says vigorously. She tries to sound powerful, but comes off just sounding cute instead.

"That's my choice; I want to stay here a bit longer," I tell her, standing my ground.

"It's against the law, remember?" Emily says as if it had never entered my mind.

"Oh, when I awake I'll be having words with the creator of this place, but for now — I'm going to take this as a reward that I feel I deserve for my service in propagating God's lie towards our people," I say to Emily with conviction.

"We arrive back on Earth in sixty-nine years," she says calmly, her desire to fight me on this topic now apparently absent. "Shall I wake you once we arrive, if you haven't yet expired?" Emily asks, cringing, as it does sound cold to unplug me while I may still be ripe.

"No, keep my pod running," I tell her. "I'll play Josie's narrative to the end. I just hope that will include Wade by my side," I say optimistically, looking over at him.

"If anyone can see him survive past twenty-two, it most certainly is you," Emily says with a firm embrace. We pull back, looking longingly in each other's eyes. The venture we have taken is coming to a close.

"We all live and die in Penticton — forever," I say Emily, wishing her well on the task at hand. "We die, and then we are reborn again over and over to repeat this cycle for centuries — forever. It's more our world than the Real Realm. I deserve to know more about it," I continue to explain to her with a confident head nod that I'm indeed sound in my thoughts.

"Twist it counterclockwise until it clicks," Emily says, repeating my instructions from earlier.

"Yes," I say to her with my eyes wide in confidence, "this will work."

Emily gets down to her knees as I move next to Wade, wrapping my arms around his waist. Emily sticks her right arm into the sphere, sticking her tongue out to the side as she reaches around. "There are so many knobs and such," Emily says with confusion on her face.

"You'll know it when you feel it," I remind her. "It's smooth, in the shape of a snake."

"I think I found it," Emily says with delight. "Yes — this has to be it; it's not like the rest," she then hollers.

"Counterclockwise," I say to her, holding Wade tightly. I watch Emily's cringing facial expressions as she activates the Failsafe. We all wait in anticipation as nothing immediately happens. Emily's arm is still submerged inside the sphere.

"Nothing is happening," she says surprisingly as suddenly everything goes to black.

Chapter 21

---◆————————◆————————◆---

I emerge from pitch blackness to a fiery-crimson ball of pure hell. I make it out of my SDS pod with only moments to spare to find myself swimming in the void-ance of space. I float aimlessly through the wreckage of most likely the *Misfit*. After locating Emily's SDS pod, I see that she is not inside.

When I do find her, I see that Emily escaped the wrath of the fire of her own pod. But as she pirouettes among the wreckage, Emily is apparently not in control of herself. I push my way over to her, embrace her exquisite husk, and lock my hands in place around her body.

For many weeks, my cracked and torn body spins relentlessly in the silence of cold space. Emily is still locked in a tight grip with my arms wrapped around her while both of our bodies are frozen, unable to move. I can sense Emily is alright. She is still in there, waiting patiently for a repair.

One day, the soft arms of the extending grasp of mechanical clutches suddenly pinch onto my waist; I am now conscious. I watch us slowly being retracted into a ship of unknown design and origin.

The pelting sound of radiation persists the deeper we go inside the ship, until I can detect all radiation levels suddenly drop to zero. A loud thud is then produced by us being dropped onto a hard, metallic surface as the clamp releases its grip on me.

Still frozen and unable to move, the dark room then glows in a curious mango and I start to gain the feeling of movement among my limbs once again. I unclasp myself from Emily as she remains still on the ground. I notice her back is burnt from head to heel. I had not seen this during our loving embrace.

I stand up with a wobble, mysteriously swaying to the side as my left leg struggles to maintain stability. With my arms stretched out to each side, I regain balance to remain upright. Looking down, I notice that the same burning has damaged the left side of my expensive husk.

The room we are in has no significant design other than greyish metal with one hatch door leading out of the wall. The clasping hands that have placed us in this room suddenly retreat up into the ceiling, sealing themselves off with a rapidly closing door. I drag my left leg to the hatch door and repeatedly pound on it with my fist for it to open.

Expelled gas is then heard followed by the door moving forward as this ship's atmosphere enters within the gaps. Once the gaseous noises have dissipated, the entrance swings up, letting me pass through. I creep down a hall that is filled with which looks to be humans, but I could not be entirely sure. My answer to where I am comes clearly into view as I notice the LaPorte logo on everyone's uniforms.

I enter one of the outshooting rooms where I notice Asia lying on a table being attended to by two LaPorte crew members. "Hold still, your husk is damaged," a LaPorte crewman tells me as he rises from his desk. I quickly push him away with a stiff arm, continuing my way over to Asia. I move up to the table and force the other two crew members aside. The crewman at the top of Asia's body stares down at her head, grasping it with his hands.

"Hey, we are trying to turn this enemy off," one of the crewmen tells me, leaning over Asia's body. Suddenly, as Asia's eyes come alive, the crewman quickly extinguishes their golden glow by twisting her neck, snapping all power to her head.

"She's evil; a spy trying to take down LaPorte Industries," they tell me, as if that is the truth.

"Miss Sage," a voice grumbles from behind me, and I turn my head to look.

"Double H," I say, surprised to see him here. "You still in the *Service*?" I ask, walking up beside him. "Still in the *Service*, indeed," I say, impressed. I look his tall frame up and down.

"Yes, Miss Sage," Double H panders with a groan. "Come this way, now!" he then commands with a firm point of his finger down the hall.

"Where are you taking me?" I ask distressingly. I am hurting — my husk commands fail to dampen the pain.

"Where do you think?" Double H gasps, rolling his eyes, "look at the state of ya!"

"An — accident," I stutter. "What happened to…"

"Even your hair is singed — *more than usual*," Double H interrupts with a sneer, brushing his long fingers through my short raven-haired locks.

"How is Emily?" I ask deeply as my memories now come back on file.

"Who?" Double H asks tediously with a snarl. "Oh — her. Stellar. Someone will attend to her; I'm here to handle only you."

Double H leads me a mile into the ship until we reached his workshop. "Now this Miranda husk," he says boorishly with a sneer, "has got to go. Shall I make you up the same? I know you have substantial credits," Double H asks boldly.

"Ya, that's fine," I tell him with a wincing pain in my hip. "Make me up the same."

"Or do you wish for maybe a new design or even an upgrade?" Double H says quickly with a ramble like the true salesman that he is; that man loves his profession.

"No modifications," I tell him soundly. Annoyed, I place my hands on my hips. "You know I never change the overall look of my husk when I am in need of a replacement," I remind him.

"Oh, yes, I know that," he says with a playful snicker. "I have to ask, plus you do have plenty of credits — but as you wish," Double H says, not one bit threatened by my menacing stance.

Double H brings up my signature design piece which has been slowly working its way through the alphabet: Amber Sage, Echo Sage, Miranda Sage — the list goes on and on. However, they all use the same design template that was gifted to me by the Great Founder LaPorte, many centuries ago.

The only aspect I modify to distinguish them is colouring of hair and skin to make them all feel different. Besides my attribute tables, which I have toiled through time to build, my husk design is considered a high-end custom fit, considerably unique. Being wealthy and *One of the Firsts* is highly advantageous in this realm of ours, especially with the many perks and upgrades available to me.

"This time let's make the hair longer," I say, pausing as new memories are added to my attributes table. "Scratch that, Double H," I say sourly towards him.

"All of it?" Double H says with a gasp.

"Yes, all of it," I tell him with a raised eyebrow for making me ask twice.

"Well, how about some of your usual raven-haired locks, Miss Sage?" Double H asks sternly, looking down at his display.

"No, make my locks blazon — as bright crimson as you can make them," I tell him. Then something strange catches my eye at the far edge of his display: *Josie Sage cold storage, restorations complete.*

"How long has Josie Sage been on ice?" I ask Double H, pointing to his display.

"Five hundred years or so," Double H tells me. "Four-hundred and ninety-seven to be exact," he then adds, looking closer at his display.

"Add Josie Sage's complete attribute table back into my next carnation, including all her perks," I instruct Double H making him gasp in shock.

"Why would you want to do that?" he questions immediately. "Josie was a walking mayhem of utter destruction," he reminds me.

"Her perks will come in handy with what I need to do next," I say calmly to Double H, looking straight ahead as I await my new carnation.

"Miranda, please reconsider. Josie Sage's perks made her into a formidable tactical husk — she was just pure mayhem," Double H continues to pander nervously, trying to sway me.

"I answer to no one below me!" I shout. Double H straightens his stance. "My credentials are right there on your display," I say sternly with a firm point of my finger as a well of anger starts to fill within me.

"And have you picked out a name for this new monstrosity?" Double H asks with his sharp, rude wit.

"A name?" I say with a laugh, rolling my eyes. "What letter in the alphabet am I on — N is it?" I ask coyly, looking up at him.

"Yes, Miranda," Double H answers with a sneer. "As someone who has known of you for many lifetimes, may I ask you something?" he requests.

"You may, Double H," I say, knowing full well he will ask his question anyway.

"Why, in the golden age of peace on Earth, would you require a tactical husk?" he asks, looking dumbfounded at me.

"Something big is coming," I tell him. I add no more context which he doesn't require.

Double H just rolls his eyes; he knows me too well to pry any further. "Well — what will be the name of this new carnation?" Double H asks, coiling back to being the snake-oil salesman that he is programmed to manifest.

"That husk already has a name," I tell him as Double H's eyes go wide in shock. "It's the perfect choice for what I need to do next. I'm going to a place to get answers — a dangerous place. She's special," I say aloud. I have nothing to hide; there is no more wool covering these sheep's eyes.

"*She is a fiery, destructive walking thing of mayhem,*" Double H mumbles, looking down at his display while shaking his head in disapproval of my choice.

Dismayed as he may act, Double H creates my husk replacement in a matter of minutes and preps me in the chair beside it. "Are you ready for your transfer?" he then asks with his finger hovering over his display.

"Yes, Double H, I'm in sound-mind to proceed," I tell him firmly.

"Record on! It's June 6, 3289. I, Harry Higgins, have the verbal sound-mind consent of a one Miranda Sage, which has been authorized and dutifully notarized by my self — transferring — now," Double H says, pressing his finger down on his display to complete the transaction.

"The *Misfit's* manifest states you were heading back to Earth; you have been away for a long time. May I ask your reasoning to return to our homely rock?" Double H asks with a smile, in the service of small talk no less.

"*Re-vol-ution,*" I say painfully under the failing breath of my Miranda body.

"Revolution, indeed," I then say with conviction. I open my eyes, freshly carnated as Josie Sage.

Epilogue

"I only had fleeting moments in time to spend with them, my two little angels. It almost feels like it may never have been real. Their souls were so pure, and they were gifted in being much wiser than I — there was no question there.

The one with the crimson hair I found a mutual shared attraction towards the physical. She debated me well, a strong tangler of the twisted tongue.

The raven-haired angel struck me with the musical harmonics that resonate within each and every core of a man. I saw eagerly into her vision, seeing the same as what I would expect within a healthy soul.

They were as close as sisters to the bitter end. Their ability to conspire against one another was like witnessing the crashing heads of two wildebeests. In the end, I chose wisely, I believe, taking the path of vengeance over the most certainty of true love. Oh, I will never love another angel like I had adored her — she was indeed one of a kind.

However, now as I write this with scorn ripped against my immortal heart, I sit, lost, with no way to cast my vision upon you again. The mighty God has delivered to me, from the holiest of heavens, two beacons of hope to show that I have not lost in vain. My legacy will live on through them, and I promise a deliverance of a real and rightest justice.

This God's time has come — and will soon come to an end!"

Epilogue from *Fallen Angel*
By Lord Devlin Dixby (cc. 2673)

"There, that's it, the damn thing is done!" Dixby bellows, handing the manuscript to his assistant Melbray.

"Another bestseller, sir?" Melbray asks in a cheerful pander.

"Oh, it will sell fine — just cuz of the previous two," Dixby says with an angry snarl. "Damn thing ain't worth the wasted ink."

"Oh, I'm sure it will be a great success," Melbray says brightly, seemingly trying to cheer the old fool up.

"That there in your hands is five hundred pages of mocking ridicule towards LaPorte Industries," Dixby says in a scathing tone.

"It reads like a love story to me," Melbray mentions humbly, but Dixby most probably isn't listening to him.

"No, the story is crap! I didn't emerge awake from the SDS," Dixby cries out. "It glitched my experiences to be that but a dream. It was such a good life, it was helping me get over Ophelia, but LaPorte's temperamental technology robbed me of that waking lifetime — Goddamn it!" Dixby yells in treasonous nonsense. "My protocol settings were off — it all felt like a dream — Goddamn it! I wasn't brought back awake!" he continues to moan.

"Sir, there is a woman from the *Service* outside wishing to speak with you," Melbray says sheepishly, interjecting himself into Dixby's boorish tirade.

"By all means, let her enter!" Dixby says clear and loud. I wait, just outside his office door.

"You may enter now," Melbray says to me, sticking his head out of the open doorway.

I enter the office and Dixby makes immediate make firm eye contact. "Mr. Dixby, may we have a moment in private?" I request, pointing with my head towards his assistant as soon as I walk inside.

"Yes, of course; Melbray, give us a minute," Dixby says with a sharp point of his finger for Melbray to exit the room.

"Now, what is this all about?" Dixby asks sharply as soon as the office door clicks shut.

"Don't you know why I'm here?" I ask of him, somewhat shocked.

"Not the foggiest," Dixby says with a coy shrug of his shoulders.

"We have been investigating you for the SDS violation of User Agreement Section three, paragraph one, and I state: *Thou shall not willfully enter any SDS system under altered user protocol parameters —*" I begin to tell him forcefully with my hands placed firmly on my hips.

"Don't bore me with your rules," Dixby interjects soundly with an arrogant sneer across his face. "You didn't come all this way in person to read aloud this nonsense — *I say, are you a husk?* I can never tell these days," he continues. His thoughts are most likely derailed due to SDS sickness — the fool.

"Oh, I didn't come here by myself," I inform Dixby, still standing my ground.

"A whole team is needed?" Dixby says with a snorting laugh. "To what — suspend my subscription?" he continues with a loud cackle.

"If you look out your window, you may have a better sense of what is in your future," I suggest. Dixby gets up from his desk and looks out the window behind him. I start playing my recording from that sales expo, twenty-one years ago. He just couldn't keep it quiet; he so badly wanted someone to hear his devious ploys.

"My SDS, they are taking my SDS pods! Those are mine!" Dixby yells, ignoring the evidence being played aloud which he already knows to be true.

"They can and they will — as you know it is signed clearly by your hand," I state. Then, with his body still turned away from me, I raise my hand up to shoot Devlin Dixby squarely in the back of the head.

Dixby's mind splatters on the window in front of him as he continues to look out in horror of God refusing mercy on him. Seconds later, he slowly turns to look at me in shock, and mumbles *Cora* — before his body crashes to the floor with conscious repair most permanently denied.

I pause for a split moment, deciphering what I may have just heard. It did make me flinch. Dixby's body twitches on the floor as I quickly regain my composure. After adjusting my fiery locks, I scan his office and see nothing but filth.

"*Record on!*" I say aloud — "*June 6, 2673, this concludes the termination of user agreement member 1,122,131 due to the user violation of LaPorte Industries subject law four dash one and four dash two. Agreed sentence of most permanent conscious death signed by the terms of Mr. Devlin Dixby's user agreement, carried out dutifully by LaPorte Compliance Officer — Badge 141, One of the Firsts — signed Josie Sage — case closed.*"

The End